‖‖‖ ‖‖‖‖‖‖‖‖ ‖ ‖‖‖‖ ‖‖‖‖‖‖‖‖‖‖‖‖‖‖
☞ **W9-BXY-584**

250

SECOND THOUGHTS

Kate wished she did not find him so inordinately attractive that everything about him affected her. It was quite ridiculous to let such things get in the way.

"Mrs. Kingsley, I believe you are already aware of the original terms of employment as governess to my daughter?"

Kate felt as if Lord Carismont had arrived at a sudden decision, for she detected a firm, new note in his voice.

"Original? There has been a change?"

"Yes, Mrs. Kingsley, one of considerable importance. But before I explain, let me assure you that this change has only just occurred to me, and I have not been deliberately conducting this interview under false pretenses."

"False pretenses?" she repeated warily.

"It has become clear to me that it is not the post of governess I should be offering you, but that of my wife. . . ."

SIGNET

REGENCY ROMANCE

COMING IN AUGUST

The Discarded Duke
by Nancy Butler

Ursula Roarke plans to lure the Duke of Ardsley into
marriage, thereby securing her place in society. But when
a local shepherd sparks a fire in her, Ursula finds herself
torn between the two most vicious foes of all time: love
and money.

0-451-20679-7

Lady Sparrow
by Barbara Metzger

When young heiress Minerva Caldwell buries her elderly
husband, she uncovers a disturbing secret. Now, with help
from a handsome lord, she embarks on a search that will
risk her life—and her heart.

0-451-20678-9

A Reckless Bargain
by Elizabeth Powell

Newly-widowed Kit Mallory is all too willing to help her
friend, the dowager Duchess, even if it means joining forces
with her friend's ill-reputed—but reputedly handsome—
nephew.

0-451-20551-0

To order call: 1-800-788-6262

RR303

Second Thoughts

Sandra Heath

A SIGNET BOOK

SIGNET
Published by New American Library, a division of
Penguin Putnam Inc., 375 Hudson Street,
New York, New York 10014, U.S.A.
Penguin Books Ltd, 80 Strand,
London WC2R 0RL, England
Penguin Books Australia Ltd, Ringwood,
Victoria, Australia
Penguin Books Canada Ltd, 10 Alcorn Avenue,
Toronto, Ontario, Canada M4V 3B2
Penguin Books (N.Z.) Ltd, 182–190 Wairau Road,
Auckland 10, New Zealand

Penguin Books Ltd, Registered Offices:
Harmondsworth, Middlesex, England

First published by Signet, an imprint of New American Library,
a division of Penguin Putnam Inc.

First Printing, July 2002
10 9 8 7 6 5 4 3 2 1

Copyright © Sandra Heath, 2002
All rights reserved

Ⓟ REGISTERED TRADEMARK—MARCA REGISTRADA

Printed in the United States of America

Without limiting the rights under copyright reserved above, no part of
this publication may be reproduced, stored in or introduced into a re-
trieval system, or transmitted, in any form, or by any means (electronic,
mechanical, photocopying, recording, or otherwise), without the prior
written permission of both the copyright owner and the above publisher
of this book.

PUBLISHER'S NOTE
This is a work of fiction. Names, characters, places, and incidents either
are the product of the author's imagination or are used fictitiously, and
any resemblance to actual persons, living or dead, business establish-
ments, events, or locales is entirely coincidental.

BOOKS ARE AVAILABLE AT QUANTITY DISCOUNTS WHEN USED TO PRO-
MOTE PRODUCTS OR SERVICES. FOR INFORMATION PLEASE WRITE TO PRE-
MIUM MARKETING DIVISION, PENGUIN PUTNAM INC., 375 HUDSON STREET,
NEW YORK, NEW YORK 10014.

If you purchased this book without a cover you should be aware that
this book is stolen property. It was reported as "unsold and destroyed"
to the publisher and neither the author nor the publisher has received
any payment for this "stripped book."

*For Sue Bell, my dear friend from school days,
with many thanks for her help with Cornwall
and its legends*

1

Darkly handsome and dressed in elegant style, he was seduction itself as he stood by the fireplace, gazing deep into the flames. Kate was drawn to him from that first moment at the Pulteney Hotel, and could not possibly have foreseen that soon, when it was too late for second thoughts, she would be told he had killed her late husband.

For the moment, however, she was only interested in creating a good impression so he would think her a suitable governess for his young daughter. She spoke. "Lord Carismont?"

He turned, swiftly, almost as if he had not expected her. "Mrs. Kingsley?"

"Sir."

Apart from a sleepy black cat curled up in an armchair by the fire, they were alone in the hotel's unusually quiet public drawing room. Candles were lit, for it was sunset outside. Another squally early-April shower dashed against the French windows that gave onto the wrought iron balcony above Piccadilly. Kate could see a lamplighter and his assistant attending to the newfangled gas lamps that had been installed three or four years ago, and were now to be found across London. On the far side of the street lay the undulating acres of Green Park, where deer and cattle grazed, and the trees swayed as the wind picked up.

A gray-and-white bird—Kate thought at first it was a sparrow hawk—flew onto a lamppost across the way. The sounds from outside were muffled, but she could just hear its calls as it struggled to maintain its balance in the wind. It wasn't a sparrow hawk but a cuckoo, and it was the first she had heard this spring. Inside, much more clearly, she could hear the crackle of the fire in the hearth; but above all she was conscious of the nervous pounding of her heart.

The longcase clock in the far corner of the room whirred and then began to chime the hour. Lord Carismont waited until it had finished, and then addressed her again. "I have been given to understand that you are urgently seeking a position as governess?"

"I am, sir. I have been a widow for two years now, and my circumstances do not permit a life of leisure. My last employer, a Norfolk lady, suddenly remarried and decided she no longer required me." *Because she rightly feared her new husband's roving eye.* "I . . . I have references . . ."

"There is no need for references, Mrs. Kingsley, for the lady in question happens to have the same lawyer as I do, Charles Carpenter, and she spoke warmly to him of your outstanding qualities. She provided the address of your lodgings, and after Charles had spoken to me, he wrote to you."

"I am very grateful, my lord." More grateful than he could possibly know, for Kate was at her wits' end. From being secure in employment and being able to provide a roof over her son's head for the foreseeable future, she suddenly had nothing. She desperately needed a new position, so the communication from Charles Carpenter had come as a very welcome bolt from the blue.

Lord Carismont gave a faint smile. "Do not be grateful yet, Mrs. Kingsley, for nothing has been agreed," he warned.

The cuckoo's calls suddenly became much louder,

and Kate's attention was snatched to the balcony, where the ungainly bird now fluttered on the wrought-iron railing. She was startled, knowing the cuckoo was usually a very timid bird, except when laying its eggs in the nests of others, of course, at which times it was anything but timid. Yet this one, a male she thought, was very open indeed about its whereabouts. She wondered why Lord Carismont had not seemed to even notice the bird; more, she wondered why the hotel cat was also oblivious. It slumbered on in its chair as the noisy cuckoo capered and flapped just a few feet away on the other side of the glass.

Suddenly the bird lost its balance, and fell onto its rump on the balcony. For a moment it sat there looking comically indignant, then jumped to its feet again, and flew up toward the hotel roof. It must have landed on the chimney, because its calls began to echo down to the hearth.

"Have a care! Have a care!"

The words of warning seemed to sound within Kate, for to be sure neither she nor Lord Carismont had uttered them. She glanced around the room, wondering if someone else had come in, but there was no one there. She couldn't have heard anything at all. It was her imagination.

The candles swayed and the fire flared as the wind drew down oddly into the room. A ribbon of sparks curled out of the flaming coals, twisting and coiling upon themselves in a serpentine motion. Fascinated, Kate gazed at them.

Lord Carismont addressed her again. "Mrs. Kingsley, I gather your husband left you poorly provided for, and that he died as a result of a duel?"

She dragged her concentration together again. "That is so, my lord, although with your leave I would rather not talk about him, especially not the circumstances of his death." Talking about Michael often made her cry, and that was the last thing she wished to happen now.

His dark eyes regarded her thoughtfully, but he

nodded. "As you wish. Perhaps we should speak of
your son instead. May I ask his name?"

"Justin."

"How old is he?"

"Eight.

"The same age as my daughter."

His gaze swept over her, taking in her agreeable
looks, neat figure, and simple merino gown, long-
sleeved, with a drawstring high beneath her breasts.
The gown was leaf-green, like her eyes, and the
golden-brown pattern on her cashmere shawl was the
same color as her hair. It was heavy hair, with just a
hint of natural curl, and he imagined she had worked
hard to pin it in the fashionable knot at the back of
her head. She was about thirty, neither beautiful nor
plain, neither fashionable nor entirely unfashionable,
and there was a lively intelligence in her eyes. Most
men would be happy to come home to such a woman.

He spoke again. "I trust I have not embarrassed
you by reserving accommodation here in your name?
The Pulteney is the best that London can provide, and
I wish you and your son to be comfortable."

"We are, my lord. Very comfortable." Kate had not
known such luxury since Michael was alive. Certainly
it was a vast improvement upon the damp, shabby
lodgings in Upper Thames Street, which was all her
meager savings could afford.

He continued, "Regardless of the outcome of this
interview, the rooms here are at your disposal for the
next month."

"You are very generous, my lord." She took in his
appearance as much as he had done hers. Gerent
Fitzarthur, fourth Lord Carismont, was about thirty-
five, maybe a year or so younger, she couldn't really
say. He was tall, with broad shoulders and a romanti-
cally handsome face. His dark-lashed eyes were as
gray as the winter seas of his native Cornwall, and
there was a hint of sadness about him that touched
her heart, for he had tragically lost his wife about
two years ago.

Disdain for the hothouse atmosphere of London's high society was evident in his tanned complexion; clearly he preferred a rugged, outdoor life to that of overheated, candlelit drawing rooms. His dark hair was tousled and damp, because he had been riding to the hotel from a late airing in Hyde Park when the heavy shower began. His immaculate top hat, gloves, and riding crop lay on a nearby table. The hat was specked with rain, and more such spots marked his beautifully tailored pine-green coat. An emerald pin reposed in the rich folds of his muslin neckcloth, and nothing could have been more perfect than his rose marcella waistcoat. His hips were lean, and his long, well-shaped legs were shown to advantage by close-fitting cream corduroy breeches.

Behind him, the ribbon of sparks continued to play, twisting and turning, skimming over the fire as if reluctant to flee up the chimney to the cold, darkening air. The cuckoo's noise still racketed down the chimney into the quiet room, but then the double-noted calls became a succession of furious squawks. Soot showered over the fire, and from the scuffles and other frantic sounds Kate could tell the clumsy bird had overbalanced again, this time partially falling into the chimney.

At last the cat's ears twitched, and its green eyes opened wide. Lord Carismont still did not turn to look at anything. He seemed totally unaware of either the cuckoo or the decidedly odd sparks. How could he possibly fail to hear the din in the chimney? Or see the soot that had cascaded over the hearth? Surely it wasn't all a figment of her imagination? Kate was perplexed, but had to hide a little smile as she listened to the cuckoo's furious indignation. It really was a jester of a bird.

"Plague take it! Plague take it! Why did the evil trollop have to come here? London chimneys are without a doubt the filthiest in the land!"

Kate was jolted by the angry clarity with which the sentence was uttered. But who was it? She looked at Lord Carismont. She must have allowed her attention to wander and thus not heard him properly, for *surely* he would not speak of trollops! "Forgive me, sir, I . . . I didn't quite hear what you said."

"Said? About the rooms here being at your disposal?"

"No, about London chimneys."

He looked at her as if she had taken leave of her senses. "I haven't mentioned London chimneys, Mrs. Kingsley, nor can I think of any reason why I would."

"Nor I, sir. Please forget I asked." She felt very foolish, yet she had definitely heard someone say something, the cuckoo's antics still sent soot floating down over the fire, and she was sure the mysteriously animated sparks were avoiding it. All of these things were impossible, of course. Weren't they? Oh, this was quite ridiculous! What on earth was the matter with her? This interview was of the upmost importance.

Lord Carismont arrested her thoughts yet again. "Mrs. Kingsley, you do understand that my daughter, Genevra, is not strong? She almost drowned two years ago, and has never really recovered from the ordeal." He hesitated. "I must be honest and also warn you that she has become difficult of late."

Kate noticed how he avoided her eyes, and wondered if there was more to Genevra's changed behavior than he was admitting.

He continued, "She had until recently been receiving tuition from the curate of St. Thomas's in Trezance, but unfortunately he has been in such poor health recently that he has been obliged to take the cure in Bath. I would have sought another such tutor for her, but then decided it might be more appropriate to engage a governess from now on."

"I understand, my lord."

"Mrs. Kingsley, my daughter and your son are clearly two very different children. Do you anticipate any problems because of this?"

"Problems? Why should there be?"

"As I said, Genevra can be difficult."

"All children can be difficult, my lord, and your daughter has had much to endure."

He met her gaze. "It would appear you have heard about my wife."

"Yes." Who had not? Two years ago in 1816, only a few days before Michael's death, all the newspapers had been full of the shocking demise of Selena, Lady Carismont. It happened on the last night of April— May Eve—when a high spring tidal surge washed her from the quarter-of-a-mile-long causeway that linked Carismont Island to the Cornish shore. Genevra had almost died, too, but had been rescued by her father.

Lord Carismont went to look out at Piccadilly, where the light of the streetlamps was distorted by the rain on the glass. "Mrs. Kingsley, I fear I have indulged Genevra, mayhap to a fault."

"It is understandable, given the circumstances of her mother's death."

He glanced at her over his shoulder. "With all due respect, no matter how thoroughly the newspapers may have reported at the time, you do not know the actual circumstances of Selena's demise. And like you, I do not wish to discuss it. We both suffered a loss at about the same time, and that is that."

Kate felt the admonishment, and her cheeks warmed a little awkwardly. She wished she did not find him so inordinately attractive that everything about him affected her. It was quite ridiculous to let such things get in the way. She was a poverty-stricken widow in need of employment; he was a wealthy nobleman in need of a governess for his motherless daughter. That was all.

She looked quickly away from him toward the fire, where the astonishing sparks now commanded the cat's alert and unwavering attention. There was no longer any soot falling, so she guessed the cuckoo had scrambled out of the chimney again, but she could still hear it chuntering irascibly, as if annoyed with its own awkwardness. Never before had she come across such a very unusual cuckoo. Had it been a parrot, she could have almost understood—but a *cuckoo*?

Lord Carismont turned back to face her fully. "Do you love your son, Mrs. Kingsley?" he asked suddenly.

"Of course I do."

"Would you consider sending him away to Eton?" He watched her face carefully.

"Eton?" The question took her by surprise. "That could never arise, my lord."

"It could if I were to offer to pay for his education."

Kate regarded him for a long moment. "If you made such an offer, sir, I would turn it down."

"May I ask why?"

"Because Justin doesn't want to go away to school, and I love him far too much to force such a thing upon him. So if you wish to employ me without my son, there is no point in continuing this interview."

He smiled and raised a hand. "Please don't take offense, Mrs. Kingsley, for I was merely curious to see your reaction."

His smile touched her senses, and she struggled to give no outward sign. "Well, now you have seen it, sir. And lest you think I too am an overindulgent parent, let me say that I am firm with him. I simply do not agree with sending young children away from home. I think it a cruel practice."

"There is no need to defend yourself, for I am in full agreement with your sentiments."

"You are?"

"Oh, yes. I was sent away to school, and I hated every miserable moment. I just wondered how . . . er, ambitious you are." He turned to the French window once more to watch the rain. "Mrs. Kingsley, are you aware that Genevra always resides in Cornwall?"

"At Carismont Castle? Yes."

"I reside there too, but am often obliged to come to London on business of one sort or another. It is an estate matter that brings me here now. Genevra never accompanies me, even though I have a house in Berkeley Street. Since her mother's death, Genevra has refused to leave the island, not even to go to the town of Trezance, which is only a few hundred yards away over the causeway." He exhaled heavily. "She needs to be given her childhood back again."

"I understand, sir."

"How do you feel about residing on a small Cornish island?" he asked.

"I am not fond of town life."

"And your son?"

"He prefers the countryside too. Most children do, I think."

The rain lashed the windows, and the cuckoo fluted in grumbling tones on the rooftop. Once again, the draft drew down the chimney and brightened the fire, where the green and pink sparks now swarmed like midges after a summer shower. The cat sat up, its hackles beginning to stand as it continued to watch the fire. From the corner of her eye, Kate noticed that there was one spark that was larger than the others—about an inch in diameter, she guessed. It was also lavender in color, and seemed able to hover, as if it had invisible wings. Kate closed her eyes, then opened them again, but the lavender light was still there. She was overtired and seeing things, she decided, needing to find a rational explanation. Yet, no, it couldn't be just her imagination, for the cat had noticed something too. And it was hardly an overtired feline, for the wretched creature slept nearly all the time.

Lord Carismont spoke again. "Mrs. Kingsley, I believe you are already aware of the original terms of employment?"

She felt as if he had arrived at a sudden decision, for she detected a firm new note in his voice. "Original? There has been a change?"

"Yes, Mrs. Kingsley, one of considerable importance. But before I explain, let me assure you that this change has only just occurred to me, and I have not been deliberately conducting this interview under false pretenses."

"False pretenses?" she repeated warily.

"It has become clear to me that it is not the post of governess I should be offering you, but . . . that of my wife."

2

Mayhem seemed to break out the moment Lord Carismont uttered his astonishing proposal. In the fireplace the flames leaped high above the coals, and with a sound that was almost like a high-pitched scream, the lavender spark erupted into the room. Followed by its much smaller companions, it zigzagged furiously above the furniture, as if in a frenzy of rage.

Then the cuckoo swooped down to the balcony again, fluting its customary song as it danced—what seemed to a completely bemused Kate—a little hornpipe. Wings folded, it hopped from one leg to the other, and twirled around with its tail feathers spread. If a bird could grin, this one certainly did, for it was an open-billed picture of feathered delight!

"Hey, nonny! Hey, nonny, no!"

As the voice sounded within her a third time, Kate decided she must have gone quite, quite mad. Yes, that was it. She was only fit to be locked away in the farthest corner of some bedlam! She was seeing and hearing things, and now believed she had received an offer of marriage from the most devastatingly attractive lord in England! Only a female lunatic would believe *that*!

"Hey, nonny! By Gawain's galoshes! There is some justice! There is indeed!"

Kate's expression was fixed. She wouldn't listen. That was it. She would pretend not to have heard anything at all!

Lord Carismont, who apparently was still unaware of anything at all, was puzzled by her silence. He smiled a little self-consciously. "Is my proposition so unthinkable?" he asked quietly.

"I—" Suddenly it was all too much, and Kate knew she had to *say* something. "Lord Carismont, there are some very strange things going on around us. Some very strange sparks are flying furiously around the room like a swarm of insects, and there is a cuckoo on the balcony that I could swear is dancing a hornpipe." She drew a line at mentioning voices in her head!

"Dancing a what—?" Startled, he turned to look, just as a gust of wind drove more rain against the glass, obscuring everything. But when it cleared a little, and the capering cuckoo was revealed, he only shook his head. "I see nothing, Mrs. Kingsley."

"Nothing? But it is there. Look!" She pointed.

Still, he shook his head.

Confounded, Kate hurried to fling the windows open to the wet, windswept darkness. The rain dashed her face, and the gusting air caught her skirts as she stood within two feet of the astonishing bird, which paused in its capering, cocked its head on one side to look beadily up at her, then went on with its ungainly performance. Everything about it exuded joy, as if something really wonderful had just happened.

Lord Carismont joined her and looked out, but again shook his head. "I see nothing, Mrs. Kingsley," he repeated.

Bewildered, but forced to accept that he really could not see the cuckoo, Kate closed the windows once again. "What of the sparks?" she inquired as the lavender light skimmed past her nose as if it would take the tip off.

"I see no sparks either." But this time his denial did not ring quite so true. Maybe he couldn't see the idiotic cuckoo, but Kate would have laid odds that he was fully aware of the lavender spark's ricocheting progress. However, short of calling him a liar, there was not much more she could say, so she made the door secure again. As she did so, both sparks and cuckoo disappeared. The cat stretched and yawned, then returned to the chair, curled up, and went back to sleep. Normality returned, and with it a feeling of intense foolishness for Kate.

"No doubt it is all an effect of the lights in the street reflecting through the rain," she murmured resignedly, although she knew full well that it had nothing to do with reflections.

Lord Carismont smiled. "I think you are right. However, we digress, for the subject of marriage had been raised, had it not?"

He spoke briskly, too briskly, Kate thought. He was trying to pass the moment off when he knew full well that some of what she said was true. But at least she hadn't imagined the proposal!

"Mrs. Kingsley," he went on, "I will try to explain my reason for making such an offer. Carismont Castle is very isolated, being built on a small island that is cut off from the mainland at all but low tide, and when I am absent, I wish to be certain that Genevra is in truly loving and careful hands. My thoughts in this are all of her, for it has become increasingly clear that she needs a woman's guidance. Mrs. Pendern, the housekeeper, does her best, but Genevra is too much for her along with everything else. A governess might seem to be the ideal solution, but such a person has no authority in a household. Lady Carismont, however, would have all the authority in the world."

Kate struggled to put the past few minutes behind her. "I . . . cannot deny your reasoning, Lord Carismont, but why on earth do you put this proposition to *me*? We both know that I am a very unlikely Lady Carismont. You and I spoke for the very first time only a few moments ago, so we do not know each other at all, and anyway, you are a wealthy and very eligible widower who could no doubt have his pick of London. Why take on an impoverished widow with a child?"

"Mrs. Kingsley, you are everything I require. Genevra needs a mother again, and your answers today have shown that you put your child before yourself. I don't want a wife who will expect to reside in London for half the year, or whose thoughts are all of the Season and how much of the social whirl she can force into her diary. Nor do I want a wife in every meaning of the word, just someone who can care properly for Genevra. To put it another way, I want someone who is more than a governess, but less than a complete wife. You will have your own accommodation at the castle, and I will never demand a husband's rights, but you *will* be Lady Carismont, with all the authority, privilege, and respect that the title warrants. All I ask in return is that you care for my daughter as if she were your own, and bestow upon her as much as you can of the love that you give your boy. I am desperately anxious for her, and must do all I can to save her from—" He broke off, clearly thinking twice about what he had been about to say.

"Save her from what, sir?" Kate prompted.

"Oh, nothing. It was just a figure of speech."

Again, she did not believe him. Handsome and charming as he was, Lord Carismont was not entirely honest. She could not think why he was being so sparing with the truth, but then there was much about him that defied explanation, not least his desire to have Kate Kingsley as his wife! "And if I refuse your proposal?" she inquired.

"Then I will look for someone else. I am afraid that marriage is now essential." The sound of the rain on the glass seemed inordinately loud in the silence that followed. He watched the expressions on her face. "If you accept, you may be assured that Justin will be well provided for, as indeed you will too. There will never again be a need to worry about where the next farthing is to come from."

Rightly or wrongly, she knew she wanted to take Lord Carismont's incredible offer. She had nothing to lose and everything to gain from such a marriage—and so did Justin. But if she accepted, would her son understand? He had loved his father very much—too much for her to make this decision without consulting him first. "My lord, I . . . I feel I should speak with my son before I give any answer."

"Of course."

"What of Genevra? Should you not . . . ?"

"Consult with her. In a perfect world I would do just that, but there is no time. I have to be back at Carismont for the whole of the last week of the month, and I wish to be married before leaving London."

Kate's eyes widened. "So quickly? But—"

"The matter is not open for discussion, Mrs. Kingsley. If you decide to accept my proposal, we will be married within the week, and will leave for Cornwall immediately afterward."

"But a wedding cannot be arranged so—"

"Quickly? But it can, Mrs. Kingsley, especially if one has friends in the necessary high places. A special license will be acquired in time. As for any other arrangements, let me say that I do not plan an immense society gathering."

The April shower ended as suddenly as it had begun, and the evergreens and grass in the park glinted wetly in a flash of fading sunset. Lord Carismont crossed the room to her, and raised her hand to his lips. "I rather think I have given you enough to think about for today, so I will leave you now and, with your permission, call again at noon tomorrow?"

"You will have my answer then."

"Good night, Mrs. Kingsley."

"Good night, Lord Carismont."

He picked up his things from the table, and went to the door, but there he paused again. "Perhaps there is one more thing I should tell you before you make any decision."

"Yes?"

"Most gentlemen have a favorite hound that accompanies them wherever they go. I am a little different, for at Carismont I keep a tame leopard."

"A . . . leopard?" Kate repeated faintly.

"Yes. He is called Belerion, which is the old Cornish name for Land's End, and he has the full run of the castle and island." He smiled again, and then left the room.

As the door closed behind him, Kate opened the French windows and stepped out onto the balcony. The April darkness was chill and damp, and filled with the promise of more showers to come. The wind still blustered, and the sound of wheels and hooves on cobbles was interspersed with the splash of puddles. Late pedestrians hurried to their destinations while they had the chance, a newsboy shouted the latest headline, and a woman selling flowers importuned passersby to buy her "sweet daffydillies." Piccadilly was always busy, no matter what the weather or time of day.

Directly below her, at the hotel steps, a rain-soaked groom in the Pulteney's livery was holding the reins of a superb—but equally wet—cream Thoroughbred. As she looked down, Lord Carismont emerged from the main entrance and flicked a coin to the groom, who immediately removed the blanket. Lord Carismont mounted, gathered the reins, and rode away eastward along the street.

As Kate gazed after him, it suddenly seemed that the hooves of his horse were the only ones she could hear in the crowded street. Then the London night fell away, and she was watching him from a north-facing oriel window set high in a castle wall. She knew it faced north, because the sun was beginning to set to her left. The castle was on a rocky hill in the middle of oak woodland, where the birdsong was shrill and glorious. A long clearing, bright with wildflowers, stretched away from the foot of the hill, and at the far end of it, there was . . . Kate could not quite see, for everything in the distance shimmered in a haze, but she thought she could just make out an inlet or creek, and a sailing vessel of some sort.

Lord Carismont was riding away from her along the clearing. Suddenly the lavender light darted toward him out of the distant haze, and Kate felt a stab of alarm. He was in danger! He should turn back! Now! Immediately! She pressed her hands to her cheeks, wanting to scream a warning to him, but no sound would come. The light skimmed closer, but then, just as it seemed it must achieve its goal, a leopard bounded from somewhere below the oriel window. Growling and snarling, it hurled itself forward, and the light sheered away as if afraid.

Kate was sure she heard a high-pitched shriek of fury as the light tried to fly at Lord Carismont from a different angle, but then the cuckoo appeared as well. It jabbed the light with its curving, pointed beak, then joined with the leopard to pursue it back along the clearing toward whatever was lost in the hazy distance. Kate was sure she glimpsed the glint of water. Maybe it was a river.

She continued to stare along Piccadilly, observing a scene that she knew could not possibly be there.

"Mama?"

She whirled about with a start as Justin spoke behind her. "Oh, Justin! I . . . I didn't realize you were there!"

He came out on to the balcony, and looked curiously in the direction she had been staring. "What were you looking at?"

"Oh, it was nothing," she said quickly, and ran her fingers fondly over his blond hair. He was a handsome boy, blue-eyed and golden, just like his father. *But please let him grow up to be indifferent to the temptation of cards . . .*

"Did Lord Carismont offer you the position?" Justin asked.

Her glance fled along Piccadilly again, but all she saw now was the crowded thoroughfare. Lord Carismont had passed out of sight in the throng. "Yes, he did, but I haven't made up my mind yet," she replied, and ushered Justin back into the room.

She closed the French windows, and the silence of the hotel folded over them both as the boy frowned. "Haven't made up your mind? But I thought you *had* to take the post, Mama."

"There is a condition." On impulse she crouched before him and took him gently by the shoulders. "Justin, Lord Carismont doesn't just want me to be a governess, he wants me to be his wife as well. So his daughter, Genevra, will have a mother again."

Justin drew back slightly. "But you can't be her mother, you're *mine*!"

"And I will always be your mother, my darling, but—"

"You can't be his wife, either, because you're Papa's wife!" Tears sprang to the boy's eyes, and he tore from her grasp and ran from the room.

Kate gazed regretfully after him. She should have thought a little more before telling him. As it was she had been too blunt. A gentler, more roundabout approach would have been far wiser. Slowly she rose to her feet. Well, it was done now. She would leave it for a while, and then speak to him again.

Standing there on her own in the room, she began to realize how very much she wanted to accept Lord Carismont's proposal. She barely knew him, yet she wanted to be his wife. She closed her eyes, as if on opening them again she would be restored to sanity. But the hope was in vain, for the desire to take that wild leap into the marital dark was still there. She turned to look at the fire. It was just a fire, glowing coals and gently licking flames, but in her mind's eye, the sparks still performed their serpentine dance, coiling and uncoiling, glittering and flashing, as they followed their lavender leader.

3

Kate saw the woods again that night. It was well past midnight, and she turned in her sleep as another fierce April shower rattled the window of her bedroom at the front of the Pulteney. She remained asleep as a hackney coach passed along Piccadilly, but in her dreams she awoke because the cuckoo was in her room. More than that, it was actually on the bed!

She sat up with a gasp, and found herself in a different bedroom entirely from the one in which she had gone to sleep. She was in the castle again, for she recognized the oriel window, through which streamed bright spring sunshine. Several casements were open, but instead of the sounds of Piccadilly, she heard the piercing clamor of birdsong. The Pulteney's neat, un-canopied fawn-and-white-striped bed had become a huge four-poster, and was extravagantly draped with gold-embroidered ruby velvet. Built of dark, heavily carved oak, with a mattress so deep and soft that it felt like swansdown, she guessed it dated at least back to Tudor times. There was someone sleeping beside her, but she could not see who it was.

The cuckoo had been perched on the footboard, but now fluttered on to the tapestry coverlet. She stared at the bird, knowing that no matter how real all this seemed, it was actually only a dream. She was asleep in the Pulteney, and what she was looking at now was the work of her imagination. The cuckoo hopped toward her, and she automatically held out her hand. As the bird jumped lightly onto her wrist, gripping through the gathers and frills of her nightgown cuff, the voice she had heard before spoke in her head again. Just one word this time. *"Window."* With the cuckoo still on her wrist, she got out of the bed and went to the oriel.

The view outside was the same as before, with the clearing through the oak woodland, and the distance still blurred by a heat haze. She knew the sea was somewhere nearby, and was sure that it reached narrowly into the land at the far end of the clearing. The only thing that was distinct at that point was the lavender light. Somehow, in spite of the sunshine, it was clearly visible, hovering just on the edge of the haze, as if someone with a colored lantern had just emerged from a bank of mist.

The cuckoo cocked its head and stared toward the light, and another word entered Kate's head. *"Wicked."* Did the voice belong to the bird? No, that was impossible. Parrots spoke, and mynah birds, as well as a few others, such as starlings. But cuckoos? No, definitely not.

Then her attention was drawn out of the window again as she heard the slow hooves of a single horse approaching at a walk. *"Protect! Protect!"* The cuckoo wobbled and flapped on her wrist as she leaned out of the nearest casement to look down at the steep, rocky incline of the hill. She saw no castle entrance, just a curtain wall broken by small arched windows. At the foot of the wall, curving around from the left—or west—there was a narrow track that made its precipitous way down toward the clearing. Lord Carismont rode into view on his cream horse, the leopard padding beside him. As before, she feared for his safety.

"Protect! Protect! Protect!" the voice insisted inside her, and the cuckoo fluttered with such urgency on

her wrist that she was *sure* the voice belonged to it. The urgency of the repeated word intensified her fear for Lord Carismont. He mustn't go into the woods, he mustn't! She called down to him. "Gerent! Please stay! I beg of you!" His first name came as naturally as if she had known him all her life.

The cuckoo took to its wings, its two-noted song echoing along the wall as it swooped down past the horse and rider. Lord Carismont glanced up at the oriel, and as his eyes met Kate's, she felt the shock of her own raw emotion. Love for him pierced her like a lance, and she was desperate to save him. From what, though? She didn't know, but words spilled from her lips anyway. "Don't go, Gerent! Stay with me! She means you harm! Great harm!" she cried, but he looked away again, and continued to ride down the steep, dangerous way.

The cuckoo fluttered onto the leopard's back, fluting earnestly, as if pleading for the big cat to do something, but the leopard merely flattened its ears and padded on. Furious to find itself ignored, the cuckoo flew onto the track ahead of Gerent, and rushed forward a few steps, cuckooing and flapping as it tried to make him turn back the way he had come. But he rode on in such a way that the aggrieved bird was forced to hop aside or be trampled under hoof. Unaccustomed to such treatment, it jumped peevishly back onto the track behind Gerent, and directed some decidedly abusive notes after him, his horse, and his unhelpful leopard.

Kate was still distraught about the man she loved. "Come back, Gerent!" she pleaded. "If you go, you will never return! Please, Gerent! For pity's sake, *listen* to me!"

But he rode steadily on, and was now nearly at the foot of the castle hill. The breeze stirred, and the wildflowers of the clearing nodded seductively. The lavender light glided toward him, and Kate heard a woman's voice, soft and bewitching. *"You're quite safe. No harm can befall you. Come to me, my beloved, and know only happiness."* As the light reached him, it wove around his face as if caressing him, and there was something so beguilingly beautiful about it that Kate was transfixed.

Then there came a frightening new sound that stilled the birdsong in the woods. Even the cuckoo fell silent at the crashing, foaming rush of approaching water. Kate's fleeting moments of torpor vanished, and were replaced by increased panic. There was so little time! So little time! She had to *make* Gerent turn back before it was too late! She screamed his name over and over, her voice catching with sobs.

The cuckoo flew at Gerent, trying to snatch the light in its beak, and at last the leopard snarled. Leaping up at the light, it swiped at it with unsheathed claws. Kate was *sure* she heard a squeal of fear—or was it a cry of rage?—then the light broke away and fled back along the clearing toward the misty horizon. As the cuckoo and leopard gave chase, the roaring water grew louder than ever, although Kate couldn't see where it was coming from.

At last Gerent reined his horse in, and turned to look at the oriel. "Kate?"

"Ride back, Gerent! You haven't much time!"

"But, I must save Genevra—"

Kate didn't hear any more because at that moment Justin's voice echoed over his words. "Mama? Mama, please come inside!"

Everything began to spin—lights, sounds, sensations—then with a sickening jolt she awoke and found herself standing out on the hotel balcony above Piccadilly. It was dark and cold, and she felt the rain on her face. She could have wept with frustration and dismay, for not only did she not know the outcome of what she had just witnessed, but a very unpalatable fact had to be faced; she had walked in her sleep again. Just as happened so often during her childhood, she had left her bed and wandered around in her sleep. After all these years being blessedly free of it, suddenly it had returned.

For a moment her thoughts were in such confusion that she resisted Justin's imploring hands as he tried to pull her back inside. Then she managed to collect herself, and glanced into the unlit hotel drawing room. To her further dismay she saw people in the doorway, their figures brightened by the night-light in the corridor behind them. There were servants in their nightclothes, and fellow guests, all staring at her as if she were a lunatic. Mortified color rushed hotly into her cheeks as she stepped reluctantly in from the balcony.

A footman carrying a candlestick came hesitantly toward her. "Are you all right, madam?"

"Yes . . . I'm afraid I walked in my sleep."

"Do you require a doctor, madam?"

"No, of course not. I'm perfectly well."

A guest whose slumber had been interrupted by Justin's anxious calls, cleared his throat grumpily. He was an elderly military gentleman with a black skullcap on his balding head, wearing a scarlet brocade dressing gown that brushed the floor. "Madam, if you are given to marching around in your dishabille, I suggest you make sure you cannot open your door of a night."

"I will do so, sir, but I was not aware that I would do such a thing. It was a childhood trait that I believed to be long over and done with."

"Well, it *isn't* over and done with, and what's more, you screeched like a banshee. I don't know who in the devil you were dreaming about, but—!"

Kate interrupted. "You have made your point, sir. I apologize for having disturbed you, and I will do all in my power to ensure that it does not happen again."

"Good." With that he turned on his heel and stomped away, his Turkish slippers slapping on the polished floor. The others went back to their rooms as well, leaving Kate and Justin alone in the drawing room.

Justin looked uneasily up at his mother in the faint light from the open doorway. "Are you sure you're all right, Mama?"

"Yes, of course," she said reassuringly, and crouched down to take him by the arms. "Did I frighten you very much?"

"Well, just a little," he confessed. "I heard the door of your room open, and you just walked out in your nightgown. Your eyes were open, but you didn't seem to hear me when I spoke to you. You left the suite without putting on your robe or slippers, and I became quite alarmed. I followed you down here. You went out on to the balcony and began to call out to someone. You called really loudly and seemed to be terribly upset with whoever it was." The boy hesitated. "I . . . thought you called 'Gerent.' Isn't that Lord Carismont's name?"

The color rushed back into her cheeks. "Oh, I'm sure you must have misheard. I can't remember what I was dreaming about, but I wouldn't have spoken so familiarly to Lord Carismont."

"No, I suppose not." Justin looked at her. "I didn't know you sleepwalked when you were small."

"I'd forgotten all about it. It happened when I was just a little older than you, and it was quite a nuisance for a while, but then it stopped as suddenly as it had begun."

"Why has it started again?"

Kate straightened. "I wish I knew. Anyway, I will make sure I don't leave our rooms again. I'll lock the door and give the key to you. We don't want to disturb General Grumpy again, do we?"

This last was said lightheartedly, and Justin grinned, relaxing visibly as he perceived his mother to be fully herself again. Then he returned to seriousness. "Mama, do you really want to marry Lord Carismont?"

"I want to provide us both with security," she replied, knowing she wasn't really answering the question. If she were honest, she'd say yes, she *did* really want to marry Lord Carismont . . . or Gerent, as she could not help thinking of him now. There was a great deal she could not help about herself where that gentleman was concerned, especially now that her dreams had intervened. Her sleeping self loved him to distraction; maybe her waking self was halfway there too. Love at first sight? Possibly. Certainly something had happened to her when she first saw him by the fireplace . . .

Justin was still perplexed. "But what of Papa? And how can you be someone else's Mama as well as mine?"

"Oh, my darling, I will never forget your Papa, but he has gone now, and will not come back. As for me being someone else's Mama, well, I will be Genevra's *stepmama,* which isn't quite the same. She had a mother of her own too, but lost her, as you lost Papa. I will never be her mother, merely her stepmother. And if I marry Lord Carismont, he will be your stepfather, not your father."

"A sort of next-best-thing, you mean?"

She smiled. "Something like that. No one can ever take the place of the person you've lost. What happens is they make a place of their own in your life. A new place for a new person."

"What do you think she is like? Genevra, I mean," he asked.

"I really do not know."

"Will I meet Lord Carismont tomorrow?"

"Yes, if you wish to."

"I think I ought to, don't you? I mean, if he's going to be my stepfather . . ."

It was consent, and Kate smiled. "Are you quite sure you agree to this, Justin?"

"Yes. If you think it is a good idea, then I do too."

She hugged him tightly, then they returned to their suite. Later, she lay awake in her bed, pondering the strangeness of the hours since Gerent Fitzarthur entered her life. Things had developed within a minute or so of speaking to him, commencing with the odd sparks in the fireplace. As a child, she had become accustomed to sleepwalking and peculiarly vivid dreams. But that was as a child; she really did not want to start all that again now! Maybe today was just an isolated occurrence, brought on by the tensions and worry of her impoverished situation. She was so desperate to be secure again that she was in a pother. "Yes, cause and effect," she told herself firmly.

But her fingers were crossed beneath the bed-clothes.

4

At noon the following day Kate waited nervously with Justin in the Pulteney's public drawing room. She wore the leaf-green merino again, but wished she had put on the daisy-embroidered white muslin instead. It was too late now, however, and the green would have to do.

Unlike the evening before, other guests were in the room today. Kate had been conscious of a lull in the conversation and a few exchanged glances when she and Justin first entered the room. Evidently word had spread of her eccentric peregrinations during the night, but thankfully the fleeting stir was now at an end. Some guests wrote letters, while others read newspapers, but the largest group by far was a chattering party of Yorkshire gentry, all related and all possessed of a loud, braying way of talking. They sounded, Kate decided, like overexcited donkeys anticipating a feast of carrots.

The black cat again graced the fireside armchair, comfortably asleep instead of being about its proper business of catching hotel mice. The French windows were closed, muffling the noise of Piccadilly, but Kate could just hear the jaunty music of a hurdy-gurdy by the lamppost opposite. It was playing the old English round song, "Sumer Is Icumen In." There was no cuckoo this morning, nothing out of the ordinary at all, it was just a beautiful April day, and the park looked very green and fresh indeed after all the rain.

Justin shuffled his feet. "I do hope Lord Carismont is on time," he said.

"So do I."

The boy fidgeted, picking at the brass buttons of his short maroon tailcoat, then tugging his top boots, which had a tendency to wrinkle over the shins. He was wearing what he termed his "grown-up" clothes, rather than his more usual waist-length jackets and frilled, wide-collared shirts. "Is there *really* a leopard at the castle?" he asked.

"That is what Lord Carismont said to me." And it is true, for I have seen it in my dreams, she thought.

"Do you think I will be able to touch it?"

"Only if Lord Carismont says you may, and certainly only if it is tame enough to be trusted."

"I will ask him," Justin vowed, and then changed the subject yet again. "Mama, you were not the only one to have a strange dream last night."

"Oh?"

"Yes. When I went back to sleep, I dreamed about Lord Carismont. He and I were at the lake in Green Park, and there were lots of other boys there with sailing boats of all sorts. He had given me a fine model that was a little like a Viking longboat, but not quite. It was painted gold, with silver oars and a crimson sail, and was at least two feet long. It sailed magnificently, and all the other boys were jealous."

"It sounds an agreeable dream."

"It was, and it was so real that I felt I was actually there. Lord Carismont was dressed in a charcoal coat, I remember, with beige pantaloons, and there was a gold pin in his neckcloth."

Kate was uneasy. Yet another strange thing. Justin very seldom remembered his dreams, so for him to recall anything at all was odd, let alone that it should so vividly concern Gerent Fitzarthur!

The cat growled suddenly, and Kate turned quickly to see the animal staring at the fire. The little sparks had appeared again, among them the single lavender light that had been so malevolent in her dream. They all rose out of the fire like a flow of tiny stars, and the cat prepared to pounce, as if they were a gathering of impudent mice. The sparks recoiled slightly from the feline threat, but then continued to snake their patterns above the flaming coals.

Kate swallowed. "Justin? Do you notice anything peculiar about the fire?" she asked, for no one else had even glanced at the fireplace, yet to her the sparks were only too bright and obvious.

"The fire?" Justin turned. "No. In what way do you mean, Mama?"

"Don't you see any dancing lights?"

He looked curiously at her. "What dancing lights?" he asked.

"Oh, it doesn't matter."

A footman entered the room and came over to her. "Lord Carismont has arrived, madam. Shall I conduct him here?"

"Yes, if you please," she replied, and when he had gone, she immediately began to tweak and smooth her gown.

Justin grinned. "Don't worry, Mama, for you look splendid."

"Splendid is one thing I am *not.*"

"You are to me," he insisted, and gave her a quick hug.

She looked at the fire again. The cat was standing now, its back arched threateningly, but then Gerent was shown into the room. And he was dressed exactly as Justin had dreamed, in a charcoal coat and beige breeches, with a gold pin on the knot of his unstarched neckcloth.

Justin was absolutely thunderstruck. His lips parted, his eyes widened, and he gaped as if at a ghost. Kate was startled too, but at the same time a little resigned.

Mysterious things seemed bound to happen when this man was near.

He bowed to her. "Mrs. Kingsley."

"Lord Carismont." Her pulse had begun to race, and a rare excitement ran through her. She was conscious of all the sensations of new love, as intense and affecting as if she were in her teens again. She drank in the perfection of his face, and knew that love at first sight *did* happen; it had happened to her yesterday . . .

Gerent looked at Justin. "Master Kingsley, I presume?"

"Sir."

He turned to Kate. "Have you an answer for me, Mrs. Kingsley?"

She made herself meet his eyes, so steady and clear, so unfathomable. Again, she found herself thinking of the gray winter seas, except there was nothing cold or bleak about him. "Yes, Lord Carismont, I have an answer for you. I accept your proposal."

The lavender spark leaped from the fireplace as if a log had collapsed, and Kate distinctly heard a woman's voice shriek a single word. *"Never!"* The cat leaped at the light as if at a mouse, and as happened the evening before, mayhem broke out in the room. Or perhaps it would be more accurate to promote the situation to outright pandemonium. A hectic pursuit commenced as the cat hurtled everywhere after the fleeing light. A gentleman's cup was jolted into his lap, a lady screamed as the cat ran between her ankles, and an elderly clergyman almost fainted as the animal landed foursquare in the middle of *The Times,* which he held open to read. While all this took place, the spark's fury was audible; at least, it was to Kate. *"Curse you! Leave me be this instant! Leave me be, I say!"*

But the cat had no intention of leaving anything be. Yowling and spitting, it kept at the hated spark as if nothing else mattered, although no one else could see that was what it was doing. To everyone except Kate, the cat merely seemed to have taken leave of its senses. She glanced at Gerent, and knew by his expression that he could see the lavender spark. So there are two of us, she thought, for although Justin was curled up with mirth, she knew the boy was only seeing the cat, not the light it was pursuing.

For a while uproar ruled supreme in the hitherto polite drawing room, but then the maître d'hôtel and several footmen came running. The unfortunate cat was grabbed in no uncertain manner, and as it was borne from the room—still yowling, spitting, and clawing—the relieved lavender light fled to the safety of the fireplace, where it hovered in a way that strongly suggested to Kate that it was gasping for breath. The maître d'hôtel fussed around his guests, doing all he could to placate and reassure them, and when calm had been restored, he and the remaining footmen departed.

Justin ached with laughter. "Oh, how splendid that was. I wonder what was wrong with the cat?"

"I have no idea," Gerent replied.

Kate looked at him, but said nothing.

He smiled, and changed the subject by suddenly taking her hand and drawing it to his lips. "Before we were so rudely interrupted, I rather fancy you had just accepted my proposal, Mrs. Kingsley."

"Yes."

The lavender light pulsed brilliantly above the flames, and Kate distinctly heard its voice, female and vindictive. *"You can't do this, Gerent!"*

He still gave no sign of hearing or seeing anything, instead he spoke to Kate again. "Perhaps it would be more appropriate to call you by your first name? Kate, is it not?"

"Yes."

"You must call me Gerent."

"I . . . I will try." They gazed at each other, and with each beat of her heart, she was further lost to his spell. She felt bewitched by him, and it was a very agreeable feeling.

"Oh, how sweet! How affecting! How unutterably nauseous!" breathed the voice.

Gerent ignored it. "There are arrangements to make, Kate."

"I will not permit it!"

"Arrangements?" Kate managed to say. "Yes, I suppose there are. I . . . I confess I had not considered beyond the moment of acceptance." She tried to marshal her thoughts, but it was very difficult when the disembodied voice kept interrupting. Whose voice was it anyway? she wondered. Beyond knowing that it was a woman, she could even begin to imagine further.

He went on, "As I said last night, I wish the wedding to take place as quickly as possible, for it is imperative that I return to Carismont in time for the last week of April."

"You are wrong if you think you can thwart me. I will have my way, Gerent, and I think you know it."

He continued, "I have anticipated somewhat, Kate, and have already arranged the ceremony for next Monday. I have been promised by all the relevant authorities that the legalities of license and so on will be accomplished in good time."

The light pulsed almost white-hot. *"There isn't going to be a wedding!"* it breathed.

Kate struggled not to show any reaction at all. "I . . . am quite happy with that date, my lord . . . I mean, Gerent."

"Gerent, she can be as happy as a fool in paradise if she likes, but it will avail her of nothing! Not if I have anything to do with it!"

Gerent smiled at Kate. "You will soon be Lady Carismont, then you and Justin will be safe and secure once more. I feel—"

"Safe and secure is one thing she will not be!" the voice interrupted.

He ignored it, and finished what he was saying to Kate. "I feel sure that we will do well together."

At that the voice began to sing tauntingly, and the song it chose was the same old English round song that the hurdy-gurdy had played in Piccadilly. *"Sumer is icumen in, Lhude sing cuccu! Groweth sed and bloweth med, And springth the wude nu. Sing cuccu! Sing cuccu!"* The singing broke off into laughter as a nerve flickered at Gerent's temple. He gave no other sign that he heard anything, but the owner of the voice knew he did, and so did Kate. She also knew the modern English translation of the words. *Summer has come in! Loudly sing cuckoo! Grows the seed and blooms the mead, And springs the woods anew. Sing cuckoo. Sing cuckoo.* As well as being very old, it was also very appropriate to the season, for everything was growing and blooming anew, and the cuckoo was indeed to be heard now!

The laughter died away, and the light flew off up the chimney. It hummed as it went, for all the world like a spiteful woman who was satisfied she had gained the last word. Kate was relieved that the horrid thing had gone, for there would be no more interruptions. Well, for the time being at least.

She couldn't help wondering if beating a retreat was the wisest course for Kate Kingsley as well. Perhaps she should simply grab Justin's hand and go as far away as possible from enigmatic, devilishly attractive, apparently haunted Gerent Fitzarthur. But all the foolishness of fierce new love made her stay.

She hadn't responded to his last remarks, so Gerent cleared his throat. "Kate?"

She gave a self-conscious start. "Forgive me. I . . . I was wondering where the ceremony would take place?"

"In my house in Berkeley Square. I do not intend to announce it across London, so there will be no one from society in attendance. I assure you that this does not signify any disrespect toward you, nor does it mean that I am in any way ashamed of the step we are to take, rather as an indication of my immense reluctance to face society's clacking tongues. Let them clack when we are safely away in Cornwall."

She was relieved that the wedding was to be so quiet,

but Genevra was on her conscience. It seemed so unfair that Justin had been consulted, but Gerent's daughter would not know anything until she was presented with her new stepmother. "Lord Carismont . . . oh, I mean Gerent. Forgive me, but I find it difficult to be so familiar when we hardly know each other. What I wish to say is that I cannot help thinking Genevra should be consulted before we take any irrevocable step."

He smiled at her. "Do not worry about Genevra, Kate. Believe me, she will accept you."

Justin spoke up a little anxiously. "Will she accept me too, sir?"

Gerent crouched in order to reassure him face-to-face. "I am certain that she will, Justin. She has been very lonely, and is in grave need of a friend."

"I will try to be her friend, sir."

"Thank you. It is my earnest hope that she will soon be yours too."

"Sir . . . ?"

"Yes?"

"Do you really, truly have a leopard at Carismont?"

Gerent laughed. "Yes, I do. I call him Belerion."

"How did you get him?"

"Well, twelve years ago there was a shipwreck in the Carismont Bay. Belerion managed to swim ashore. That is all I know of him. He rather adopted me, and has been with me ever since. He never leaves the island, though."

"Is he fierce?" Justin inquired, his eyes wide with fascination.

Gerent smiled and ruffled the boy's hair, then straightened again. "Only with those he does not like. I will introduce you to him, and make certain that he knows you and your mama are my friends."

"Will you really?"

"Of course. Tell me, is there anything you wish to do before leaving London? Anywhere you wish to visit, perhaps?"

"Actually, sir, I really would like to see the Tower of London, especially the Royal Armory."

Gerent looked at Kate. "Would that be in order, Kate?"

"Why, I . . . yes, of course.

He smiled at Justin. "Then the Tower it is. Would you care to go there tomorrow?"

Justin was delighted. "Oh, yes, sir, if you please!"

"I will call for you both in my carriage at eleven." Gerent's face assumed a teasing expression. "Now, in order to insinuate myself still further in your good books, Justin, I have sent a gift up to your suite. It awaits you now."

"Really?" Justin's face brightened with anticipation, and he looked pleadingly at Kate, who nodded.

"Yes, you may go."

"Thank you, Mama!" Justin almost ran off, but remembered his manners in time. Solemnly he bowed to Gerent. "I am pleased to have met you, Lord Carismont."

"And I you, Justin."

As soon as the boy had gone. Gerent conducted Kate to a sofa, and when she was seated, he joined her. "Your son is a credit to you, Kate."

"Thank you." She looked intently at him. "Gerent, are you quite, quite sure you want this marriage? I am perfectly well aware of the advantages to me, and to Justin, but I have yet to be fully convinced that there are many for you."

"Oh, there are, believe me. You are my perfect bride, Kate."

And you are the sort of husband any romantic maiden would dream of, she thought. No, he was more than that, for he was the sort of husband *any* woman would be glad to dream of. Handsome, charming, thoughtful, wealthy, and titled; what more could any bride desire?

"Is there anything you wish to ask me?" he inquired.

Oh, a thousand questions, but the only one she felt able to ask was, "What do you wish me to wear for the wedding?" How lame and stupidly female, she thought.

"You may wear whatever you choose."

"My wardrobe is hardly à la mode."

"Does a fine wardrobe matter to you, Kate?"

"Well, it would be nice to have one, but I am quite accustomed to making do."

"Lady Carismont does not need to make do, Kate. Selena . . . my late wife . . . used to attend Mrs. Camberton in Golden Square, and was always very well pleased with her work. You may go to any couturiere you choose, of course, but I am willing to send word to Mrs. Camberton that she is to expect you. Do you wish me to do that?"

"Yes, please."

"Consider it done. Order as many gowns and whatever as you wish, and they will all be sent on to Carismont. It will take time, of course, and in the interim—"

"And in the interim I will continue to wear what I have now. I fear you will have a very unremarkable bride, sir . . . I mean, Gerent."

"There is nothing unremarkable about you, Kate," he said softly.

Time seemed to stop, and she felt as if he had leaned forward to put his lips to hers. It was a sensation so intense and real that she was sure she could feel his breath upon her cheek. His mouth was soft and yet firm, his kiss knowing and yet tender, stirring emotions she had suppressed since Michael's death. Yet he wasn't kissing her at all. He had not even leaned toward her. Instead he was speaking of other arrangements that had to be attended to before they could set off for Cornwall.

But the imagined kiss still burned upon her lips.

Later, when Gerent had gone and she returned to her suite, Kate found Justin sitting on his bed, playing delightedly with the gift Gerent had given him—a

golden boat about two feet long, with silver oars and
a crimson sail. It was something like a Viking longboat, yet it wasn't.

Justin looked at his mother as she appeared in the
doorway. Neither of them spoke, and a small shiver
ran down Kate's spine. It wasn't a shiver of fear, but
one of excitement and anticipation. Something momentous was beginning, and she did not know what it
was. But as it beckoned, so she followed . . .

5

The Tower of London was at the very eastern edge of the capital, where the land rose to a low hill on the north bank of the Thames. Surrounded on three sides by a moat, and on the fourth by the river, it nestled within a great wall that showed just how formidable a fortress it still was. It comprised an assorted collection of buildings, the most important being the great Norman tower. A great many visitors came each day, to see among other things, the royal jewel house, the armories, and the menagerie. There was already a crush of carriages as Gerent's coachman drew the team of roans to a halt.

Gerent alighted first, and paused to straighten his tall hat. He wore a gray coat, gray-and-black-striped waistcoat, and cream pantaloons, and there was a silver pin in his neckcloth. He carried a cane, and the shine on his Hessian boots was evidence of much elbow grease on someone's part. Everything about him smacked of such fine style and good taste that Kate doubted there could be a more handsome man anywhere in London—perhaps in the whole of England. It was hard to believe that he was not only her escort today, but was about to become her husband. Surely she would awaken in a moment, and find she

was still the hard-pressed Kate Kingsley of a few days
ago, still in desperate need of a new situation in order
to support herself and her son. However, as she
alighted, her hand in his, she knew it was really
happening.

She wished she had something wonderfully fashionable to wear, instead of a peach marguerite gown that
was too high at the waist and too clinging at the skirt,
and a brown fustian pelisse with military tassels and
frogging, both purchased during the freezing January
of 1814. Her brown hat, acquired at the same time,
was of equally military style, and the wry and unflat-
tering thought had crossed her mind that it looked as
if she had stolen it from a barracks!

The entire ensemble had seen three more Januaries
since that first one, but in spite of her sterling and
successful efforts to keep everything in pristine condition, no amount of care could conceal the fact that
she was definitely *not* à la mode. In the spring of 1814,
she had earned many an admiring glance; in the spring
of 1818, the only glances that turned her way were of
astonishment that one such as she should be on the
arm of an arbiter of fashion like Lord Carismont. She
couldn't help wondering how far their jaws would
drop if they knew she was about to become Lady
Carismont. Some of them would no doubt swoon away
from the shock!

Justin ran on ahead as they strolled toward the
Tower gateway. She found herself thinking about the
journey from the hotel. They had stopped at the Lud-
gate Hill premises of the firm of jewelers that was
always patronized by the Fitzarthur family. The elderly assistant who attended them, an owl-faced man
with a tonsure of white hair and a quill tucked behind
his ear, had known Gerent for many years, and was
surprised to hear of his imminent remarriage. He
wished them both every happiness, and raised Kate's
hands to his lips. If he thought her an unlikely and
strangely unfashionable choice for an aristocrat like
Gerent, he gave no indication.

By tradition, all Fitzarthur brides wore rings of the same design, a band of rich red-gold cut with a pattern of roses and oak leaves. A spare ring was always kept in stock because Gerent's great-grandmother had once lost hers while staying on an estate somewhere in the Scottish Highlands, so there was no problem at all in supplying the exact wedding band that was needed. It was a little large, but the jeweler assured her that it would be the correct size in time for the ceremony.

Gerent had then conducted her out to the carriage, where Justin was waiting impatiently for them to continue to the Tower. However, instead of climbing in with her, Gerent had suddenly remembered something and gone back inside. Through the window she had seen him take a slip of paper from his pocket, and place it on the counter. The assistant had inspected it, and nodded. Gerent then came out to the carriage again. He did not say why he had gone back inside, nor did she ask, but she wondered greatly.

Justin's footsteps echoed on the cobbled way as he ran ahead beneath a gateway into a courtyard where yeoman warders in Tudor costume waited to conduct visitors on tours. Of all the things on display at the tower, Kate was most looking forward to the crown jewels, but Justin was so eager to see the armories that they went there first. It was all surprisingly absorbing, so that for a while Kate quite forgot the strangeness of the past day or so, but a sharp reminder was not far away. It happened when they were in the Horse Armoury, a long room that was lined down one side with eerie mounted effigies of past monarchs. Their suits of armor shone in the light from the barred and latticed windows opposite, and the walls and beams were hung with helmets so close-packed that they looked like a huge necklace. Shafts of sunlight lay brightly across the dusty floor, and the voice of a yeoman warder droned as he conducted his party beyond a stand of medieval lances at the far end of the room.

Something, she didn't quite know what, made Kate

turn suddenly to look back at the door through which they had entered. The door gave onto a spiral stone staircase lit only by arrow-slit windows, and for a moment she thought there was nothing there, but then the lavender light bobbed into view. It hovered by the staircase, and she heard its taunting voice inside her.

"If you are wise, you will not dare to fight me!"

It was as clear as if the unknown woman herself stood there, but all Kate could see was the solitary dancing spark, light, star, or whatever it was. She glanced at Justin and Gerent, who had strolled on to listen to what the yeoman warder was saying about the equestrian statue of William the Conqueror.

"Do not imagine Gerent is going to be yours. You aren't worthy, nor do you have the right!" breathed the voice, and the lavender light seemed to become more intense.

The tone goaded Kate. She wasn't about to put up with being spoken to in such a way! Just who or what did this . . . this *thing* imagine it was? Well, it could be the Queen of Sheba for all Kate Kingsley cared. Throwing caution to the winds, she marched back toward the staircase, intent upon a few choice words of her own. She halted about two feet away from the light, which didn't shrink from her, but hovered there almost belligerently. "I am beginning to find you tiresome! Just what is it you want?" Kate demanded, keeping her voice low.

"I want what is mine."

"I take nothing that belongs to anyone else—" Kate broke off as the cuckoo suddenly appeared at one of the arrow-slit windows, and squeezed through into the stairwell. There was a glint in its eyes as it perched on the sloping embrasure and cuckooed at the top of its voice. The fluting sound reverberated up and down the staircase, but when Kate glanced hastily back into the Horse Armoury, no one else seemed to have heard anything.

The moment the cuckoo appeared, the lavender light recoiled in dismay. *"Oh, no! Go away!"*

A second voice now sounded in Kate's head, and

now she was certain it belonged to the bird. *"Ha! So you're at it again, eh? By Mordred's mittens, you're a pesky persistent wench, and no mistake!"* With that the cuckoo launched from the window to try to snatch the light in its claws.

"No! Leave me alone!" the unlovable spark shrieked, as it darted aside to escape.

The cuckoo paid no heed, but lunged again and again, and when it became clear it would not succeed in such a confined space, it contented itself instead with jabbing at the light with its sharp, curved beak. *"Have at you! Come here, you scheming strumpet!"*

Kate watched in amazement, for it was a pantomime worthy of Sadler's Wells, and the curtain only closed when the light finally had the wit to shoot out through the little window. The cuckoo hurled itself after it, and the last Kate saw was an undignified feathered posterior scrambling and squeezing through the narrow slit. Then both hunter and hunted had gone.

Silence returned, with just the yeoman warden's voice holding forth about armor in the reign of Edward I. Numb with amazement, Kate stared at the window, telling herself she could not really have seen what just happened. It was too *mad* to be believed!

"What are you doing back here, Kate?" Gerent asked suddenly. He had come to see what was claiming her attention. Justin remained with the rest of the party on the tour.

Realizing Gerent had seen and heard nothing, Kate summoned a quick smile. "Oh, I'm not doing anything really. I . . . thought I heard someone stumble on the stairs, but there's no one here."

He smiled. "It is to be hoped no one lost their footing, for it's rather a long way to the bottom!"

"That's what I was thinking," she replied, managing a laugh.

Suddenly serious, he looked into her eyes. "Are you having second thoughts, Kate?"

"Second thoughts? No, none at all. If you fear I mean to try to take Selena's place . . ."

"You will make your own place, Kate," he interrupted softly, and suddenly put his hand to her cheek. It was an unexpectedly tender gesture, an intimacy that came from nowhere, but went to every inch of her body.

"I will try to be a good wife, Gerent," she whispered.

"And you will succeed." He stroked her cheek with his thumb, and before she knew it he suddenly bent forward to put his lips to hers. There was nothing imagined this time, he really did kiss her.

She responded. How could she not when he exerted such a bewitching spell over her? She felt him hesitate, but then he took her by the waist and pulled her to him. His kiss became more intimate and searching, more needful. Excitement spread richly through her. Her skin felt warm, the blood seemed to rush along her veins, and a luxurious ache yearned deep inside her. He held her tightly to him, his lips moving over hers in a way that seemed to be the very essence of magic. Wild feelings began to tingle over her, wonderful, gratifying feelings that she had not known in such a long time. Pleasure. Such pleasure. And all from a kiss . . .

He drew back, his eyes dark as they met hers. For a moment there seemed only warmth and desire in his gaze, but then something else was there too. Unease? Alarm? Whatever it was, he let go of her as if he had been apprehended in a crime. "I . . . should not have presumed. Forgive me, and rest assured that it will not happen again."

"Gerent—"

"It was a transgression, Kate, and broke the assurance I gave when I asked you to marry me. I trust you will forget all about it."

Forget it? She didn't *want* to forget it! It had been the most exhilarating, magnificent, exquisite kiss she had ever had in her entire life, and far from wanting to pretend it had never happened, she wanted it to happen again! But he had brought the matter to a close, and his embarrassment told her he had drawn a line beneath the incident.

He summoned an awkward smile. "I think we should return to poor Justin, who will shortly wonder if we have overlooked him." Drawing her hand over his sleeve, he led her back along the Horse Armoury.

6

The day of the wedding arrived in what seemed no time at all. There had not been any further peculiar visions or dreams, sleepwalking, lavender lights, inner voices, or capering cuckoos; in fact, everything seemed almost conventional. Late afternoon came at last, and the April shadows lengthened. In a few minutes it would be time for Kate to go down to the carriage that was waiting to take her from the Pulteney Hotel to the ceremony at Gerent's town house in Berkeley Street.

She looked at herself in the floor-standing glass in the corner of her dressing room. She imagined the stir if word had escaped about Lord Carismont's surprising nuptials. But no one knew. The jeweler and Mrs. Camberton, the couturiere, had observed the discretion that had been requested of them, and so had the various persons in authority with whom Gerent had to consult regarding the hasty marriage. As a result, there was not a single person of consequence to see Kate Kingsley, a complete nobody, become the wife of one of London's most eligible and attractive lords.

Kate could just imagine how ladies of the *ton* would react to her clothes, for her wedding outfit was comprised of a walking dress and matching pelisse that had been fashionable three years ago. Both garments were just plain apple-green silk, and without embellishment except for some pretty piping. The gown had a low, square neckline, and its waistline was fixed high beneath her breasts by a belt of the same material, with an oblong gilt buckle. The sleeves, long and full, were gathered in a frill at the wrists. As always she had spent an age on her hair, but more so than ever today, so that pretty honey-brown curls framed her face under a cream straw bonnet that was decorated with forget-me-nots from her bridal posy.

Justin had bought the posy from the flower seller outside the hotel, and the freshness of the little blooms drifted pleasantly in the warm room as Kate donned one of her few remaining pieces of jewelry, the dainty diamond eardrops Michael had given her as a betrothal gift. Kate's thoughts wandered back to that time.

She had been a minor Herefordshire heiress, and ecstatically happy to be loved and claimed by one of the county's wealthiest, most dashing young men. Kingsley Park was a beautiful estate that dated back to Jacobean times, and in Michael she had a loving husband. He seldom bothered with London, being content to stay in the country with his wife and new son. But then it had all gone wrong. On an unexpected visit to the capital, he fell in with a fast crowd that spent its nights in gaming hells. Almost overnight Michael became more concerned with the turn of the next card than anything else, and he extended his stay in town.

Nothing had ever been the same again. Justin saw little of his father, whose fortune was slipping away like sand. Michael never stopped loving her, or their son, but could not break away from the lure of cards and dice. The circle he moved in now was composed of gentlemen who all drank heavily and lived dangerously, and one night at the beginning of May, in 1816, in a Thamesside tavern, he fell foul of a dangerous stranger. A challenge had been issued, and just after dawn the next morning, they faced each other on Putney Heath. Michael's anonymous opponent, cool, calculating, and conscienceless, fired before the call was given, then slipped from the scene and disappeared. Michael died that night. He had not even left a note for his wife and son, and Kate only learned she was a widow when a brief letter arrived at Kingsley Park from one of his friends, a man named Denzil Portreath, who himself had only heard of the duel by chance.

Those terrible events two years ago had been just the beginning of Kate's difficulties, for as if being widowed were not bad enough, she had also been left with debts that forced the sale of the estate. To provide for herself and Justin, she had then been obliged to seek employment. That was how things had remained. Until now.

She regarded herself in the glass again. What sort of path was she about to follow? A pretty way carpeted with primroses, or a thorny track scattered with sharp stones? Her resolve faltered suddenly. Was she doing the right thing? Or should she have second thoughts? Now before it went any further.

Justin tapped at the door. "Mama? The carriage is here."

"I'm ready," she replied, then glanced down at the fourth finger of her left hand, where the gold of Michael's wedding band still glowed. For a moment the old sadness welled up once more. Part of her would always love Michael Kingsley; but part of her was angry with him too. Everything that had gone wrong had been his doing. Slowly she removed the ring, and placed it on the nearby dressing table. From today Michael would be more in the past than ever, for Gerent was in her life now. Donning her white silk gloves, she picked up her posy and left the room.

Half an hour later, amid the luxury and exquisite good taste of Gerent's blue-and-gold drawing room at Berkeley Street, Kate Kingsley became Lady Carismont. Only Gerent's servants were present, but Kate felt as if other eyes were watching too. She had the strongest feeling that someone was standing by the ivory silk drapes of the farthest window. Once or twice she even turned to look, but there was no one there. Nor were there any sparks or strange lavender lights. The fire was calm and gentle, just amiable little flames bobbing above glowing coals. It was almost as if earlier events had been a fantasy after all. Kate almost hoped they were, for she had no desire for their return.

The ceremony over, Gerent kissed his new bride briefly on the cheek, bade her make herself completely at ease in the house of which she was now mistress, then left the house. To say that Kate was nonplussed by this would be a considerable understatement, for it was the very last thing she had expected him to do. She was upset, even though he had made it plain that theirs would be a marriage of convenience. In truth, Kate didn't know whether or not to be relieved that he had gone out, because now that his ring was actually on her finger, she felt curiously ill at ease with him. But it was too late now. The time for second thoughts had been before she left the Pulteney, not after she had made her vows. She really did not know what to expect of this unusual marriage, and ideally would have liked to use this unexpected time alone to try to assemble her thoughts. This, however, was not to be. First, there was Justin, and second, it soon became clear she would have to assert herself over the servants.

In the eyes of Gerent's Berkeley Street household, his decision to go out on his wedding night reflected poorly upon his new bride, whom the servants had discovered had recently been a governess. This Kate realized with dismay when she overheard two maids giggling about it on the stairs. They ridiculed her wedding clothes, and made it plain they thought she was no better than they were, so she knew she had to put them firmly in their place. She had been mistress of Kingsley Park, and so knew perfectly well how to go on. The mark of authority was in her every sharp word, and the maids scuttled away to the kitchens to warn the other servants that governess or not, she wasn't to be trifled with. After that, when Justin had gone to bed and she was alone at last, the attitude of the footman who brought her a cup of hot chocolate was all that was polite and deferential.

She was in the drawing room, where earlier she and Gerent had been married, but now she was completely alone as she read a book while awaiting his return. It was difficult to know what to do really. Should she retire to her own room? Or play the new wife and await her bridegroom's return? To be honest, she hardly knew what was expected of her at all. She had rushed into this marriage without clarifying anything, except that she was to be a wife in name only. Perhaps she should put her rash actions down to the moon, she thought wryly, as she glanced around the candlelit room for what seemed the hundredth time.

Like the rest of the house, it was furnished in classical style, and thus very fashionable. But it was impersonal, she thought, comparing it unfavorably with the uneven Jacobean coziness of Kingsley Park. Here everything was so precise and balanced that she felt the symmetry was ruined by her presence. Only if she stood in the very middle of the room could balance be maintained, so the fact that she sat here in an armchair beside the fireplace, with her back to the door, quite spoiled the effect.

It was a masculine room too, she decided, with no evidence at all of there ever having been a first Lady Carismont, either here or in the rest of the house. Everything suggested a bachelor residence, which Kate could have understood if Gerent's first wife had always stayed in Cornwall with her daughter, but that was not the case. Kate knew from the newspapers and ladies' journals that Selena, Lady Carismont, had been one of the *beau monde*'s most dazzling adornments, and there had even been whispers that she would become a lady patroness of Almack's. So she had often been here in this house, but for some reason had not left her mark. There wasn't even a likeness of her, although there were paintings and drawings in abundance. In this room alone Kate noted several views of Athens, various drawings of Greek gods and goddesses, a sylvan landscape with nymphs and satyrs, and two interpretations of Daedalus constructing the labyrinth, but not a single portrait of anyone. Come to that, she hadn't seen a portrait anywhere in the house, not even of Gerent's daughter. Maybe it was simply that he did not like portraits.

Kate removed her new wedding ring to examine the pretty design. It was still far too loose, because even though the jeweler had made it smaller, he had not made it small enough. She was sure that unless she was very careful indeed, sooner or later it would slip from her finger without her knowing. As she turned it in the candlelight, she suddenly noticed that it was engraved on the inside as well, not with more roses and oak leaves, or even with a motto, but with five tiny symbols: ᚤᚦᚷᛉᛋᚲ

Unsure if she was seeing them or not, she leaned closer to the lighted candle on the little table by her chair. Yes, they were definitely there, five shapes, each one carefully cut. What were they? They looked vaguely familiar, and yet she could not quite place them. After puzzling a little longer, she replaced the ring on her finger and tried to resume reading the book.

Time passed. There was not much noise in the Mayfair street, just the occasional private carriage. The ticking of the glass-domed clock on the mantel made her drowsy. She was hardly aware of her eyes closing or of the comforting arms of sleep. The candle beside her guttered and went out, and because the tall back of her armchair was toward the door, a maid who glanced in thought she had gone to her bed.

All was quiet, and Kate was deep in a dreamless

slumber when she was suddenly disturbed by the sound of Gerent's raised voice in the room behind her. "For pity's own sake, leave me to live my life! *Please!*"

Kate's eyes flew open, but she did not turn in her chair. The room could not have been more dazzlingly bright had half a dozen grand chandeliers been ablaze, yet she knew there was only one chandelier, and it had not been lit that evening. As the vestiges of sleep began to unravel and flee, she became conscious of something else . . . her new wedding ring was burning into her finger. It felt inordinately tight too, as if her finger had swollen to twice its size while she slept. What was happening? Was she still asleep and dreaming? Even as she thought it, she knew it was not so. This was no prelude to sleepwalking, for she was truly awake.

Gerent spoke again, his tone more measured this time, as if he were resisting something he found sorely tempting. "That will not work either, madam, so pray do not think it will. The time for kisses and caresses is past."

He was with a woman! Pangs of hurt and anger stabbed through her as she remained silently in her chair. They had been married this very day, yet he brought someone else to the house! Was this his way of making sure his new bride did not presume too much? Her thoughts were torn in all directions at once. What was the blinding light? And why was her wedding ring now so tight and hot that she feared it would stop her blood?

The woman must have whispered something in his ear, for he responded with trembling emotion. "Why must you torment me so?" he breathed. "You *know* it is done with. The die is cast, and you must accept it." He exhaled slowly, with a sensuousness that told of caresses received and not entirely spurned.

Kate was in a quandary. He had every reason to think she had retired, and that he was therefore alone down here with his temptress, whoever she was. An old love, it seemed. This situation was likely to arise again and again, and although it was something Kate had not foreseen, it was clearly something to which she had to become accustomed. How should she deal with it?

She was aware that the longer she sat here like the proverbial mouse, the more difficult and embarrassing it would be when she eventually made her presence known. Yet she could not bring herself to stand, speak, clear her throat, yawn as if only just awakening . . . anything that might alert her husband and his ladylove to the fact that they were not alone in the room! All the new Lady Carismont seemed capable of was just sitting there, "like two penn'orth of God help us stuck on a stick," as her old aunt was wont to say. Kate leaned her head back against the chair, and as she gripped the arms, her ring seemed hot enough to brand her. She bit her lip to hold back a cry of pain, then closed her eyes against the brilliance of the light.

Again, Gerent's lady friend must have whispered to him, because he sighed anew. "Dear God, have you no conscience? I did not seek what happened, nor was I at fault. It was all your own doing, and now you think to reassert your hold upon my heart?" For a few moments there was silence, then he whispered, "It has to be over now. The happiness you offer is of no interest to me, for my duty lies here."

Kate was confounded. If that was how he felt, why on earth had he brought the woman to the house? And what did he mean by "duty" anyway? His duty as a husband? If so, that was nonsense to begin with!

Suddenly there came the sound of fluttering in the chimney. The cuckoo! She heard a familiar double-noted call, then a shower of soot fell down, and with a cry of alarm the cuckoo tumbled down as well. Flapping and fluting, it hopped hastily out of the way of the fire, then shook its feathers and stood there hunched, looking at her, as if waiting for her to do something. But Kate could only meet its gaze, for she really did not have any idea what was expected of her.

The bird's unconventional and—to Kate's ears—noisy arrival passed unnoticed by the two other people in the drawing room. Was it possible that only she could see it?

"Well, don't just sit there! By the power of Percival, must I do it all?"

It *was* the cuckoo speaking. When she met the bird's bright eye, she suddenly knew for a fact what she had only guessed before. But couldn't the silly bird tell that if she knew what to do, she wouldn't just be sitting here?

Gerent addressed his lady companion once more. "How many times must I tell you it is over? Your fate is sealed, but mine is my own, to do with as I please. The same must be said for Genevra. It pleases us both to stay here, not go to you."

Kate found such sentiments unacceptable. How could he be so pompous as to tell the woman it was over, when he had just brought her here? He was playing silly games, and as a consequence plummeted in his new bride's estimation.

But even as she thought this of him, he exclaimed again. "No, damn it all! I do not want this! My life is going to be my own once more!"

The cuckoo cocked its head and eyed Kate. *"Come on, come on! Now is not the time to dither! Get on with it!"*

Kate was in wholehearted agreement. Gerent was in the wrong to bring another woman back to the house on his wedding night. It didn't matter that his marriage was one of convenience only, for there was a principle at stake. The second Lady Carismont was not about to meekly accept a constant procession of his former loves, present loves, future loves, or passing *belles de nuit*! Released from the frozen immobility that had shackled her, and incensed beyond all thought of discretion, Kate leaped to her feet to confront him.

The second she moved, the blinding light was extinguished; no, not quite extinguished, for she was aware of it diminishing at speed to become the lavender light, which skimmed toward the fireplace. But it reckoned without the vigilant cuckoo, which caught it in its beak. The light screamed and tugged so frantically that it managed to tear free, and in a trice had hurled itself up the chimney. The cuckoo followed. Soot scattered and the fire smoked, and Kate heard the bird's furious scrabbling. Suddenly the soot stopped falling, and she knew the cuckoo had escaped into the night.

But now was not the time to dwell upon such things, for she must face Gerent. She mustered her concentration. The room was candlelit and mellow once again, her wedding ring felt comfortable and slightly too large, and Gerent was alone by a table, leaning upon his hands. His head was bowed and his eyes closed, as if some great torment were upon him. He seemed completely oblivious to anything having happened. He certainly did not yet know she was there. "Gerent?" she ventured hesitantly.

"No, I say!" The bitter words were wrenched from him, his head jerked up, and he whipped around toward the sound of her voice. For a moment his eyes were iron-bright, but then they changed. "Kate? I didn't realize you were . . ." He didn't finish.

"I was asleep in the chair, and heard voices. What's happening? Who were you talking to?"

He didn't answer immediately, then gave a slight laugh. "No one. I fear you were confused by sleep. I always talk to myself after a surfeit of cognac."

She knew what she had heard and witnessed. He had definitely not had a surfeit of cognac, anymore than she herself had.

He smiled. "You should not have waited up for me, Kate."

"It . . . seemed the right thing to do," she replied a little lamely. His smile affected her as much as his anguish of a moment ago.

"There is no need for such wifely diligence. We may be married now, but we lead separate lives."

"I know, it's just . . ."

"Yes?"

She regarded him. "Gerent, what is the lavender light?" she asked quietly.

His lips parted slightly, as if he was dismayed to realize she was aware of such a thing, but then he shook his head. "I don't know what you mean."

The denial was level and unequivocal, but lacked truth for all that, and he met her eyes in a way that brooked no further questions. Somehow she managed to give a slight smile. "I . . . will retire to my rooms now. Good night."

But as she tried to walk past him, he caught her arm. "Kate . . . ?"

"Yes?" Their eyes met again, and in his she saw uncertainty and unhappiness, twin emotions that reached out to touch her heart. "What is it, Gerent? What is wrong?"

"Never take off your wedding ring."

"My wedding ring? Why, Gerent? Please tell me what—"

"There is nothing to tell," he interrupted, releasing her.

She hesitated. "You do know that you can trust me?"

"Yes, I know I can." He smiled. Only faintly, a softening of the lips and eyes that far from merely touching her heart, rent it completely asunder. Then he bent close and brushed his lips gently over hers. "Good night, Kate," he whispered.

She caught up her skirts and hurried out.

7

Atrocious weather caused the journey to Cornwall to take much longer than usual, so that instead of Gerent being back at Carismont for the whole of the last week of April, as he wished, it would be the twenty-ninth before they eventually reached their destination.

First there was torrential rain that made the roads difficult and very dirty, then came a heavy mist that closed visibility to such an extent that it was impossible to see more than twenty feet in any direction. The latter prevailed as the carriage crossed a particularly bleak and dangerous part of western Dartmoor, so rather than press on to his usual comfortable inn in Tavistock, Gerent reluctantly decided to halt instead at an isolated wayside inn that as a rule he would have passed by. He was impatient with all the delays, and seemed really very anxious indeed to be at Carismont. Kate wondered what was so very important about the last week of the month, but he gave no indication what it might be.

The hostelry stood at a lonely crossroad, and was huddled to the rising land as if trying to keep a low head against the unkind gales that often swept over the moor. It was called the Falcon, although that was not what Kate thought when she glanced up at the inn sign that hung motionless and dripping in the mist. The bird she saw depicted on the weather-beaten board was most definitely a cuckoo, and as the carriage drew up in the yard, she naturally imagined that to be the hostelry's unlikely name. She was to discover she was wrong, and that she was the only person who could see a cuckoo on the sign. As she alighted, however, she thought the painted cuckoo was a disconcerting coincidence, and that all things strange had not been safely left behind in London.

For the first time in two years, she was à la mode again. She wore a fashionable new olive silk bonnet, high-crowned and richly adorned with lace and lemon ribbons. With it she wore an olive velvet spencer and a white muslin gown sprigged with lemon flowers. The gown's ankle-length hem was lavishly stiffened with rouleaux and bows of the same ribbons as her bonnet, for Mrs. Camberton had spared no effort in the swift production of at least some of the lucrative new order for Lord Carismont's second bride. Some of the requested garments had been delivered the day before setting out from London, and were now carefully packed on the carriage. The rest of the order was set to follow as and when it was ready.

The inn's taproom was low-beamed and sparsely furnished, with settles by the inglenook fireplace and upturned casks for seats at the tables. Late April or not, a fine fire roared in the hearth, and the smell of roast dinner emanated from the kitchen. Few people had ventured out in such a mist, and the only other travelers were a party of farmers on their way home to Crediton from Tavistock. They were laughing and talking good-naturedly as they played shovelboard and dominoes.

The innkeeper was tending one of the barrels behind the trestle at the back of the room, but straightened attentively as he saw the grand new arrivals. Hastily wiping his hands on his long apron, he hurried to greet them. He was a thick-set countryman in his late forties, with ruddy cheeks, light brown eyes, and rough hands that were clearly used to hard work. His neckcloth was tied in a loose granny knot, and there was a daffodil pinned to his leather jerkin. His straight brown hair was tied back with a crisp brown ribbon. "Welcome, zur, madam, young zur," he said in his broad Devonshire accent.

Gerent inclined his head. "I am Lord Carismont. This is Lady Carismont, and Master Kingsley."

A lord and lady? The innkeeper's eyes widened at such an unexpected honor, and he swept a respectful bow. "My name is Daniel Livesey, and I'm the land-lord of the Falcon."

Kate was taken aback. "The . . . Falcon? Oh, but—" She broke off, suddenly sensing she might again be alone where cuckoos were concerned.

Mr. Livesey looked inquiringly at her. "Is somethin' wrong, madam?"

"Er, no, it's nothing." She colored a little, and re-frained from saying anything more, but now knew for certain that the weird goings-on had not after all re-mained in London as she had hoped.

Two comfortable rooms were soon provided for them, one for Kate and Justin, the other for Gerent on his own. If Mr. Livesey had thoughts as to why Lord and Lady Carismont should sleep separately, he was too experienced an innkeeper to reveal it, but Kate felt embarrassed, because she knew how odd the arrangement must appear. She and Gerent were man and wife, and quite obviously got on well, yet they slept apart.

That night, after a hearty repast of roast mutton and early greens, followed by sweet batter pudding and raspberry preserve, the three weary travelers from London were glad to retire to their beds. Gerent saw his wife and stepson safely to their door, and then went on to his own room. There was a washstand behind a little screen in the corner of Kate's room, and after washing in chilly water from the jug, Justin climbed thankfully into the capacious bed and fell asleep almost immediately.

Kate washed as well, then extinguished the candle and after getting into bed, lay listening to the sounds of the inn. A creak here, a scratching sound there, voices, a door closing, a dog barking. Drowsily she raised a hand to push her hair back from her face. It was her left hand, and she noticed she had forgotten to replace her wedding ring after washing. But she was too warm and comfortable to get out to put it on again. She'd do it in the morning.

She watched the fire shadows on the beams, and at last began to drift into sleep. Except . . . her sleepy eyes wandered toward the fireplace just as the little sparks emerged from among the flames. Glittering and spellbinding, they coiled and snaked toward the bed. Her heart quickened unpleasantly, but she couldn't move; she couldn't do anything!

The lights danced around her, seeming to find their way into her hair and beneath the bedclothes. She tried to awaken Justin, but her voice would not obey her either. The sparks began to twine around the fourth finger of her left hand, where the wedding ring should have been. Then she saw the lavender light gliding toward her, and she was sure she heard a woman's low laughter.

Suddenly the lights vanished, and the room was just as it was before, but outside there was an abrupt and considerable change in the weather. At least she thought it was abrupt, because she hadn't been aware before of the strong wind that now moaned in the eaves by the window. Confused and a little frightened, she glanced swiftly around the shadowy room. Justin slept on at her side, his breathing deep and reassuringly steady.

Then she heard a woman calling in the distance outside. Who was it? Rain dashed against the glass, keeping time with the gusting wind, which now howled like a banshee around the moorland inn. Again the woman called, and Kate sat up with a start as she realized it was a cry for help. She slipped from the bed and went to the window, a small dormer that peered out of the rambling roof. The catch was difficult and resisted at first, but at last the window opened. The wind roared in, snatching at her nightclothes and hair, and the rain spattered her face as she leaned out.

The night was very dark, with heavy clouds obscuring the stars and new moon. She couldn't see anything, except the wet inn sign as it swayed violently on squeaking hinges. It was still a cuckoo, she noticed fleetingly, but her attention was on the distance, where the pale glimmer of a signal lantern swung to and fro. Someone was trying to attract attention! She heard the woman calling again. *"Help! Help me, please! Oh, please!"*

Kate closed the window again, and went to quickly put on her peach woolen dressing robe, then she hurried from the room, intending to arouse Gerent. But although she knocked several times at his door, there was no reply. It was the same at every door she tried, so in desperation she hurried downstairs and then out of the inn. Rain sluiced down, trickling along gutters and splashing into puddles, and all the time the wind keened ferociously around the inn and its outbuildings. The smell of wet earth, gorse, and heather filled her nostrils, and she could hear horses stirring restlessly in the nearby stables. There wasn't anyone around, not even a groom. The woman continued to call, a sob of desperation now entering her voice.

"For pity's sake. Help me!"

"I'm coming! I'm coming!" Kate shouted back, and caught up her skirts to run blindly on to the dark, storm-swept moor.

The distress lantern waved to and fro as she stumbled over soaking hummocks of heather. Her clothes caught on gorse thorns, and she was soon soaked through, but still she struggled toward the lantern. The woman cried out again and again, *"Can't anyone hear me? Help! Please!"*

Kate forced herself to continue, but each step was taken in increasing trepidation. Something did not seem right, and at the back of her mind she thought

of wreckers on the coast, luring stricken ships ashore
during storms . . . She didn't know why she thought
of such a thing, yet somehow a seed of doubt was
sown. She glanced back at the inn, which was lost in
the murk and darkness, without even a light to show
its whereabouts. A sense of foreboding crept over her.
There was danger close by, she could *feel* it!

The woman sobbed and implored. *"Help me! I need
you! Please! Someone is badly injured . . . !"*

Kate was spurred on, but suddenly there came a
familiar double-noted call, and the cuckoo flew down
behind her. It grabbed her hem in its beak, dug its
claws into the wet ground, and tugged as if determined
to make her turn back.

"Help me! Come to me!" A new edge of anger entered the woman's voice, and she no longer implored,
but commanded.

The cuckoo tugged frantically at Kate's hem, almost
falling over itself in the battle to stop her from taking
even one step more. Kate yielded as the bird wanted.
"All right, all right, I'm not going farther!" she cried,
and the relieved bird released her clothes. It plumped
back on a tuft of heather, as if quite worn out by the
struggle, and its thankfulness could not have been
more eloquent had it possessed a handkerchief with
which to mop its brow.

The unknown woman gave a shriek of unutterable
fury. *"Come on, Kate! Face me if you can! Fight for
him if you dare!"*

Kate's attention flew back to the lantern, as—too
late—she recognized that voice. To her dismay she
saw not one, but numerous lanterns! Small and bright,
they were swooping and whirling toward her, led by
the lavender light. A frightened gasp was torn from
Kate's parted lips, and the cuckoo leaped to its feet
with a dismayed squawk. But then, just as the advanc-
ing lights were almost upon her, someone gripped her
fiercely by the arms. "Kate! Wake up!"

Her eyes started open, and there was just the silence

of a misty Dartmoor night. "Wake up, Kate." Gerent was holding her shoulders from behind, and the only light came from a lantern held high by the landlord, Mr. Livesey.

She turned in confusion, and Gerent looked urgently into her eyes. "Kate, you must not take another step, for you are at the edge of a drop to a deep pool."

Bewildered, she stared at him, trying to grasp what was real and what was a dream. Where was the storm? The lights? The cuckoo? The voice . . . ?

He saw the tumult in her eyes, and spoke more gently. "You've been sleepwalking again."

She found her tongue. "No . . ."

"I fear so."

"But I hadn't even gone to sleep." Yet even as she protested, she knew he was right. Everything that had just happened had been an illusion, the effects of another sleepwalking dream. "I . . . I thought I heard a woman calling for help," she whispered. "It was so real, and yet . . ."

"And yet?"

She fell silent, for how could she explain that even as she experienced the illusion, she had known there was an otherworldly quality about it?

"You were dreaming, Kate."

She looked where the swaying lantern had been, but there was nothing, only a thick veil of cold, clammy mist. "But it was a stormy night, with a gale and driving rain, and I was soaked through . . ." She glanced down at her clothes. They were a little damp from the mist, but certainly not wet, except perhaps for the hem, where she had pushed through the grass and heather. Heather. She looked quickly at the tuft where the cuckoo had seated itself so suddenly. In the light from Mr. Livesey's lantern, she saw a single gray feather lying there.

"There was no storm," Gerent said, and tried to pull her toward him, but she resisted.

"How do I know I'm not dreaming now?"

Mr. Livesey chuckled. "You'm not dreamin', my lady, you'm in danger of breakin' your pretty neck. Green Pool is a notorious guzzler of unwary souls."

"Green Pool?"

"Take a step or so farther the way you was goin', my lady, and you'd 'ave found it quicker'n you knows. There's a sheer drop of at least twenty feet, right into water so deep no one knows the bottom."

A horrid shiver ran over her as she glanced where he indicated. Sure enough, the ground suddenly ended, and when she ventured to peep nervously over, she saw the lantern light reflecting on the pool. She gasped, and Gerent drew her swiftly away from the edge, wrapped his cloak around her, and held her close for a moment. "It's all right now, Kate, you're safe."

"How did you know I was out here?"

"I awoke when I heard someone calling 'I'm coming! I'm coming!' I recognized your voice, looked out, and saw you hurrying onto the moor, so I grabbed some clothes, awoke Mr. Livesey here, and we came after you as quickly as we could. We caught up with you in the very nick, for to be sure you would certainly have fallen over the edge."

No, she wouldn't, for Kate knew what he didn't— that the cuckoo had already saved her. What was it all about? Why had the cuckoo come to her rescue? Whose voice did she hear when the lavender light appeared? Selena's?

Even as the incredible thought struck her, she knew it was right. Gerent's first wife had been the unseen woman at Berkeley Street, and had also lured her out here tonight!

8

As Gerent and Mr. Livesey ushered her back to the inn, Kate was still stunned with the realization about Selena. She noticed as they reached the inn that the sign was now most definitely a falcon, but she was really too distracted to do more than observe the fact in passing.

It was warm and comforting inside after the horror of what happened on the storm-swept moor . . . except, of course, that there had not been a storm at all, only in Kate's dreams. In reality the night was calm and still, and the other guests slept on, unaware of the drama that had just overtaken the second Lady Carismont.

The kitchen was as rambling as the rest of the inn, with whitewashed walls and a red-raddled floor. The ceiling boasted a number of heavy beams from which were suspended hams wrapped in muslin, dried herbs, a sugar loaf in a cradle, and strings of onions, while above the lime-washed back door there were a number of cheeses tied in cloth. Beside the door was a stone sink, with a newfangled hand pump that raised water from a well just outside in the yard.

Opposite the door there was a huge dresser that stretched from floor to ceiling, its shelves laden with blue-and-white crockery. The fireplace was very large indeed, and numerous pans stood neatly on the hearth, awaiting use the next morning. The door of a bread oven was set into the whitewashed wall amid an array of gleaming copper pans, and the smell of bread seemed to be part of the room; maybe it was, for the oven had no doubt been in use for several generations.

Gerent made her sit on the carved oak settle by the fire, then lit some candles before trying to poke some life into the fire. As soon as some new flames began to flicker, he rammed another log on the coals and applied the bellows until the fire licked noisily around the dry bark. He had dressed so hurriedly that he wore only his shirt, pantaloons and boots. He was in need of a shave, and his hair was tangled and uncombed. She thought he looked tired and strained—surely not on her account?

Mr. Livesey extinguished the lantern, placed it on a shelf, and then went to the pantry to pour milk into a pan, which he brought back and placed carefully on the fire to heat. He still wore his nightshirt, over which he had flung on a coat, and his bare feet had been hastily shoved into calf-length boots that he had not had time to lace. As he waited for the milk, he addressed her. " 'Tis very dangerous to go on the moor of a night, my lady, especially 'round 'ere," he said earnestly. "Green Pool 'ave claimed more'n one life, so if you'm likely to wander around in your sleep again, you'd best make sure your door is firmly locked."

The milk began to rise in the pan, so the innkeeper whisked it away and poured it into two blue-and-white cups from the dresser. Then he muttered something about having to be up with the larks in the morning, and left them alone. Gerent waited until the door closed behind him, then pressed one of the cups upon Kate. "Drink, it will help you to relax."

She looked up at him as she took the milk. "I know I am in your debt for coming after me tonight."

"Hardly in my debt. You are my wife."

His wife? Selena held that title; the second Lady Carismont was merely a cipher. Kate had to avoid his gaze, knowing she desired more from their contract than he was prepared to give. The intimate side of marriage was something she had missed greatly since being widowed; the comfort of Michael's presence beside her in bed, the way he sighed as he turned over, the joy of his lovemaking . . . Not that there had been a great deal of the latter toward the end, for he had always been in London, driven by his devils . . .

Gerent went to the fire, and rested a boot on the fender and a hand on the mantel. "Have you sleep-walked before, Kate?"

She drew a deep breath. "I have not done so since I was a child, and I thought I never would again, but it happened at the Pulteney. And now again here." She paused. "Gerent, about tonight—"

"With luck you will not do it again," he interrupted quickly, and she knew it was an attempt to prevent her asking awkward questions.

"Gerent, I know you do not wish to talk about it, but nevertheless . . ."

"You walk in your sleep, Kate, that is all."

"No, it isn't all, as you are perfectly well aware." She regarded him steadily. "The very first time I saw you at the Pulteney Hotel, you were looking into the fire as you do now. But unlike now, there were lights playing above the flames, like tiny stars, dancing and twisting. There was one light in particular, it was lavender and—"

"Inferior coal, no doubt," he broke in dryly.

"Mock me if you wish, but I am telling you the truth."

"I'm not mocking you, Kate. Dreams can be very vivid."

"I was not asleep when you interviewed me," she pointed out quietly, then she sipped the hot milk and allowed silence to fall. Sleep might have something to do with some of the things that had happened, but by no means all. Apart from the interview, she had been very much awake the first time she stood on the balcony above a dark, wet Piccadilly, and watched him ride into a sunlit woodland. She had also been wide awake at the Tower of London.

Gerent exhaled slowly, then his shoulders slumped a little, and he nodded. "Oh, Kate, forgive me for all of this. I admit there is much I have not told you, and now I fear I may have drawn you into something that no one can possibly be equipped to deal with."

Her heart leaped. He was going to tell her about it!

He gazed into the fire. "But you have to believe that I truly thought I had made you safe."

"Safe? From what, Gerent?" she asked quickly.

Reluctantly he met her eyes, but as his lips parted to answer, his glance slid to her naked left hand. "Your ring! Where is it?" he demanded.

"I . . . I took it off when I washed, and forgot to put it on again."

"So that's it! Kate, you must *never* take it off! Especially while the April moon is waxing!"

"The April moon? Gerent, I—"

"Just do as I say, Kate," he interrupted. "Keep the ring on at all times."

"But . . . why? What is so important about it? And what are the little symbols inside it?"

"Symbols?" He repeated the word reluctantly.

"Please don't pretend to know nothing of them, for I am not a fool. You asked the jeweler to put them there when you went back into the premises, didn't you?" The realization had come so clearly that she marveled she had not seen it before. She got up and went to crouch by the hearth, where she used her finger to draw the symbols in the ash dust. "They look something like this," she said.

He nodded reluctantly. "They are runes, Kate."

"Runes! Yes, of course! What do they mean?" She straightened.

He hesitated, then explained. "They are only a Cornish good luck charm. At least that is what my old nurse swore. ᛖ is Ehwaz, the strongest rune for protection. ᛏ is Tiwaz, to give inner strength. ᚷ is Gebo, which will help love and friendship to grow. ᛋ is Sowilo, to enhance the soul. And ᚲ is Kenaz, to show the way through uncertainty. I did indeed have them put on the ring, as well as on the gold locket I purchased at the same time for Genevra." He reached for her hand and drew the palm to his lips. "Trust me, Kate, for now that I know you did not have the ring on tonight, I am able to see why certain things happened to you."

Her fingers closed around his. "Tell me what all this is about, Gerent," she begged.

"Give me a little time . . ."

She let go of his hand. "Then at least answer me one thing, even though I know it is none of my business, and you may think less of me for asking." She looked up into his eyes. "Did you love Selena very much?" she asked softly.

He didn't show any anger at a question he might easily have regarded as impertinent. "Why do you wish to know?"

"After all that has happened tonight, I think you know the answer to that as well," she reproved gently. "The lavender light I mentioned earlier has something to do with Selena, doesn't it?"

He didn't deny it, but still did not answer her question. "So, you wish to know about my love for Selena because of what has been happening? Not because . . . ?"

"Because what?" She looked deep into his winter-sea eyes.

For a long moment he simply met her gaze, then he turned away. "When I married Selena, I loved her with all my heart. Does that satisfy your curiosity?"

"A little." How could she answer otherwise, when he so obviously qualified his answer? He had loved Selena at first, but maybe not toward the end. She wanted to ask him so much, needed to know so much, but suddenly she could not put anything more into words. "I think I should go to my room now. My clothes and slippers are damp . . ."

"Yes, of course." He stepped quickly aside.

Embarrassment hung in the air, but then she glanced at the fire and saw the sparks emerging. Bobbing and skimming, spiraling and swooping. Gerent saw them too, and she heard his sharp intake of breath. Then he spoke urgently to her. "Go now, Kate."

"But—"

"Go!" He grabbed a lighted candle from the table and thrust it into her hand. She hurried out without another word, but as the door began to swing to behind her, she turned to glance back. He was standing where she had left him, his head flung back, his eyes closed as the lights, especially the one that was lavender, twined around him. She saw how tightly clenched his fists were, and how his lips moved as he whispered something, she knew not what. Then the door closed, and she saw no more.

But as she turned to walk away from the kitchen, the lavender light suddenly swept beneath the door and attacked her. *"He's mine, do you hear? Mine! Before this moon is done, he will have come to me forever, and you will never see him again!"*

Kate cried with pain and alarm as the light pricked and stung with such ferocity that she fell sobbing to her knees. The candlestick fell with a clatter, and the flame was extinguished so that darkness engulfed the passage. Then Gerent flung the door open, and light flooded out once more as he bent to pull her up into his arms. The light's fury was intense. *"No, Gerent! You belong to me, not her!"*

He ignored it as he held Kate tightly to him. His fingers slid tenderly into her hair, and he whispered in her ear. "Don't be afraid, Kate, for I have you safe now."

With a flash of brilliant white light, the lavender spark disappeared, and suddenly Kate and Gerent were alone. He stroked the nape of her neck. "I will walk you back to your room now, Kate, and I will see you put the wedding ring on your finger once again. It can only protect you if you wear it."

She raised her eyes to his. "*Please* tell me what is happening . . ."

"I will, I promise. But not yet. Trust me, Kate, for I am certain the runes will protect you."

"From Selena?"

He didn't answer, but his lips pressed together with such bitterness that no further answer was required. It was indeed Selena. "Gerent, at least admit that much!"

"You have my word that I will tell you when I am ready. Until then, just remember that if there is something you think you see, but which seems strange in some way, then it is likely to be false. If night seems turned to day, winter to summer, mist to storm, whatever form it takes, then do not trust your own eyes. With the ring upon your finger, you are safe. Something will always come to your rescue, as happened tonight on the moor."

"The cuckoo? Is that what you mean?"

He looked mystified. "I know nothing of a cuckoo, Kate."

She was taken by surprise. "But—"

"I really don't know about a cuckoo," he repeated, then looked earnestly at her. "As to everything else . . . Please don't press me for an explanation now, for I am not ready to speak of it. But I will tell you soon, you have my word of honor upon it."

She had to be content with that. "Gerent, you do know that I want to help you, don't you?"

"Even though the world may think I am totally mad?"

"If you are mad, then so am I," she pointed out. She even managed a smile. "I am the cuckoo who sees cuckoos, remember."

He smiled too, and gazed into her eyes. "You will never know how great a comfort it is to have you near, Kate. I had no right to embroil you, no right to expect anything of you now, but—"

"No right? Gerent, you are wrong if you think I entered this marriage for solely selfish reasons. I made vows to you, and I will stand by them. I will stand by *you* . . ."

He gazed at her. "Shakespeare wrote words that might have been for this moment, although shrew you most certainly are not," he said softly, then quoted from *The Taming of the Shrew*. "The prettiest Kate in Christendom; Kate of Kate-Hall, my super-dainty Kate, for dainties are all cates: and therefore, Kate, take this of me, Kate of my consolation . . ." He took her face in his hands, and kissed her on the lips.

With that her fate was sealed beyond all redemption. He already had her love; now she was prepared to give her life as well.

9

A few days later, in glorious afternoon sunshine, the carriage drove down from a gorse-clad Cornish moor that was far gentler than the bleak grandeur of Dartmoor, and entered a leafy little valley that wound down toward the sea. Down and down the road plunged between raised verges where cowslips, bluebells, and ramsons grew thickly beneath overhanging hawthorn hedges that were so thick and frothing with sweet blossom that they almost met overhead to form a tunnel of flowers.

It was four o'clock on the last day of the month, a Wednesday, and the sun was dazzling. Cornwall in late April was something to behold, Kate thought, as she inhaled the sweet air. She sat facing the way they were going, and the carriage windows had been lowered, allowing her senses to be assailed by the sounds, scents, and warmth of a peerless spring afternoon. When everything was as utterly normal, tranquil, and reassuring as this, it was hard to believe that she had recently experienced such a very different side of the coin.

Kate leaned her head back against the carriage upholstery, but did so with great care to protect the olive silk bonnet she wore again. Throughout the journey she had been conscious of looking after her new clothes,

and the olive velvet spencer and white muslin gown were
as pristine now as they had been at the outset in Berkeley Street. She gazed dreamily out of the window, for
the scented air was both warm and drowsy.

Nothing more had happened to her since that night
at the Falcon, and Gerent had yet to confide anything
more in her than he had admitted already. She knew
that he would, for she had his word, but it was very
difficult to hold her tongue and wait for him to find
the moment. In the meantime she had been very con-
scientious about wearing her ring. It had not left her
finger from the moment Gerent watched her put it on
again at the Falcon.

The carriage swayed over the uneven surface of the
road, and from time to time a gate in the hedgerow
allowed Kate a glimpse of the valley slopes. On a
knoll she saw a circle of Scotch pines, in the center
of which rose yet another of the many standing stones
she had seen since arriving here in the far southwest
of England. Each stone had been an eerie reminder
of the mysterious past, but this one caught the sunshine in such a way that she could see it was carved
all over with ancient symbols. Runes! As she looked,
a cuckoo flew from one of the pines to perch on the
stone. Somehow she knew it was her cuckoo, but then
the dense hedgerow closed the view again. She didn't
say anything as the carriage drove on.

Now that the indifferent weather had gone, and
London was well over two hundred miles behind
them, she knew beyond all shadow of doubt that she
had done the right thing by marrying Gerent. How
could such a thing *not* be right? The sensations that
passed through her now were almost magical. Things
were going to be good from now on, she just *knew*
they were . . .

She longed for the moment he confided in her, for
she *needed* to help him all she could. Love blazed
through her like a flame, consuming her body and
soul. She stole a glance at him as he sat opposite. His
coat was a shade of gray-blue that emphasized the

color of his eyes, and the ruby pin in his neckcloth glinted now and then as the sunlight stole through the canopy of hawthorn. The perfect fit of his tight gray silk waistcoat allowed it to lie in gentle ripples over his lean but muscular chest, and the cream stuff of his pantaloons clung to his slender hips and long thighs like a second skin, leaving very little of his anatomy to conjecture.

She had to face up to the fact that she was fiercely drawn to him. He aroused feelings she had tried to suppress since things had gone wrong between Michael and her; now those feelings were with her all the time, but *still* she had to suppress them, even though the man she desired so much was her new husband. What irony there was in the situation. She was his wife, and she knew he was not indifferent to her because of the kiss at the Tower. There was nothing at all to prevent him from coming to her bed; but he left her to sleep alone.

Embarrassed color entered her cheeks, and as she looked quickly away again, her glance fell on the seat beside him, where Justin's model boat lay. Its gold paint and silver oars shone, and its crimson sail was a bright splash of hot color amid the cooler shades of springtime.

Justin was next to her, deeply engrossed in a book of stories about old Cornwall, but suddenly he looked earnestly across at Gerent. "Sir, is it true that Carismont was once part of the mainland, and not an island at all?"

Gerent regarded him with interest. "What makes you ask?"

"Well, it says here that Robin Hood, Tristan, and some of King Arthur's knights came from Lyonesse, a fabulous sunken land that once stretched from the Isles of Scilly in the far west, to Carismont Bay in the east."

Gerent smiled. "Carismont Bay was certainly once land, and at very low tides even today it is possible to see the remains of tree trunks from an ancient forest that covered the area. The land upon which the castle stands is an island now, but a long time ago it was merely a hill that rose out of the trees. Whether or not it was Lyonesse, or whether the likes of Robin Hood and Tristan came from there, I cannot say with such authority." Gerent smiled, but Kate thought she saw a shadow in his eyes. Why?

Justin was agog to hear more. "It also says here that sometimes it is possible even now to hear the tolling of church bells from beneath the sea, ghostly bells from the drowned land."

Kate shivered. "Oh, don't, Justin, that's quite horrid."

Gerent smiled again. "There are those who claim to have heard such bells. There is a belief that they are heard for several days on either side of a particularly high and fierce tide."

Like the one that drowned Selena? Kate wondered.

Gerent elaborated on the subject of the bells. "Some people have even sworn they've seen submerged steeples far out in the bay, but I have to admit that it is usually the result of too much rum and shrub at the Merry Maid inn in Trezance."

Kate did not wish to talk of such things as drowned churches. "What is rum and shrub?" she inquired in a clumsy attempt to deflect the conversation.

"Rum sweetened with an alcoholic cordial made from spices and herbs. It can be very potent, especially the Merry Maid's brew."

Justin frowned. "I've never heard of an inn called the Merry Maid before."

"But I'll warrant you've come across several called the Mermaid. It's just the Cornish way of saying it," Gerent explained.

Justin sat forward, with a look on his face that alerted his mother to more talk of eerie sunken bells, so she spoke first. "What house is that?" she asked, pointing toward a large gray-stone building that stood in the lee of a hill. It was surrounded by a windbreak of evergreen trees, but its crenellated towers were visible above the treetops. The entrance to its drive was flanked by two more of the standing stones, and this time she clearly saw the runic symbols on them.

Gerent's face hardened. "That is Polwithiel."

Carismont Castle and Polwithiel were clearly not on amiable terms, Kate thought, and she would have left the subject forthwith, but Justin was not so wise.

"Who lives there, sir?" he asked.

There was silence.

"Who lives there, sir?" he asked again, in that innocent but persistent way children have.

Gerent had to respond. "A man I once regarded as my friend, but who is now my most bitter foe. His name is Denzil Portreath."

Kate's eyes widened. Denzil Portreath? Could it be the same man who had written to her about Michael's death? Was such a coincidence possible . . . ?

Justin, who knew nothing of the letter from his father's friend, at last saw wisdom, and fell silent. Kate was obliged to do the same, even though she now had yet another burning question to ask. Maybe there would soon be a more opportune time, certainly not now.

The valley widened just a little so that small fields appeared on either side of the road, then suddenly a vista opened, and about two miles ahead they saw the great turquoise horseshoe of Carismont Bay, with the little town of Trezance hugging the water's edge. Just offshore rose a steep rocky island, about two hundred feet high. The lower slopes were cloaked by magnificent gardens, but the summit was crowned by the most romantic castle Kate had ever seen. She knew from Gerent that it had been built in the twelfth century as a Benedictine priory, and that after the Reformation it had become the home of the Fitzarthur family. Over the centuries it had been enlarged and improved to its present astonishing beauty.

An hour later the carriage clattered into Trezance, and drove down through narrow cobblestone streets to the quayside, where the first thing Justin noticed was the erection of a colorful maypole in the middle of a wide area that seemed to be marketplace, town square, and waterfront all in one. Teams of men heaved the bright pole into place with ropes, and excited children clapped and cheered as it became perpendicular, its long ribbons fluttering and shivering in the sea breeze. An old one-legged man with a penny whistle was playing a tune. *Sumer Is Icumen In* . . .

The tide was in, covering the granite causeway that connected the island to the mainland, and Gerent told Kate and Justin that they would halt awhile at the Merry Maid to wait for the ebb, which he reckoned would be passable at about sunset. The waterside was very busy, with carts, barrows, fishermen, their womenfolk, children, dogs, and even a cat or three basking in the sun. Kate saw fishing boats of all description moored alongside, fore-and-aft-rigged luggers, seine boats, and schooners. It was very noisy as the carriage threaded its way past piles of netting, crab and lobster pots, coils of rope, upturned rowing boats, barrels, and crates, to draw up at the inn. Seagulls wheeled and screamed excitedly as a newly arrived lugger unloaded its catch, but Kate's awareness reached beyond the immediate clamor to the island, rising silent and mysterious out of the bay.

Justin craned his neck to look up at the Merry Maid. It was a three-story, weather-boarded building, with gables and twisted chimneys, and its faded sign depicted a rather ugly mermaid combing her hair and looking at herself in a hand glass. After a moment he whispered to Kate that it must be a smuggler's haunt. Privately she was in agreement, but she told him that she was sure it was far too respectable a hostelry to be used for such things. How prim she sounded, she thought as Gerent assisted her down from the carriage at the inn's entrance.

Amid the noise of the quay and the racket of the seagulls, there suddenly came a familiar call. Kate turned sharply toward the sound, and saw the cuckoo glide down to the mainmast of a lugger, where it wobbled awkwardly for a moment before folding its wings. Then it tilted its glossy gray head to one side, and eyed Kate earnestly. She immediately felt uneasy, for she had come to associate the bird with danger. Was the lavender light nearby? Was it about to attack her again?

A fisherman was examining a net on the deck of the lugger, and his small brown-and-white terrier had been sitting quietly beside him until the cuckoo arrived. The sight and sound of the bird seemed to goad the dog, which immediately rushed to the base of the mast, barking excitedly. It stood on its hind legs, pawing at the mast, making such a din that the fisherman became irritated. Kate heard him chide the animal. "Hush up! There's nothin' up there!"

The cuckoo's warning voice suddenly echoed through Kate. *"Beware!"* Beware of what? she wondered, looking around with redoubled urgency.

Gerent spoke to her. "Shall we go in?" he suggested, offering her his arm.

But just as they started to enter the Mermaid, a gentleman emerged, momentarily blocking the entrance. At least it would have been momentary had he not come to a startled halt on seeing Gerent. The man was tall, with blond hair and cold blue eyes. His eyebrows were so light as to be almost invisible, his pale skin was dusted with freckles, and a scar ran diagonally across his right cheek to the corner of his mouth, giving him a lopsided appearance. His clothes were unexpectedly fashionable and stylish, however, for his pine-green coat and white riding breeches smacked of Hyde Park rather than the streets of a remote Cornish port. Kate found him disturbing, and knew without further telling that he was the reason for the cuckoo's warning.

The man's cold eyes were upon Gerent. "Well, Carismont, what brings you home at this of all times? I would have thought there was little attraction here now."

"What I do and where I go are none of your business, just as your activities are no longer of any interest to me. Except, perhaps, when it comes to still finding you on this side of the tide."

Kate looked curiously at him. On this side of the tide? What a very odd expression.

Gerent continued, "Is it a case of severe second thoughts? Or have the flames of love perchance turned cool?"

"I choose to be here, not there."

Gerent gave a cold smile. "Be honest for once in your miserable life, Portreath. You are simply too lily-livered to take that awesome leap into the unknown."

Portreath? The owner of Polwithiel, and possibly Michael's good friend? Kate looked more closely at the stranger. Somehow he did not seem the sort of man with whom Michael would have been friendly. Michael had always been warm, amusing, and sometimes painfully unguarded; this decidedly guarded, seemingly humorless man seemed made of ice. Nevertheless, she would have asked him about Michael, except that Gerent's simmering, ill-disguised loathing prevented such a social inquiry.

Portreath's glance flickered to her. "Where are your manners, Carismont. Aren't you going to introduce me to your charming companion?"

A smile glimmered on Gerent's lips. "As you wish, Portreath. Allow me to present my wife, Lady Carismont."

Portreath's face changed. "Your *wife*?"

Gerent turned to her. "Kate, this is Denzil Portreath of Polwithiel, who is not a man to like, trust, or rely upon; indeed, treachery is his middle name."

Portreath slammed his top hat on his head, and without another word pushed rudely past them. But Kate saw how his steps faltered as he passed the open door of the carriage. He glanced at Justin's golden boat on the seat, but then he tugged his top hat even more firmly on his blond hair, and marched on to where one of the inn's grooms was holding the reins of a rangy chestnut hunter. He mounted, kicked his heels, and rode recklessly away up the street in the direction of Polwithiel.

"Good riddance! Good riddance!" the cuckoo cried after him.

Justin didn't hear the bird, but was in agreement with its sentiments. "What a rude man," he observed.

Gerent nodded, then looked apologetically at Kate. "Forgive my own display of ill manners, Kate, but so much lies between that man and me that civility is impossible."

"It concerns Selena?"

"Oh, yes, it concerns Selena, and it is all part of what I know I must tell you."

Justin was growing impatient, and looked urgently up at her. "Can we go in, please, Mama? I'm terribly hungry, and I'm sure I smell hot Cornish pasties inside. I really like them."

Gerent laughed, and ushered him into the Merry Maid. Kate started to accompany them, but then the cuckoo's exasperated screech broke in once more.

"Silence! You useless racketmonger! You iniquitous cur! Oh, by Sir Kay's codlings, silence!"

On the lugger the terrier had now become almost frenzied, and its hubbub had proved too much for the irritated bird. The fisherman had heard enough barking as well. "Darned varmint, what's up with thee? Seein' buccaboos an' piskies now, eh?" With an old Cornish oath that probably did not bear translation, he snatched up a pail of water and flung the contents at the overexcited dog. The terrier yelped and retreated out of range to the bow of the lugger, from which relatively safe distance it continued to bark.

By now the cuckoo was provoked beyond endurance. Taking to its wings, it glided down over the terrier's head, and did something exceedingly unmentionable as it passed. Its aim was perfection, and a certain deposit landed directly between the dog's ears. Silence abruptly ensued, and thus the cuckoo achieved the desired effect. "In one smell swoop," Kate murmured wryly to herself, wondering if only she and the unfortunate terrier were aware of the grave insult that had just been delivered.

Then she followed Gerent and Justin into the inn.

10

Gerent was right about the tide, for it was almost eight o'clock and the sun was setting before the sea had retreated sufficiently to drive to the island. The commencement of the granite-paved causeway was marked by a carved standing stone that greatly reminded Kate of the one they had passed on the knoll. The ebbing water was as calm as a millpond when the carriage drove down from the quay onto the raised road, which at the highest point of the tide had been submerged beneath four or five feet of water.

While waiting in the Merry Maid, Kate had wondered why the moored fishing vessels did not keel over as the tide withdrew. From the inn window it seemed that the revealed land of sand, pools, and seaweed-strewn rocks came right up to the stone quay. Now she saw that the entire quay was built along a narrow channel of deep water that curved to the east and then south toward the open sea.

When she commented upon it, Gerent nodded. "Centuries ago, when the bay was still land, there was a creek just here, and that is why Trezance is where it is. It was the head of safe, navigable water."

Kate's heart beat a little more swiftly. Carismont was now a castle on an island, but in the very begin-

ning it had been a castle on a hill. From the Merry
Maid she had already observed that Carismont possessed a north-facing oriel window like the one she
had looked out of in those strange events at the Pulteney. If Gerent's castle was where she had looked
out of, then this causeway followed the line of the
woodland clearing, and this creek at Trezance was the
water she had felt so sure lay in the haze.

She looked at Gerent. "To what room does the oriel
window belong?" she inquired, pointing.

"My bedchamber, as it happens. Why?"

"Oh, nothing. I . . . I just thought it a splendid
feature," she murmured. She felt his curious glance
upon her, but didn't meet his eyes as she recalled
that in her sleepwalking dream she had awoken in a
sumptuous bed hung with gold-embroidered crimson
velvet. Someone had been lying beside her in that bed
when she got up to look from the oriel window . . .

The causeway dipped lower toward the island, and
soon the carriage drove into the inch or so of sea that
had yet to ebb completely from the granite surface.
The hooves and wheels sent ripples over water so
smooth that Kate found it difficult to believe that two
years ago—the anniversary was tomorrow night—a
sudden surge of turbulent incoming tide had swept
Selena to her death. Kate wondered where on the
causeway it had happened. She glanced at Gerent. He
had his back to the island, and was gazing back the
way they had come. She thought he was looking
toward Polwithiel, and by the set of his mouth sensed
his lingering anger from the encounter with Denzil
Portreath.

The carriage passed into the shadow of the island,
which now shut off the sunset. Justin spoke suddenly.
"Where is the submerged forest, sir?"

"You cannot see it at the moment. Actually, the
tide will not be low enough for that until well into the
summer, and maybe not even then, because the tree
remains are quite a way out from the shore. Right
now, with the moon almost full and the vernal equinox

not long over, there is more likely to be a surge tide that will cover everything even more than usual.''

Like the tide that drowned Selena, Kate thought.

Justin was disappointed about the drowned forest, but was quick to perceive another possibility. His eyes lit up hopefully. "A surge tide? So I will probably hear the drowned bells instead?"

Kate shuddered. "I sincerely hope not," she said firmly.

Gerent did not say anything more, but his glance moved over the darkening, oddly motionless water that had yet to retreat from the bay.

Closer and closer they drew to the island, the shadow of which lent a chill to the air that had hitherto been warm and balmy. Through the lowered windows the fragrance of the castle gardens was suddenly almost heady. It was a blend of spring flowers that, if contained in a bottle of scent, would surely be desired by every woman in England. Kate could detect the cool freshness of daffodils and narcissi, the warm, spicy sweetness of wallflowers, and above all the rich perfume of the beds of hyacinths at the foot of the castle walls. There were trees in blossom, others in full leaf, and still more that had yet to produce a bud of any sort, but Kate did not doubt they had all been chosen for their rare beauty. Even hawthorn seemed somehow exotic in this enchanted place. Enchanted? Under the circumstances, was that word perhaps a little too close for comfort?

Suddenly the wheels and hooves no longer splashed through water, but clattered on dry land as the track led off the causeway onto the island. Almost immediately there came the creak of tall wrought-iron gates, and then commenced the winding climb to the castle. Kate turned to look back, and saw that the gates were set in a high boundary wall that encircled the entire island. There was a lodge beside them, and a keeper who stood in the road watching the carriage drive on.

"It is necessary to keep Belerion safely here on Carismont," Gerent explained, following her glance. "I allow him to roam free, so it would not do for him to get loose to cause alarm in the streets of Trezance."

The road up to the castle stayed mostly on the landward side of the island, because the seaward side was an almost sheer drop into the water. The carriage had negotiated half the ascent when suddenly Justin pointed out excitedly. "Oh, look, Mama! It's Belerion!" he cried.

Kate saw the leopard bound past an arbor of rowan trees, one of which seemed strangely denuded, as if someone had gathered almost all its branches. But she hardly gave it a thought as she watched the leopard approaching the carriage. As it fell into a lope alongside, Kate heard a new voice, which she had little choice but to believe belonged to the leopard.

"Great thundering paddy-paws! I'm getting too old for this 'welcome home' rushing around!"

So, Kate thought resignedly, there was a spiteful lavender light with a penchant for uttering unpleasant threats, a garrulous cuckoo, and now a talking leopard as well? She hardly dared wonder what else might await at Carismont. Would the castle cat prove to be an unconscionable chatterbox? The dogs fluent in French? And what if the mice were given to midnight choral practice! Anything now seemed possible.

At last the tired horses were urged along the final stretch of the drive, where it led beneath the oriel window and around to the entrance on the western side. All was ablaze in the full flood of light from the sunset. There was an imposing sixteenth-century barbican, and a drawbridge over a narrow scoop in the rocky ground.

Kate expected Belerion to stay with the carriage, but instead he sheered away again. *"That's enough exercise for today,"* he muttered as he disappeared back into the gardens.

The carriage rumbled over the drawbridge and then echoed beneath the barbican. Suddenly they were in a wide quadrangle, where long shadows lay over close-tended lawns and flower beds as the slanting sunset pierced the barbican behind them. An ornamental pool with a fountain was adorned with new water lilies, which were being carefully planted by an elderly gardener and his young assistant. Both straightened and snatched off their hats as the carriage appeared.

Kate tried to forget everything else and concentrated on meeting the servants for the first time. Gerent had assured her that the carriage's arrival at the Merry Maid would have been observed from the castle. Sure enough, the staff waited in a line by the elegant porte cochere in the southwestern corner of the quadrangle. As the carriage halted, Kate could only ponder their astonishment when they realized Gerent had brought a second wife and a stepson with him.

But even as she steeled herself for the stir she was bound to cause, she couldn't help noticing that the doors into the castle were all decked with boughs of hazel, hawthorn, and rowan. Why would that be? she wondered. Stranger still were the bay leaves that had been lavishly scattered on the three shallow steps that led up from the porte cochere to the doors. Was her existence known after all? Was it some sort of hasty bridal decoration put up because someone from the Merry Maid had rowed over to the island to warn them they had a new mistress?

Gerent, who hadn't yet looked at the doors, smiled at her before alighting. "Welcome home, Lady Carismont," he said softly.

Home? Was it? Would it ever be?

As he climbed down, a middle-aged woman in a gray linen dress hurried to greet him. Her wispy hair was tucked into a mobcap, and she had a pleasant face with the pink-and-white complexion of a countrywoman; but her face was anxious, and she was twisting a handkerchief in her hands. "Oh, my lord, my lord, how glad I am that you are here at last!" she cried.

Suddenly he noticed the greenery. "What's happened, Mrs. Pendern?" he demanded, "Why have you put up such protection?"

Protection? Kate's lips parted.

"It was all I could think of, my lord," the housekeeper replied. "Oh, I have been so worried since the moon began to wax again. I was sure you would have been home in good time, but when you didn't come . . . Well, I've guarded all doors into the castle with boughs like these. You know what is said. *By three hazel, hawthorn, and rowan; by four is bay against evil sowan.*"

Gerent replied patiently, but with a definite edge in his voice. "Yes, yes, I know the couplet well enough, but what I wish you to tell me is *why* you have resorted to this. What exactly has happened?"

"The bells were heard as soon as the new moon appeared, sir, just like this time last year and the year before. Then, the night before last, Miss Genevra went in the sea again, my lord."

In the ensuing silence Kate thought she heard the cuckoo in the distance. The first part of the housekeeper's statement had made Justin's eyes brighten excitedly, but the second part alarmed him. Genevra heard the ghostly bells and actually went into the sea? Kate put a quick hand on his arm and squeezed reassuringly, which earned her a grateful smile.

Gerent's momentary shock deserted him, and he spoke sharply to Mrs. Pendern. "Genevra went in the sea?" he repeated.

"Yes, my lord. For the same reason as before," the housekeeper whispered.

"Dear God, is there nothing that . . . that *creature* will not do to have her way?" Gerent breathed.

The housekeeper was anxious for her own as well as the other servants' accounts. "Please believe that it did not come about through anyone's neglect of duty, my lord. Miss Genevra went out at night, and no one knew she had gone. If it were not for the leopard . . ."

"Belerion?"

"He set up a racket fit to raise the Old Boy himself, and it was soon realized Miss Genevra had gone. The leopard led us down to the little landing stage. She was in the water right up to her waist, just standing there, calling for her mama. Oh, the poor little mite was in such a way. One of the men waded right in to get her, and we brought her back here right away. I made her drink a glass of chamomile tea, and she was put into her bed."

"Is she all right now?"

"Well, yes, my lord, I . . . I think so."

"You only think so?"

Mrs. Pendern became a little flustered. "She is in one of her tantrum tempers, my lord, but that is not new."

Gerent nodded. "And apart from this one incident, nothing else has happened?"

"No, sir. Like I said, the bells have been heard for a few days now, and the moon will be at its fullest tomorrow night, so I know there's another big tide on the way, like the one that's come with the April moon for the past two years. What with that, your absence, and Miss Genevra's talk of her mama, all I could think was I must put up the proper greenery. So at first light yesterday, I sent some men to gather it from the gardens. They were silly enough to take most of the rowan from the one tree, which has been quite spoiled as a consequence. I told them off right well, my lord, but at least the castle is protected according to the old ways. I hope I did right?"

In the carriage, Justin gazed in puzzlement at Gerent and the housekeeper. Greenery as protection? That was silly! Castles were protected by things like cannon and men at arms, not branches of leaves! Kate was scarcely less bewildered. Superstition had been evident in every word, but what shocked her most of all was to hear Gerent refer to his daughter as "that creature." At least she supposed it was Genevra he referred to. Gathering her skirts, she alighted, and Justin followed with his boat.

As they stepped down, there was an immediate stir among the watching servants. Mrs. Pendern was caught so unawares by there being anyone else with Gerent, that she stepped back involuntarily before remembering her manners and dropping a hasty curtsy. "Why, welcome, madam, young sir. Forgive me, I . . . I did not realize you were there."

Gerent acquainted her with Kate's rank. "Mrs. Pendern, this is Lady Carismont, whom I wish you to address as such."

The gathered servants gasped audibly, and a rustle of whispers broke out among them. Mrs. Pendern was so thunderstruck, she could only gape.

Then Gerent calmly introduced Justin. "And this is my new stepson, Master Justin."

The housekeeper stared at Kate. "My . . . my lady. Master Justin. A . . . a new Lady Carismont?" she said then. "I never thought I would see the day . . ."

"Well, see it you have," Gerent said. "Now, then, I think I should see how Genevra is after her ordeal." He remembered the other servants and turned to acknowledge them. "Thank you for welcoming us home."

The little assembly managed a hodgepodge of bows and curtsies, and then Gerent looked at Justin. Seeing the apprehension on the boy's face, he offered him the opportunity to postpone the moment of meeting his new stepsister. "Justin, I think maybe it is best if I introduce Genevra to your mama on her own first. Unless, of course, you would particularly like to be there . . . ?"

"Oh, I think you and Mama should go alone, sir!" Justin broke in hastily. He much preferred the chance to sail his boat on the ornamental pool to the prospect of Genevra and her tantrum tempers.

"Mrs. Pendern will look after you for a while."

"Yes, sir."

Gerent offered Kate his arm, and together they entered the castle. As they disappeared from view, a babble of conversation broke out among the servants.

11

The sound of Genevra's tantrum was audible long before Kate and Gerent reached the little girl's rooms. Her sobs and screams, and the anxious imploring of her harassed maid, echoed along the beautifully furnished, white-plastered passages where long ago black-cowled monks had gone about their daily devotions amid bare stonework. In the Carismont Castle of today, no expense had been spared to make it as luxurious and comfortable a residence as any to be found throughout the land. Elegant furniture was in every room and passage. There were also stained-glass windows, exquisite paintings, tapestries, and curtains. The view from every window Kate passed was utterly glorious. It was a place one could only love, she thought, and in which one could only wish to be loved.

On reaching the open doorway into her new step-daughter's rooms, Kate waited for Gerent to precede her. Genevra was in bed, screaming, kicking her legs, and beating at her hapless maid with clenched fists. It was a monumental outburst of passionate emotion, and the little girl was so in its grip that Kate doubted she knew why she was doing it, or how to stop. Kate had seen such a display before, when Justin had behaved the same way for a while after Michael's death.

In his case it had been a combination of grief, fear, vulnerability, and a need for his remaining parent's undivided attention. If Kate had to make a spur-of-the-moment judgment about Genevra, she would have said that the little girl's behavior resulted from the same things.

She watched as Gerent hurried to his daughter's bedside. The tearful maid was glad to be dismissed, and hurried out past Kate without even noticing her. The moment Gerent gathered Genevra into his arms, the tantrum dissolved into gentle sobs. The little girl clung to her father tightly, as if she wanted to disappear into his comforting presence. For several minutes her stifled weeping and Gerent's soothing voice were all that could be heard.

It was impossible to see what Genevra looked like, except that she was as dark as Gerent, with long ringlets that were in a terrible tangle because she had threshed around so on the bed. Kate could not help admiring Gerent's gentleness and understanding. Only too many fathers would have ranted and railed at a child for such misbehavior, but he remained kind and loving. More and more was he a man after Kate's own heart. And more and more she realized too that in his remark to Mrs. Pendern—"Dear God is there nothing that . . . that *creature* will not do to have her way?"— he had not been referring to Genevra. To whom then?

From the doorway, Kate had an excellent view of the rooms, which faced due south over the open sea. The arched casement windows stood open, and she could clearly see the bay sparkling and glinting like molten metal that had spilled from the furnace that was the sky. The windows were set high above a precipitous drop to the sea, which was always deep this side of the island. Through a doorway to her left there was a washroom, and through another to her right there was a dressing room, with a large and rather cumbersome wardrobe that Kate imagined had once been a medieval livery cupboard.

The bedroom itself was predominantly primrose and

white, with Chinese floral curtains at the windows and on the four-poster bed. The floor was covered with a fine Wilton carpet, and to one side of Kate stood a lacquered screen, adorned with beautiful Chinese scenes. A fire burned in the hearth, and on either side of it were armchairs upholstered in navy-blue brocade. A bookcase containing various children's volumes stood against a wall, and in a corner was a table laden with everything necessary for drawing and painting. Genevra did not lack for toys, either, for there was a handsome dollhouse, a rocking horse, a number of dolls, and a pink velvet cat that looked as if it had been much cuddled and loved. The rooms were those of a little girl who was adored and provided for, and who lacked nothing at all . . . except her mother, and the constant presence of her father.

As Gerent at last took Genevra by the arms, and held her gently away from him, Kate saw that the little girl was pretty, with a dainty face and large hazel eyes that Kate guessed must be like Selena's, for they were certainly nothing like Gerent's. He took out the locket he had brought for her, and placed it around her neck. "There, a present for you from London. Wear it all the time."

"All the time?" Genevra sniffed, wiping her eyes on her nightgown sleeve.

"Yes. Never take it off."

Genevra looked curiously at him, but nodded. "I promise I won't, Papa," she said, still not noticing Kate in the doorway.

He brushed her ringlets tenderly back from her hot forehead, then cupped her face in his hands. "What has upset you so, sweeting? What's wrong?" he asked gently.

"I . . . I'm going to die, Papa," she said solemnly.

It was such a terrible thing for a child to say that Kate's lips parted. Gerent was shocked too. "No, sweeting, of course you're not going to die. Whatever gives you such a notion?"

Genevra's lips pressed together, and she didn't reply,

but Kate noticed how her dark eyes crept toward the window, peering out to the glittering sea.

Gerent was determined upon an answer. "Genevra, did someone say you were going to die? Was it your maid? I cannot believe it was Mrs. Pendern . . ."

"No, it wasn't either of them."

"But someone did say it?" he pressed, still kindly.

"Yes, but I can't tell you who, Papa. It's a secret."

At that he drew a heavy breath, and lowered his hands from the child's face. "Well, now I think I know who it was, sweeting, and you must not believe her. She is not telling you the truth."

"She is, Papa, truly she is."

"No, dearest. Promise me you will not listen to her anymore."

"But—"

"Promise," he interrupted firmly.

For a moment Genevra looked a little rebellious, but then she nodded. "All right, I promise. At least . . ."

"Yes?"

"I will *try* not to listen."

"I must be content with that, I suppose," he murmured, then smiled and stroked her cheek with his thumb.

Genevra quickly put her little hand over his. "Are you staying at Carismont now, Papa?"

"For a few months."

"Please stay always. I hate it when you go away."

"I have to go away from time to time, darling. Business affairs must be attended to." Gerent smiled. "And at least when I go away, you can be sure I will bring you a present. This time I brought you a beautiful gold locket."

Genevra lowered her eyes. "I know you bring me presents, Papa, but I am always afraid . . ."

"Yes?" he prompted.

"I am always afraid you will not come back."

"Of course I'll come back," he said firmly.

"Mama didn't," she reminded him.

Gerent drew his hand away, and got up from the bed. He looked quickly at Kate, and she saw the question in his eyes. Was this the right moment to introduce her? But even as the glance was exchanged, Genevra suddenly saw her anyway.

"Who are you?"

Kate stepped hesitantly into the room, and Gerent cleared his throat. There was no painless way of imparting such news, no gentle whisper that would make it easier to absorb. He had to just say it. "Genevra, this is my new wife, your stepmother . . ."

Genevra stared at Kate as if suddenly perceiving cloven hooves beneath her embroidered muslin hem.

Gerent became uneasy. "Genevra?"

"No!" The girl screamed suddenly. "No! She can't be your wife! Or my mother! I hate her! I will not have her here!" She flung herself facedown into the pillows, weeping hysterically.

Gerent was rooted with dismay, but Kate knew what to do. She nodded at him to leave the room, which he did reluctantly. She closed the door behind him, and then went to Genevra's bed and sat down. She said nothing, but allowed Genevra to continue. Her silence led the child to think she too had left the apartment, so that when the sobs suddenly stopped and Genevra sat up again, it was with something of a shock that she saw Kate.

The child's mouth opened to begin sobbing again, but Kate spoke first. "By all means continue if it makes you feel better, but I believe you are tired of screeching."

"I don't like you!"

"I understand how you feel. Justin was exactly the same when he heard your papa was to be his stepfather."

Suspicion clouded Genevra's dark eyes. "Who's Justin?"

"My son. He is the same age as you." Kate went to hold a candle to the fire and brought it to the little table by the bed, for the sunset was fading fast now. Then she sat down again on the edge of the coverlet.

Genevra gave her a mulish look. "Why would Justin feel like me? He has my papa, whereas I only have—"

"You only have me?" Kate smiled. "Well, that's true, of course, but when I said Justin felt like you, I did not mean about having a stepfather, although I admit he wasn't very pleased at first. No, I mean that he felt like you when his papa died. He loved him very much, you see, as much as I'm sure you loved your mama."

Genevra hesitated, searching Kate's face with big, uncertain eyes. "I love my papa," she said then, which seemed to Kate rather an odd response. Given Genevra's mood, a fierce claim to have loved her mama more than Justin could *possibly* have loved his papa seemed more likely. Instead there was just the simple statement of loving Gerent.

Kate felt her way carefully. "Justin was angry when his papa died. He was so unhappy that he wouldn't do anything I asked him, and it was all because he was afraid he was going to lose me as well. He wanted me to be where he could see me, so he knew I was safe. Is that what you want your papa to do?"

Genevra didn't reply, but fresh tears wended down her flushed cheeks.

"There is nothing wrong with feeling that way, you know," Kate said gently, taking a handkerchief and pressing it into the child's hand. "We all need to feel secure and loved, even when we grow up."

"Do you feel like that?"

"Oh, yes."

Genevra wiped her eyes. "I badly want Papa to stay here," she admitted then. "Whenever he leaves, I think it will be the last time I ever see him."

"Why don't you go with him," Kate suggested.

Genevra recoiled. "Oh, no, I can't do that."

"Why not? I'm sure he would not mind."

"I can't leave the island."

"Why not?" Kate asked curiously, remembering that Gerent had said Genevra refused to leave the island since Selena's death. Was it simply that she was afraid of the causeway?

"I just can't. I have to stay here." Genevra regarded her. "Is Justin here too?" she asked suddenly.

"Yes."

"I hope you do not think I should be nice to him?" The question was a gauntlet thrown down.

"Well, I hoped you might, and I rather think your papa hopes so too, but no one will *make* you do anything. Justin is on his own like you, and is quite able to play by himself. I think he would like to spend time with Belerion."

Genevra didn't like that. "He can't!"

"Why not?"

"Belerion belongs to Papa."

Kate smiled. "Well, maybe when you're feeling better, you will have second thoughts about Justin. Maybe then you will want to show him what he can and cannot do."

"Oh, yes, I'll show him all the things he *can't* do."

Kate hid a smile. "But what if you and he get on together? I mean, you would have someone to talk to, someone who really does understand exactly how you feel. You could help each other."

"Because he has lost his papa?"

Kate nodded. "Yes, and because his mama has married your papa. Justin would much prefer to have his real papa back again, you know, just as I'm sure you would like your real mama again."

Genevra's eyes widened. "Oh, no . . . ! I mean, I . . ." She put her hands to her head, and closed her eyes tightly, as if unable to deal with all the conflicting thoughts running through her mind.

Kate touched her gently. "I'm sorry, Genevra. I really did not mean to upset you." It was becoming obvious that the thought of Selena's return appalled her daughter. "Look, I know you are feeling very out of sorts tonight, but—"

"I'm not coming down to dinner!" Genevra broke in quickly, determined not to meet Justin until she absolutely had to.

Kate smiled. "If that is what you wish, then of course no one will *oblige* you to join us. Perhaps in the morning, after a good sleep, we can all meet properly at breakfast? You may find that you like Justin."

"I won't."

"Your papa would like it if you did. He loves you very much, you know." Kate paused, thinking it best to broach the matter of school lessons. She was a great believer in putting all cards on the table at the outset, for then everyone knew where they were, and each card could be picked up at leisure. "Genevra, I met your papa because he interviewed me for the post of governess to you."

Genevra gaped. "You mean, you're a *governess*?" Had Kate been a three-headed toad, the child's horror could not have been greater.

"I was for a while. When Justin's father was alive I was mistress of a grand house like this, but things were difficult when he died, and I had to provide for Justin and myself. Then I met your papa, and he asked me to marry him. But although I am his wife now, and your stepmother, I am also to give school lessons to you and Justin."

Genevra was mollified by the mention of a grand house, but still pulled a face. "Lessons? Oh, no . . ."

"I'm afraid so." Kate hid a smile, for there was something very natural and straightforward about the little girl's reaction. She got up from the bed again. "I will go now, and let you rest, for I am sure you have much to think about." She went to the door, and then paused to look back. "Genevra, why did you go out into the water the night before last?"

"Because I heard the bells, and then Mama called me" came the simple reply. Genevra pointed at the window. "She was out there among the trees, I saw her."

Kate went to the nearest window and leaned out a

little to look. There were no trees at all, of course, only the sea . . . and the cuckoo wheeling over the shimmering gold of the water. Darkness was approaching fast, and the air had a quality she had not known before. A strange, magical quality that made the hairs at the nape of her neck tingle.

Genevra spoke again. "Something woke me up, and I went to the window. Mama was beckoning, then she called me to go out to the forest with her. So I went."

"But there is no forest, Genevra," Kate said slowly.

"Oh, yes, there is. Lyonesse is out there. It's where Mama lives now."

Kate did not know how to reply to this, but thankfully was spared the necessity because the little girl, clearly exhausted from her tantrum, snuggled down in bed to go to sleep.

Kate decided to remain until Genevra fell asleep, which happened soon enough. But then, just as Kate turned from the window, she heard the dull, booming toll of church bells coming from out in the bay. Muffled and distorted, the sound seemed to issue from deep below the waves, and it sent a shiver through Kate. How many bells were there? Three? Four? As if it were Sunday morning in several nearby villages. Drowned villages.

The cuckoo suddenly glided toward the windowsill, and Kate drew back hastily to prevent herself from being flown right into. The bird, clumsy as ever, landed so awkwardly that it was forced to grab the curtain with its beak to prevent itself from slithering right into the room. For a desperate moment its tail swayed up and down, but at last it perched safely, shuffled its wings neatly, then eyed her.

It was close enough to touch, but Kate did not reach out. Somehow that did not seem the thing to do. But, rather oddly, speaking to it *did* seem the thing. "By Sir Kay's codlings, you aren't the most agile of birds, are you?" she observed.

The cuckoo seemed utterly taken aback, and its eyes popped. *"You can hear me that well?"* it gasped.

"Oh, yes. And I can hear the lavender light and Belerion."

The cuckoo stared at her. *"Upon my soul and Lancelot's liver pills!"* it breathed, greatly impressed by her prowess.

"What do you want? Why am I the only one to see and hear you? Except for the fisherman's unfortunate dog, of course."

The cuckoo looked sleek, clearly relishing the memory of the dog's punishment. But then it eyed her again. *"You must take great care."*

"Why? Am I in danger?"

"Oh, yes. So be on your guard at all times."

"But—"

Before she could say anymore, the strange cuckoo launched itself from the window with a sort of flapping, legs-thrust-forward leap that was anything but graceful. It flew away into the remains of the sunset, and disappeared against the brilliance of the sun's rim.

12

Leaving Genevra soundly asleep, Kate slipped out of the apartment to find Gerent waiting anxiously in the windowless passage, where a lighted candle now stood on a console table, next to a small Sevres bowl filled with primroses.

Belerion had been sprawled on the carpet at his feet, but got up as she appeared. *"So you can hear me too, can you? Good, for that means less work,"* the leopard observed. Then it yawned, stretched its front paws before it, and walked slowly away along the passage. *"Why I've had to stay here all these years, I don't know,"* it grumbled. *"That fool of a cuckoo should have been called upon before now. Why should it all have been up to me? It's most unfair. Yes, by my spots and whiskers! Most unfair."*

Still muttering, the grumpy leopard disappeared around a corner, and Kate looked quickly at Gerent. "Did you hear that?" she asked.

"Hear what?"

"Oh, nothing . . ."

The candle swayed gently, blushing the creamy primroses to pink, and at the same time reflecting in Gerent's eyes as he asked about Genevra. "How is she?"

"Sleeping."

He turned away with a sigh of relief. "These episodes always distress her."

"I am not surprised. Gerent, she is a very unhappy little girl. Losing her mother makes her fearful of losing you as well, especially when you are away for any length of time."

His shoulders slumped a little, and he nodded. "I know," he said quietly. "But you know as well as I that a landlord must attend to all manner of things that keep him away from his country home."

Oh, yes, she knew well enough, for toward the end Michael had seldom been at Kingsley Park. But that had been on account of his addiction to gambling, not because estate business required his presence in London. "Gerent, you keep telling me that business matters keep you in London for weeks at a time, but is that entirely true? Forgive me, but as you have pointed out, I do know about the running of an estate. I certainly know that you do not need to be away for such long periods. Why do you really stay in London?"

He turned, regarding her rather quizzically. "How suspicious you sound, Kate. Do you wonder if I keep a woman in some discreet high-walled villa?"

She flushed a little. "No, that had not crossed my mind."

He smiled ruefully. "I am disappointed. I wondered if perhaps such a possibility had made you jealous."

"Do you wish me to be jealous?"

He nodded. "Yes, I rather think I do."

The conversation had taken a sudden and very unexpected turn, and she felt a little flustered. "We . . . were speaking of your absences."

"So we were. In truth, Kate, I stay in London to escape from disagreeable . . . er, memories, here. Genevra will not accompany me, and so I go alone. I need to be away from here, and all that goes with it."

There was something behind his words, but Kate could not think what it might be; except, of course, that it must concern Selena. Well, it didn't matter what it was, for Genevra must come first. "Gerent, you must promise to stay here much more."

"Am I being lectured, my lady?"

Was there an edge in his voice? Kate could not tell, but she held her ground anyway. "Yes, my lord, you are. You married me so that I could take proper care of Genevra. That is what I am doing now."

"My idea was that you would look after her in my absence," he murmured.

How typically male, she thought. "Well, the best laid plans can go awry, sir, as in this case, for I am not about to view my duties as intermittent." Nor, Gerent, should you, came the silent addendum.

She delivered the rebuke quietly, but meant every word. For a moment he continued to gaze at her as if undecided whether to be angry or not, but then he gave a hint of a smile. "I consider myself duly chastised, Kate, and I admire your resolve."

"It is not resolve, Gerent, it is a matter of conscience. I entered this marriage on the understanding that I would look after Genevra as well as I look after Justin. This I will do to the very best of my ability, and if it means pointing out things that you will not like, I am afraid that it is too bad."

He laughed a little. "Good heavens, my lady, you have turned into a veritable dragon, and it is too late for me to have second thoughts about our union," he murmured.

"You know that isn't true."

"What isn't true? That you are a dragon? Or that it is too late to think again?"

"Neither is true, for I am definitely not a dragon, and as this is a marriage in name only, you could walk away from it if you so wished. I imagine non-consummation is grounds for annulment?"

"I wouldn't know, but have to point out that you are as free to walk away from your vows as you think I am." He became more serious. "*Do* you wish to walk away, Kate?"

"No."

"Nor do I, which rather dispenses with any earnest debate about non-consummation." He ran a hand through his dark hair. "Before we become too embroiled in this diversion, perhaps I should ask if there is anything else you wish to say to me concerning Genevra?"

"Well, she will join us for breakfast tomorrow, on which occasion she promises to tell Justin what he may *not* do."

"That I can believe," he responded dryly.

"Well, he is more than capable of standing up to her, so I think we may expect fireworks. Unless, of course, they find they like each other after all. They will probably unite when it comes to the business of lessons, about which I have also told her." She paused. "Gerent, there is one thing I want you to promise me."

"And that is?"

"That you will spend some time alone with Genevra tomorrow morning."

"But I have much to do tomorrow, Kate. My agent is coming to—"

"Please, Gerent. You are going to have to consider her needs more than your own, and more than Carismont's needs too. It's important, and you owe it to her. You owe it to yourself as well, for I can tell how very much you love her. So just be with her for a while tomorrow, then promise her you will spend more time together later in the day. And the day after that, and the day after that."

He gazed into her eyes. "Yes, of course."

"You promise?"

"Yes. Now, is there anything else you think I should know?"

Was this an opportune moment to venture into more mysterious matters? "About Selena. Genevra told me that—"

He held up a hand. "I am not ready to speak of Selena," he interrupted, his manner and tone such that

Kate had to fall silent. He clearly felt he had been a little harsh, for he gave her an apologetic smile. "Forgive me, I did not mean to be abrupt, or indeed unhelpful."

"Oh, Gerent . . ." There was something about him in those few seconds that tore at her very heart. Oh, *how* she longed for more from this marriage. How she longed to lie in his arms, and . . .

Someone—a woman—was heard approaching along the passage. Another candle flickered, and for a brief moment Kate feared it would be Selena, come to lay claim to her husband, but it was a maid that came around the corner.

Gerent turned. "Ah, Kate, this is Bessie Portreath, who is to attend you."

"Portreath?"

He nodded. "Yes, it is a widespread family in these parts. She is second or third cousin to Denzil Portreath."

Bessie reached them, and dipped a respectful curtsy. "My lord, my lady." Fluffy blonde hair peeped from beneath her mobcap, and she had wide-set hazel eyes. She was of medium height, with a tidy little figure that clearly benefited from running up and down the winding castle stairs. Her dress was made of green-and-white-checked gingham, and her white apron was stiff with starch.

Gerent addressed her. "Bessie, you know what is expected of you, so please attend to Lady Carismont." He turned to Kate again. "I will go to find Justin now. I rather think he will be in the quadrangle."

"Sailing the boat? Yes, I'm sure you're right."

He gave a quick smile. "Bessie will tell you about arrangements for dinner, which is usually at eight but obviously will be much later tonight." He inclined his head, then walked swiftly away.

Kate looked at Bessie. "Hello, Bessie."

"My lady. I will do all I can to be a good maid to you."

Kate smiled. "And you will succeed, I'm sure."

"I am to take you to her ladyship's apart—I . . . mean, to your apartment."

A shock ran through Kate. She was to have *Selena's* rooms? The thought simply had not occurred to her, even though on reflection it was rather obvious this would be the case.

"Is something wrong, madam?" the maid inquired, seeing her expression.

"Er, no, of course not." Kate plucked inspiration from the air. "I was wondering where my son's rooms are to be?"

"Master Justin is to have the apartment above Miss Genevra, madam. The staircase leading up to them is just along there." The maid pointed farther along the passage. "Mrs. Pendern thought Master Justin would like those rooms, which were his lordship's when he was a boy. They are right at the top of the castle, partly in a turret, but are very comfortable, and the view from there is much better than anywhere else."

"They sound excellent."

"Oh, they are, madam." Bessie curtsied again. "If you will come this way," she said then, and turned to conduct Kate to her predecessor's apartment.

13

Bessie's candle smoked and flared so much that she had to protect the flame with her hand as she led Kate through the castle.

With the day now at an end, Carismont had become a place of shadows, with recesses, looming shapes, and odd corners that might lead anywhere. Heavy arras curtains flanked doorways, fine paintings and dusky tapestries adorned walls, and ancient chests stood in alcoves. There were vaulted chambers, stone staircases, great iron candleholders, immense fireplaces, and Gothic tables and chairs that could well have come from the original priory. It was•atmospheric in a way Kate had not experienced before; and all the while there was the presence of the sea, which she occasionally glimpsed in the faint remains of the sunset.

Selena's apartment was approached along a wide gallery that was lined on one side with studded oak doors, and on the other with cloisterlike stained-glass windows that overlooked the quadrangle. When Kate paused to look through the uneven lozenge-shaped panes, she saw Gerent and Justin sailing the boat. Or rather, watching the boat as it sailed around and around the pond. There was something odd about its movement, although Kate could not think what it was.

As she looked, Belerion padded from the darkness of the barbican and approached the pool. The leopard took a drink, and then lay down on the grass, watching the boat as it glided past within reach. Gerent took Justin to the great cat, and introduced him. Lying down evidently took the edge off Belerion's cantankerousness, for much to Justin's delight, the leopard rolled over for his belly to be tickled.

Bessie shuffled a little at the end of the gallery, and Kate caught up her skirts to walk on. At last they reached Selena's apartment, which faced toward the lights of Trezance. The lilac-and-gold rooms were warm in the glow of firelight and candles, and it was all very much to Kate's taste. If only it were not so very much Selena's domain, she thought as she glanced around. Various shades of lilac dominated— or maybe it was lavender. Yes, lavender, Kate decided, the fact not lost upon her that the mysterious little light was the same color. The light and Selena were synonymous, and Kate would have been prepared to lay odds that lavender was that lady's favorite color.

The brocade coverlet on the four-poster bed was lavender, so were the various armchairs, and even the wall silk and carpets. A good fire had been kindled, but as yet the air was still a little cool. Maybe it was because this side of the castle faced north, Kate thought, shivering slightly.

"Are you cold, madam?" Bessie asked.

"Only a little," Kate replied, going to hold her hands out to the fire. The logs shifted, and sparks flew up the chimney. Just sparks, pale and golden, as sparks should be. . . .

"Shall I build the fire up more?"

"No, that won't be necessary." Kate watched the sparks.

"Is something wrong, madam?"

"No, thank you, Bessie."

The maid came hesitantly toward her. "Do you wish for a French maid, madam?"

"A *French* maid? Why do you ask?" Kate was a little puzzled.

"Her ladyship . . . I mean, the first Lady Carismont . . . had a French maid."

"I see. Well, I'm quite happy with you, Bessie."

The maid was pleased. "Thank you, madam. No one liked the Frenchwoman. She was always complaining, so I told her France was a vile country, where the people ate frogs and drank ditch water."

Kate laughed. "Good for you, Bessie."

"She had no business complaining about Carismont, for it is a place of magic."

"Magic?" Kate looked intently at her.

"Oh, yes. Everyone knows the island was conjured from beneath the sea, and that it can sometimes disappear again for a while. It can happen twice a year, at midsummer and midwinter."

Thoughts of lost lands and sunken bells edged in, and Kate shivered again. "How very disagreeable if one happens to be here at the time," she remarked.

Bessie nodded. "But we'd all be safe, madam, for we'd turn into fairy lights."

Kate's interest quickened. "Fairy lights?"

"Yes, madam. They're often seen on the coast here. They can appear in a fog, when they're called hoopers, and they can be just on their own. Some people believe they are piskies, but most reckon they are people from Lyonesse, come to see how we live."

Bessie went to draw the curtains across the windows, and arranged them carefully on the spacious, cushioned seats that formed the sills. "My cousin says they are definitely from Lyonesse and that we must all stay well away from them if we know what's good for us," she said, plumping up one of the cushions.

"Your cousin? Would that be Mr. Denzil Portreath?"

"Yes, madam. The lights are always being seen up at Polwithiel. That's his big house on the way to—"

"Yes, I know Polwithiel, for I saw it among the trees as we drove to Trezance."

"A great drafty place it is, and I know I wouldn't

want to live there. Not that it is likely to happen, for Cousin Denzil has fallen out with just about everyone in the family. There's only my brother Jan who has anything to do with him now, and he works up at Polwithiel."

"And your Cousin Denzil has fallen out with Lord Carismont too?" Kate ventured, hoping to find out exactly what had caused the bitter quarrel between Gerent and Portreath.

But the subtle pumping did not draw water, for Bessie looked suddenly guilty. "Oh, madam, I'm not supposed to mention my cousin. His lordship has forbidden his name to be spoken here. Please don't tell him I've been so indiscreet."

"You weren't indiscreet, Bessie, for I was the one who mentioned him." Kate did not press more. No doubt Gerent would tell her himself . . . eventually. In the meantime she would be left to wonder in what way the two men would fall out over Selena. The obvious conclusion was that the first Lady Carismont had an affair with Denzil Portreath. Anything was possible, although why any woman would turn from Gerent to a man like Portreath, Kate could not begin to guess.

Bessie cleared her throat. "Shall I begin unpacking your things, madam? I believe the luggage has all been brought up here now."

"Yes, by all means, Bessie," Kate replied. "Oh, you will find an apple-green silk gown. I will wear it for dinner."

"Yes, madam." The maid hastened through into the adjoining dressing room, then stopped when she saw how few trunks there were. "Oh, I . . . I think there must be more to come up here after all . . ."

"No, that is all I have with me."

Bessie turned in astonishment. "All? But—"

"The rest of my wardrobe will come from Mrs. Camberton," Kate explained, rightly guessing that the maid would recognize the name of Selena's dressmaker.

Bessie's eyes cleared. "Oh, I see, madam," she said, and went to begin her tasks.

Kate wondered what the maid's thoughts would be when she found the unmodish, rather ordinary apple-green silk, which was hardly what would be expected of a Lady Carismont, and certainly could not be attributed to a couturier as superior and sought after as Mrs. Camberton of Golden Square! The truth about Gerent's new wife having recently been a governess was bound to come out, for the coachman who had driven them here would have heard all the gossip at Berkeley Square. He was hardly likely to keep silent about such a thing. It would already be spreading through the castle like wildfire!

With a sigh, Kate untied her bonnet and placed it on a table. Then she studied the rooms again, only too sensitive to the fact that they had been Selena's. She felt a little like a fly that had become caught up in the web of a very large spider. Suddenly she wanted to be able to picture that spider a little more clearly. "Bessie, are there any portraits of the first Lady Carismont?"

"Portraits, madam? Oh, no. His lordship wanted her to sit for one, but she did not hold with such things."

"May I inquire what she looked like?" Kate asked, hating herself for interrogating a servant, but if she wished to know more, what other option was there? She wasn't about to ask Gerent.

Bessie came to the archway. "She was the loveliest thing I have ever seen, madam, with a cloud of red-gold curls that tumbled right down her back, and big lavender-blue eyes that were the shape of almonds."

Now, why am I not surprised? Kate wondered.

"She did not have a single freckle, in spite of her hair," Bessie continued, "and lavender suited her greatly, on account of her eyes, so she always wore it in one shade or another. That was why she has these rooms decorated like this."

Kate vowed never again to wear lavender—either as a color or a scent. She would even avoid it in gardens!

Bessie gasped suddenly. "Oh, I almost forgot, madam.

Mrs. Pendern said I was to especially ask you if you would like a hot bath after your long journey."

"It depends how long it is until dinner."

Bessie came into the room to look at the ormulu clock on the mantel. "Another hour yet."

"Then, yes, I would like a bath."

Bessie beamed. "I will attend to it directly." Snatching up her skirts, she hurried out.

Silence descended over the rooms, and Kate's attention was suddenly drawn to the bed. She gave a start, for without her having heard anything, the gilded cords that held the hangings to the posts had been undone, and the bed was now fully enclosed. Had someone entered the room? No, it was impossible! And yet . . .

"Justin? Are you playing games?" she demanded. There was no reply. She took a hesitant step toward the bed, but then the fire shifted. A shower of sparks fled up the chimney. She hesitated, then continued angrily to the bed, seized the curtains, and flung them back. There was nothing there, but she thought she heard Selena's low laugh echo faintly down the chimney.

14

It was time to go down to dinner, and all lights in the apartment had been extinguished except the candle Kate intended to use to find her way to the former refectory that now served as the castle's dining room. She and Gerent were to eat alone, Genevra having already decided to stay in her rooms until breakfast, and Justin now electing to enjoy supper in his exciting turret bedroom, from where in daylight he would have a panoramic view over the bay.

She smoothed the apple-green silk gown, glancing down at it in the candle's thin glow. How dull and dated she felt after Mrs. Camberton's white muslin sprigged with lemon flowers. Yet she knew the pale, delicate shade of green suited her particularly well. It was a regrettable fact that having been at the height of Golden Square fashion for the journey from London, she found it very hard indeed to slip back into Kate Kingsley's old clothes.

She tweaked the square neckline, and then fluffed out the frills at the cuffs. It would have to do, because the sprigged muslin was in definite need of refreshing after the rigors of traveling. At least she was satisfied with her hair, for Bessie was surprisingly good with comb and pins. When the very latest London styles had been described, the maid had soon achieved a creditable froth of honey-colored curls at the front and a tumble of delightful ringlets from a knot at the back. Now Kate felt as ready as she was ever likely to be, but could not help imagining how Selena would have looked right now. With her cloud of red-gold hair, incredible beauty, lavender eyes, and an exquisite dinner gown by Mrs. Camberton, the first Lady Carismont would no doubt be breathtakingly perfect. "Well, Kate, you're a very poor substitute," Kate murmured to herself.

Waiting for the clock on the mantel to strike the hour, she went to a window and held the curtain aside to look out. The tide had now ebbed almost completely, leaving rocks, pools, and stretches of rippled sand where at high tide there would be quite deep water. The lights of Trezance shone on the shore opposite, the fishing vessels still afloat on the channel of the creek. She could clearly see the heights of the moor beyond the town. The sky was cloudless, with what seemed a million stars, and the almost full moon was already up, pale, enigmatic, and serene.

The clock began to chime suddenly, so she went to pick up her shawl, which was prettily patterned with cream, green, and rose. Draping it over her arms, she took the lighted candle and went out. Before dismissing Bessie for the night, she had asked for directions to the refectory so that she would be able to find her way.

The candle fluttered, and her footsteps seemed to echo eerily, even though she only wore satin slippers. She found herself glancing back from time to time, because the echo was so strange that it sounded as if someone were behind her. When she reached the end of the passage to Genevra's apartment, the sensation of being followed became so strong that she whirled about. But the passage stretched away into darkness, the emptiness broken by a heavy oak chest and several tapestries. But for one split second, so swift that she almost thought she had imagined it, she heard another footfall. Then silence.

"Who's there?"

There wasn't a sound. She swallowed nervously, then turned sharply to the front again as from the corner of her eye she saw candlelight leaping down the twisting stone steps from Justin's room. "Justin?" she called. There was no answer, but the light descended steadily, and then she heard the swish of a woman's skirt, accompanied by a chinking sound. "Who is it?" she cried in growing alarm.

"It's only me, my lady," Mrs. Pendern answered, and a moment later came into sight. The chinking sound came from her keys, which brushed the steps as she descended.

"Mrs. Pendern! Oh, you did give me a fright!" Kate gasped with relief.

The housekeeper smiled. "Forgive me, madam, but my hearing is not always as sharp as it might be, and I did not realize you were down here. I have just been to see if Master Justin requires anything, but he's fallen asleep on his bed. So I've just taken off his boots, covered him over with an eiderdown, and left him. It's the sea air after all that traveling, I think."

"You are sure he's all right?"

"Oh, yes. Have no fear of that, madam. I will go up a little later and see if he has awoken. If he is hungry, I will make sure he has something nourishing to eat, but I think he will sleep right through to morning." The woman smiled again. "The pasties at the Merry Maid are hearty enough to feed a horse, and no mistake, so he'll not lack sustenance if he sleeps on. So please do not fret now. You go on down to dine with his lordship. Cook has prepared a very fine meal for your first night here."

"Has she? Please be so good as to thank her for her kindness."

"I will, madam."

"I wish to thank you too, for looking after Justin."

"It is no trouble; indeed, it is my duty." The housekeeper smiled. "You are very welcome here indeed, Lady Carismont. This castle needs a lady, and his lordship needs a bride."

Even if a bride was until recently a lowly governess? Kate wondered.

The housekeeper seemed to read her thought. "Madam, may I speak frankly with you?"

"Yes, of course, Mrs. Pendern."

"You may think I am out of turn, but I wish to reassure you if I possibly can. The coachman has relayed the gossip from London, as no doubt you knew he would. That is the way of it with servants. But no one here thinks any the less of you for having had to earn a living, indeed we admire you for it. So please do not fear that anyone at Carismont will behave like those foolish maids in London. Here you will be respected for the lady you were, and the lady you still are. The governess in the middle is of no consequence to us."

Kate was quite touched. "Why, thank you for saying that, Mrs. Pendern."

The housekeeper smiled, then inclined her head respectfully, and hurried away, her skirts still rustling.

Kate glanced up the staircase. All was quiet, so she continued toward the refectory, hurrying a little more because it was taking longer than she anticipated. She reached the gallery, from where the deserted quadrangle was silvery in the moonlight. Suddenly Gerent walked from beneath the barbican, and Kate halted to watch him.

He was dressed for dinner, in a formal deep-purple coat—velvet, she thought—and white silk breeches. Th jeweled pin in his lace-edged neckcloth flashed in the light of the moon as he paused to look back. Belerion padded into view as well, and went to nuzzle his hand like a tame dog. There was something almost dreamlike about the scene; the man so handsome and swathed in mystery as to be the very personification of romance, and the great cat so lithe, beautiful, and out of place in these surroundings. Kate felt almost as if she were looking into a private room through a slightly open door, or had just turned a page and discovered an illustration for a poem . . . perhaps Lord Byron's *Don Juan*, with its tortured hero and melancholy secrets. She was unable to do anything but watch. If Gerent glanced up he would see her because of her lighted candle, but she did not extinguish it or do anything to conceal her presence.

There was something so fascinating and almost erotic about watching him that she did not really care whether he observed her or not. She drank in the perfection of his face. Every line, every curve, and every feature was a temptation she could not resist. He was her husband, and his lips had kissed hers with desire, but that was all. She longed for more. To look at him was to desire him, yearn for him; *need* him . . . It was an urgent excitement, a thing of forgotten emotions rekindled, of hidden dreams brought to life, and it reached across consciousness itself to invade her flesh, and rob her of the control she had managed to exert since Michael's death. Now raw desire engulfed her, making her ache as never before; and all because she looked secretly down upon the man whose ring she wore, but who was beyond her reach.

He walked on toward the castle entrance, and passed out of Kate's sight. As he did so, she became sharply aware of her wedding ring, which seemed to become hotter and tighter upon her finger. Then Selena's voice whispered malevolently in her ear. *"You'll never have him, for he's mine!"*

With a startled gasp, Kate turned. The lavender light was there, so close that she could have reached out to touch it. But she made no move. Suddenly she was angry, and needed to trade taunt for taunt. "You've lost him, Selena. He's beyond your reach now!"

"He will never be beyond my reach. Nor will you, my sweet, Danger surrounds you, and will soon pluck you out."

Kate raised her left hand. "You can't do anything while I have this. Oh, you may be able to make it burn and tighten, but that is *all* you can do!"

"Don't count upon it, Kate dearest!" At that moment there came the distant sound of a cuckoo, and Selena started back in alarm. Kate sensed that she was glancing nervously up and down the gallery, afraid the cuckoo would flap into view. The bird's fluting notes came once more, closer now, and with a gasp Selena sped away. As the light wriggled through a slightly open window into the quadrangle, Kate's wedding ring returned to normal, and she caught up her apple-green skirts to hurry on.

15

The refectory was a lofty white-plastered chamber, with an exposed beam roof of ancient dark oak. Iron-rimmed chandeliers were suspended low above the long sixteenth-century table that ranged down the center of the stone floor, and a plasterwork frieze depicting a hunting scene decorated the wall above the arched windows. Tapestries, paintings, and a display of coat of arms and banners added bright splashes of color. The chandeliers and various candlesticks cast a warm light over everything, sparkling on the glasses and cutlery of the two place settings at one end of the table. A fire flickered in the hearth of an immense carved-stone chimneypiece. Gerent had yet to arrive, and all was quiet as Kate entered.

She put her candle down on a sideboard that must have been centuries old, as was the array of gold plate displayed upon it, then she looked around the refectory again. Gradually her attention was drawn to the chimneypiece and a particularly lavish coat of arms emblazoned there in bright heraldic colors. The lower portion of the shield showed a golden boat with silver oars and a crimson sail, on a blue background. The upper half was divided vertically into two, showing on the left a rampant golden lioness on an ermine ground, and on the right a standing cuckoo, gray and white on a silver ground. If only the lioness were a leopard, she would be looking at three elements of the mysterious events of recent days. But the rampant cat did not seem to have a single spot, and so must definitely be a lioness.

Gerent's footsteps sounded, and she turned as he entered through an archway. Belerion was still with him, and padded across to where she stood. The leopard brushed her aside quite unashamedly. *"Make way for my poor old bones,"* he muttered, like a moaning old man. Then he settled down to enjoy the fire, and squeezed his eyes contently as all cats do. *"That's better. I do like a nice fire,"* he sighed.

Gerent went to pour two glasses of sherry from the decanter on the sideboard, then came to press one into her hand. "I trust you like sherry? I fear it did not occur to me to ask first. Selena liked—" He broke off. "Er, forgive me."

"I like sherry well enough too," she said.

He went to the table, and leaned back against it. "You were studying the coat of arms?" he inquired.

She turned to look at it again. "Yes. Does it belong to your family?"

"No." He pointed toward a shield above a doorway. "That is the Fitzarthur badge, a golden sword in a silver stone, on a blue ground. It tries to link the Fitzarthurs to the Arthurian legends, but I fear we have no such claim."

"Why doesn't it have pride of place on the chimney-piece?" she asked.

"For the simple reason that the shield on the chimney-piece predates my family's connection with the island. It is said to be the coat of arms of Lyonesse, the lioness being a play on the name."

"It's not a lioness," Belerion observed. *"The spots may have gone with age, but it's a leopard all right. Great thundering hailstones, I should know."*

"You're wrong, Gerent. It is absolutely, beyond all doubt, a leopard," Kate said, sorely tempted to divulge the source of her certain knowledge, but still not being quite prepared to divulge that animals and birds talked in her head.

He smiled as he anticipated her. "I know what you're thinking, but before you identify the bird as a cuckoo, let me point out that it is a martlet, which is a mythical bird often used in heraldry. I doubt if any medieval knight would have been eager to carry a cuckoo into battle."

Belerion sighed. *"Martlet? I wish that were so, for cuckoos are without a doubt the bane of my life! They can't be trusted to do anything properly! Give me a martlet every time. Not that there are many around now, of course. They died out not long after Arthur became king. Nowadays there is just a preponderance of pesky cuckoos. Well, one cuckoo anyway . . ."*

Mrs. Pendern appeared in the archway. "Begging your pardon, my lord, but do you wish dinner to be served now?"

"Yes, if you please, Mrs. Pendern." As the housekeeper disappeared, he looked again at Kate. "This coat of arms means nothing, Kate. It may be old, but family tradition has it that it is a fake, created by the monks in order to raise money from gullible visitors. Other places had saintly relics, Carismont had the legend of Lyonesse. That is all."

"Except that you and I know Lyonesse wasn't a legend, but definitely did exist."

His eyes met hers for a moment, then he gave a slight laugh. "Would you like to claim as much in the middle of a fashionable Mayfair gathering?" he inquired dryly.

She had to smile too. "Certainly not," she admitted.

"Exactly." He put his fingers briefly to her cheek.

The touch passed through her like a shock of lightning. Oh, if only he would kiss her now, she thought, if only he would bend his head forward and put his lips to hers . . . Desire rose so sharply through her that she almost gasped. Then, incredibly, it suddenly seemed that he *did* lean forward to kiss her. Just as had happened at the Pulteney Hotel, she felt his arms move around her and draw her close, felt his body to hers, his lips warm and urgent.

Time seemed to stop, as did her heart. The sensation of being embraced was so fierce and strong that she was sure his arms *were* around her; that his lips *did* kiss her. A wild delight scattered over her entire being. It was accompanied by a wave of gratification that seemed to wash deliciously over her, making her shiver with pleasure. But he had not moved, nor had he lain a single finger upon her, let alone pulled her into his arms. It was all an illusion, an exquisitely sensual illusion that was already fleeing to the very edges of her consciousness. Yet when she looked into his winter-sea eyes again, there was a light there that hadn't been before, as if he not only knew her emotions, but shared them.

The moment was snapped in two by Mrs. Pendern's return with a footman and maid carrying the first course. The servants remained nearby throughout the meal, which meant that conversation could not touch upon anything remotely personal. Only when the liqueurs, fruit, and nuts had been served, and the housekeeper ushered the footman and maid out again, could matters of a more intimate nature be broached.

Gerent poured two glasses of peach brandy, gave one to Kate, and then took the other to the fireplace, where Belerion was now fast asleep in the warmth. Sitting on the floor and lounging against the recumbent leopard, Gerent held up the glass so the flames shone through the liqueur as if through molten amber. There were no strange sparks in the fire, no shooting stars, will-o'-the-wisps, fairy lights, call them whatever—just the flames, warm and leaping, and the man and leopard by the hearth.

Kate sipped her glass and tried not to be obvious about gazing at her new husband. Unspoken words and unacknowledged emotions hung tangibly in the air, but neither of them spoke, until at last he looked directly at her. "We are alone at last, yet it would seem we have nothing to say to each other."

She felt unaccountably embarrassed, as if she had been perceived in an indiscretion, so instead of taking the offered opportunity to bring things into the open between them, she found herself mentioning something that was really not at all important. "I . . . I would rather like to go riding now that I am in the country again."

"Riding?" He looked blankly at her for a moment, then gave a short laugh. "You are quite at liberty to do that if you wish. There are several suitable mounts in the stable. I will see that one is placed at your disposal from tomorrow."

Having stumbled into such a subject, Kate now perceived an immediate difficulty, to wit, the lack of a riding habit. "I, er, can't, actually. I . . . don't have anything suitable to wear."

He surveyed her, clearly puzzled by her choice of after-dinner conversation. "I would not normally suggest this, but as your desire to ride is evidently very keen, I will point out that Selena's wardrobe is still here. Like the horses, it is entirely at your disposal."

"Oh, I . . . I don't think I could . . ." she began, wishing the floor would open up and swallow her.

"Kate, if riding is of such importance to you, I think it a little foolish not to indulge simply over a matter of clothes. Selena had at least three riding habits, and I am sure you and she were sufficiently of a size . . ." he didn't finish.

She knew her cheeks were flushed, but it was too late now. She had dug a little hole for herself, and had to sit in it. She might as well make the best of a bad thing. "Actually, it occurs to me that if I go for a ride, maybe Genevra and Justin could come with me."

"I take it I am to be excluded from this little excursion?" He drank his liqueur, then put the glass down carefully.

"Not at all, you are most welcome to come too."

"I'm relieved to hear it, for I was beginning to feel rejected."

Their eyes met, and she had to look away. "Maybe we could ride on the moor behind Trezance?"

"Ah, well that might create a small problem for Genevra."

"Oh?"

"I think I have already mentioned that she will not leave the island. Since Selena's death she has steadfastly refused to set foot on the causeway, ride on it, drive on it, or even go in a boat. Believe me, I've tried all manner of things in the hope of persuading her. If you can persuade her to go with you, I will be eternally grateful."

"I will do my best." She looked at him again.

He smiled. "Do not be deterred from your ride if she will not come."

"Will you come?"

"Not tomorrow. After an absence of any sort I have much estate business to attend to with my agent. I have sent word to him, and he will come to the island after breakfast. I fear I shall be busy with him for most of the day. But again, that must not deter you and Justin. If Genevra will not accompany you, I will see that you have a footman to ride along. It would not do for you to get lost on your first excursion from the island."

She smiled. "Justin and I are quite capable of finding our own way around. I *hate* having a footman trail along behind me. Michael used to insist upon it, but I had my own way in the end."

"I'm sure you did," Gerent murmured, his glance lazily amused. "Now, let me see. What other innocuous subject can we discuss? Ah, yes, Carismont. What do you think of your new home, Kate?"

The color rushed back into her cheeks. "Why, I . . . think it is very beautiful."

"Will you like it here?"

"It is too early to be certain of anything."

"Oh, what an exceedingly cautious creature I have married."

His teasing tone piqued her a little. "Well, if I were to ask you if you thought I would be an accomplished Lady Carismont, what would you say?" She paused, and when he did not answer immediately, continued, "There, you see? You cannot answer, because it is far too early for you to know."

"On the contrary, I know the answer very well. You will make an excellent Lady Carismont." He held out a hand suddenly. "Enough of this shilly-shallying. Come here, if you please."

She gazed at him, uncertain how to react.

He raised an eyebrow. "Have I offended you? If so, I apologize. Please come to me, Kate."

Slowly she got up, but then hesitated to take his outstretched hand. He looked up at her. "Perhaps you are too much of a governess after all," he murmured.

"Too much? What do you mean?"

"Well, Belerion and I are relaxed and informal down here on the floor, but you are all stiffness and formality up there."

Her fingers slid into his, and she sat down as well, her apple-green silk skirts brushing his thigh. Belerion stirred a little, stretched, then gave a huge sigh and drifted back into sleep. The sensuousness of the moment was not lost upon Kate. How could it be? Both the man and the slumbering leopard were relaxed, the firelight glancing upon their bodies, and she was so acutely aware of Gerent that there seemed to be electricity in the warm air. He was virile and exciting in a very different way from Michael, and just the thought of being one with him made her blood course like the wild hunt itself.

"Oh, Kate, why do you fight against what we both want?" he said softly. He still held her hand and caressed her palm with his thumb.

"Please, Gerent . . ."

"Please what? Don't make love to me because I do not want you?"

"You know that isn't true!"

"Yes, I know it, for you want me as much as I want you." Slowly, gently, he pulled her toward him. The firelight flickered as the magical sparks began to dance above the flames. They twisted and flashed like a swarm of angry fireflies, but they did not come out into the room. It was as if they were afraid.

"Don't be afraid, Kate," Gerent whispered, "for no harm can come to you while you wear your ring. And with Belerion here too, you are quite, quite safe . . ."

The sparks began to spin, and as Selena's lavender light appeared among them, Belerion raised his head suddenly. *"Be off with you, vile witch!"* he growled. All the lights shrank back, and milled behind the glowing logs.

Gerent looked deep into Kate's eyes, as if into her very soul. "Oh, my sweet lady," he whispered, sliding his other hand into the soft hair at the nape of her neck, "A marriage in name only is not enough tonight. I need you, Kate, and you need me . . ." He drew her mouth toward his.

As their lips met, her wedding ring seemed to momentarily scorch her flesh. Selena's voice screamed out. *"No!"* Then the fire flared like a sunburst, and all the lights rushed furiously up the chimney toward the cold night sky far above.

But Selena would be back; oh, yes, she would be back. And soon.

16

Moonlight shone softly through the oriel window that Kate had seen as she drove along the causeway. It was two in the morning, and the chiming of the long-case clock in the corner of the bedchamber had just awoken Kate.

She was lying in the great Tudor bed of which she had dreamed at the Pulteney Hotel; and now, at last, she knew that the person who slept beside her was Gerent. They were in each other's arms, nakedness to nakedness, warmth to warmth, and as she put her lips to his shoulder, the scent of southernwood on his skin seemed to pervade her. She was no longer his wife in name only, but in every sense of the word. Would he make love to her again in the morning? Or would he regret the unalterable change he had brought about in their marriage? Please don't let that be so.

He stirred in his sleep, his hair very dark against the pure white pillow. He had flung the bedclothes back, and his body was smooth and virile in the silver light. She snuggled closer, feeling more happy, content, and satisfied than she had ever been before. This one night with him had opened her eyes to the sensual, seductive wanton that had always hidden deep in her soul. Now she knew herself as never before,

and was amazed at what had been revealed. The pleasure she had discovered tonight, the joys she had been
taught, and the excitement she had known. Had she
really indulged in such wickedly carnal ecstasies? Oh,
yes, she had. And it had been wonderful. Now, lying
here like this with him, she felt as if she were in her
own small paradise. It was a place she wished never
to leave.

Lazily she turned to lie on her other side, one arm
outstretched over the edge of the bed. She thought
she heard something metallic fall somewhere close by.
It rolled, then was silent. She thought nothing of it as
she glanced sleepily around the room, which was filled
with the silver of the moon. There was a tapestry on
the wall opposite, depicting a scene of medieval maypole dancing. Earlier she had noticed water reflections
playing over the fine needlework, but now there were
none. She supposed it was because the tide was out
as far as it could go.

Sleep began to overtake her once more, but as her
eyes started to close, the lavender light appeared
above the embers of the fire. It curved and swayed
to the hypnotic music playing in the distance outside.
Music? Kate's eyes opened swiftly, and sleep retreated
as she sat up with a gasp. Gerent didn't stir beside her.

The light twisted and turned, and the music grew
stronger. A flute, a drum, little bells that jingled, and
a stringed instrument of some sort. The tune was, of
course, "Sumer Is Icumen In." It was very quaint, and
something about it made her look at the tapestry with
its scene of fifteenth-century maypole dancing. Yes,
that was it, the music sounded medieval!

Slipping from the bed, she went to the window.
Ever afterward she was to wonder whether she knew
she would see the forest instead of the sea. She should
have given a start of surprise, of fear even, instead
she just accepted that she was seeing what could not
be there. The long clearing was as it had been before,
except that this time it was night, and there was no
haze in the distance. She saw a settlement of thatched

dwellings where present-day Trezance should be. Torches flickered by the creek, where she saw the golden boat, its silver oars shipped, its crimson sail furled. There was a maypole on the shore, and a crowd of people in rough medieval clothes making merry as they watched children dancing around it.

A woman detached herself from the gathering, and began to walk along the clearing toward the castle. She wore a gown that glittered so much it might have been composed entirely of diamonds, and she carried a flambeau, by the light of which Kate could see Selena's cloud of red-gold curls. Even at that distance it was possible to make out her anticipatory smile . . . and her glorious beauty.

Then Kate heard slow hooves, just as she had that night at the Pulteney. Opening the casement, she leaned out to look down as Gerent rode past the base of the castle wall. Gerent? She turned sharply to look at the bed. It was empty! Her heart lurched, and she looked out of the window again. He reined in suddenly and gazed up at her, as if undecided. She tried to beg him not to go any farther, but her voice would not obey her. Then, to her immeasurable dismay, he rode slowly on . . . into the utmost danger!

Leaving the window, she seized her peach robe, pushed her feet into the satin slippers she'd worn earlier, and ran from the apartment. Even with so much moonlight, Carismont was a maze in the darkness. She meant to go down to the quadrangle, but took a wrong turn, and suddenly found herself in a part of the castle she did not know. She hesitated, hopelessly lost, then saw a passage she thought she recognized. There was a door at the end, studded and old, and she could not recall having seen it earlier, but she supposed it must have been there. She turned the ring handle, and the rusty hinges groaned as the door opened.

It was a postern, and Kate found herself at the top of steep steps carved into the rocky face of the castle hill. Directly below was the beginning of the clearing,

and against the foot of the castle hill a shallow woodland pool filled by a spring. She could see Gerent
riding toward Selena. The night air was cold, and suddenly she could hear the music much more clearly. It
was almost spellbinding, as if luring her to follow Gerent to the creek.

Kate's fear for his safety intensified. She managed
to cry out. "Gerent! Don't go to her! Please don't go
to her!" But he didn't seem to hear. Selena's laughter
drifted on the wings of the music, and Kate's breath
caught on a sob. "Gerent, don't go on! It's dangerous!
Please, I beg of you!"

Still he rode away, not even checking his horse's
pace or glancing over his shoulder. Then Kate again
heard the tolling bells, carrying loud and clear upon
the night breeze. But as she listened, there came the
rush of fast-approaching water, and the bells suddenly
became a muffled booming. She knew Gerent was in
mortal danger, and she screamed his name for all she
was worth. Still he did not turn. With another choked
sob she began to stumble down the steep steps toward
the shallow pool.

Suddenly there came a snarling growl as Belerion
leaped past her. *"Oh, no you don't, you venomous
doxy! Great galloping cockchafers, I'll have you this
time!"*

The cuckoo could be heard somewhere too. *"Get to
it, Belerion! Oh, faster, faster!"*

"I'm going as fast as I can!" the leopard shouted
back testily. *"Where were you, you stupid bird? Preen-
ing your foolish feathers as usual? I have to do all the
hard work!"*

"Oh, do stop whinging!"

Kate hurried unevenly down the steps as fast as she
dared. The drowned bells tolled again, and she could
still hear the water, louder every second. The cuckoo's
voice sounded inside her. *"Go back! Go back where
it's safe!"* She took no notice, but blundered on down,
too intent upon saving Gerent to think of herself.

Then she heard Selena's cry of fury as Belerion bounded along the clearing, and a scream of pain as the cuckoo's sharp beak found a mark.

On reaching the bottom step, Kate was about to run along the path by the pool, when suddenly everything vanished. The music stopped, the bells no longer tolled, and there just seemed to be an inky, confusing darkness. All that could be heard was the roar and splash of the water. Closer and closer it came, rumbling, hissing, and foaming. Was it the sea engulfing Lyonesse? Was *that* what she could hear? She felt suddenly cold . . . so cold . . . She wanted to close her eyes and sleep again, but someone—or something—grabbed hold of her robe. She was terrified. What was happening? Had she fallen into the woodland pool? No, it was salt water she could taste! She was in the sea! She thought she heard Belerion again, and in the distance the cuckoo's frantic fluting.

Reality swooped sickeningly over her. She was floundering in water, and Belerion was with her. The leopard had her robe in his teeth and was trying to haul her on to a rock. She felt the draft of the cuckoo's wings as it too grabbed the robe in its claws, and tried to help pull her to safety.

"Wake up, Kate! For God's sake wake up!" Gerent seized her under the arms. "Stop struggling! I have you now!" He gripped so tightly that his fingers hurt, but he managed to drag her from the sudden inrush of tide that had almost claimed her.

There was an opening in the boundary wall that encircled the foot of the island, and a tall wrought-iron gate that gave access to more steps to a stone landing stage, the sort from where rowing boats could come and go. In her sleep she had opened the gate and gone out. The woodland pool she had seen was now below the level of the high tide and permanently filled with seawater.

Gerent pulled her well above the tide's reach, took off his coat, and wrapped it around her. Belerion scrambled out of the water as well, then shook himself so fiercely that droplets showered in all directions, drenching the cuckoo, which had paused for breath on a nearby rock. The bird took severe exception to this, and gave the big cat a look that might have withered a lesser beast on the spot. Then it waggled its tail feathers, hunched its wings, and sat on its posterior to look in concern at Kate, who knew with a plunging heart that she had walked in her sleep again. And this time it had almost cost her her life.

She tried to collect her wits as she looked at the water rushing and foaming a few feet below her. She was soaked through, her hair clung to her face and shoulders, and there was a strong taste of salt on her lips. In the moonlight she could see the tide bouncing and bubbling over the rocks and sand on either side of the causeway. As yet it was shallow and swift, but beside the landing stage there was always deeper water because of the depression where once had been the woodland pool. The spring still played into it, but was never seen now because of the depth of seawater that always lay over it. It was a place in which anyone might easily drown . . .

Gerent sat beside her and held her close. "I thought I had protected you well enough; instead I almost lost you a few moments ago. But you're all right now, I have you safe," he whispered.

She leaned against him. His arms were steady and reassuring, and the southernwood on his skin and clothes was like a balm to her fear. He had dressed hurriedly, tugging on boots and breeches, and a shirt that he had not had time to button. His lips moved against her hair as he spoke. "When I saw you step off the landing stage into the sea . . . If Belerion hadn't awoken me when he did . . ."

"Belerion woke you?" She drew her head back to look up at him in the moonlight. She had to make herself concentrate, make herself collect her thoughts and be in control of herself again.

The leopard spoke. *"Yes, it was me again, not the idiotic cuckoo that is supposed to be the lady's guard!"*

The cuckoo took exception. *"That isn't fair! I did my bit tonight!"*

"Eventually," the leopard replied pithily.

It was too much for the cuckoo, which leaped to its feet again. *"Oh, you try my patience! By Pendragon's pips, you do!"* it cried, then took to its wings and flew off into the night.

Belerion's ears went back, and his mouth turned down sourly. *"Pendragon's pips to you too!"* he muttered.

Kate heard all this, but at the same time Gerent was speaking to her. "Belerion came to the door of the apartment, making enough noise to disturb the entire castle." Gerent nodded behind, where two footmen, still in their nightshirts, stood with a lantern. She glanced up at the postern door, and saw several more lanterns shining on the faces of anxious servants. What must they be thinking? That she was mad? Her thoughts were still in confusion. Where did sleep end and reality begin? Which things could she rely upon as fact, and which were the wanderings of a dream?

"Kate, you were sleepwalking again. I awoke and realized you had gone. The door of the bedchamber was open, and I looked out to see you walking along the passage. I called, but you didn't answer, and I guessed you were walking in your sleep. So I put on some clothes and followed. You came out here, and the postern closed behind you before I could prevent you from going any farther. I had the devil's own job forcing the damned thing to open again, and by the time I managed it, you were down here."

She pulled from his arms. "I heard music—'Sumer Is Icumen In'—and when I looked from the window, I saw you riding along a clearing in the forest. At the end of the clearing, where Trezance is now, there was just a medieval village and the golden boat moored in the creek. You were going to Selena. I saw her, heard her laughing . . ."

He gave a long, resigned sigh. "It is time to tell you everything, but first I must get you inside. You will take cold if we stay out here like this." He got up and stretched down a hand to her. It was then that he realized she was not wearing her ring. "Oh, Kate! Did I not *warn* you? Where is it?"

She was caught completely unawares. The ring should be on her finger. She hadn't taken it off! "Gerent, I swear I've kept it on ever since you told me." Then she paused, remembering the sound she had heard as she dozed back to sleep.

He looked sharply at her. "What is it? Have you thought of something?"

"Yes. The ring is loose, and I think it fell from my finger. I was very sleepy, but I heard something, a metallic sound and then something small rolling across the floor."

He took her chin in his other hand, and looked urgently into her eyes. "Always check that the ring is there, Kate. If it is likely to fall from your finger, then you must wear it on a ribbon around your neck. It *must* be with you at all times. Tonight, because of Belerion, you escaped, but you may not be so fortunate again. Tomorrow will be especially dangerous, for the moon will be at its fullest." He bent forward and brushed his lips lovingly to hers. "Go to your own apartment now, for you must wash and change after being in the sea. When you are ready, send Bessie to tell me, and I will come. I promise that before dawn you will know all there is to know."

17

Kate sat in the moonlit window in her apartment. There were candles in the room behind her, but it was the moon that shone over her. She had taken another bath, attended by Bessie, and was now sipping a cup of hot milk that Mrs. Pendern had insisted she take. Her wet hair still hung about her shoulders, but at least it now smelled of rosemary and chamomile instead of the sea. She wore a clean nightgown, and the room was warm because the fire had been built up anew until flames flickered brightly. Bessie had been sent to tell Gerent she was ready, and he was expected at any moment.

Outside the sea now covered everything between the island and Trezance, except the causeway. The water had come in at first in a single swift wave only an inch or so high, but was being followed in at the more usual rate by the rest of the tide. Bessie called it a half-and-half, neither quite ordinary nor entirely a surge. The maid warned that tonight was not to be compared with a true spring surge, which could sweep in quite tumultuously, dividing in two arms around the island, then clashing together over the causeway. It was this latter phenomenon that had dashed Selena to her death, and Bessie predicted there would be another like it very soon, because the moon was right and the bells had been heard. The Lyonesse bells, she called them.

It was almost dawn now, and in these quiet hours there were few lights in Trezance. Someone was still up at the Merry Maid, and there were lanterns by an upturned boat on the quay as men worked hard to make it seaworthy after a recent mishap. In the hills behind the town there was another light, and Kate was sure from its position that it must be at Denzil Portreath's house. Thoughts of Michael crossed her mind, incongruous thoughts, given what else she had on her mind. She could not believe there were two Denzil Portreaths, and knew she had to ask him about Michael, whether or not Gerent and the master of Polwithiel had fallen out. Even now, when her heart had been given to Gerent, she needed to know all she could about how her first husband met his death.

Her thoughts slid from the past to the present as the fire shifted in the hearth, and she turned nervously. There seemed just the crackling fire. "Are you here, Selena?" she whispered, then started up from the window seat as the apartment door opened suddenly. But it was only Gerent.

He was immediately apologetic. "I did not mean to startle you, but I knocked and there was no answer."

"You knocked? I . . . didn't hear."

Belerion came in with him and trotted to the bed, upon which he jumped and then sprawled as if it were his own. The leopard exhaled with great satisfaction. *"Ah, bliss. I vow this is still the most comfortable bed in the castle,"* he declared, then closed his eyes and promptly went to sleep.

Gerent was again apologetic. "I hope you do not mind Belerion accompanying me, but if he is here, Selena will keep her distance. And I need us to be quite alone for what I have to tell you."

She nodded, and slowly he closed the door and came over to her. "What you are going to hear defies belief, Kate, but every word I tell you is the truth."

He sat her down on the window seat, then joined her, leaning his head back against the glass. "I must start at the very beginning if you are to understand properly. You see, when I told you that Belerion came ashore from a shipwreck twelve years ago, in 1806, I did not tell you that Selena came into my life at the same time. She was found unconscious on the little landing stage where you were tonight. She appeared to have come from the same wrecked vessel as Belerion, and was believed to have struck her head, because she had lost her memory. She didn't even know who she was, or so she claimed, and because the new moon happened to shine through a break in the storm clouds when they found her, I rather fancifully named her Selena. Extensive inquiries were made to identify her, but to no avail. She spoke English and was a lady, but that is all that was ever established with certainty."

Kate was surprised. "All that was ever established? But surely, if there was a shipwreck there must have been other survivors? *Someone* must have known who she was!"

"The vessel was driven inshore by a surge tide of considerable force, and was so badly shattered on the causeway that its identity was yet another mystery. There seemed evidence that it might be of American origin, but nothing was ever really known. No documentation was discovered, not even a torn invoice, and anything of value that may have survived the impact was quickly taken away by the local people." He looked at her. "Booty from wrecks vanishes into thin air in these parts," he explained. "Belerion and Selena appeared to be the only survivors, but I now know that they did not come from the shipwreck."

Kate met his eyes. "Lyonesse?"

"Yes, although it was the night she died before I knew it. Until then I had no inkling at all that there was anything supernatural about either of them."

Kate glanced toward the bed, where Belerion was now snoring. He did not seem at all like a supernatural leopard from the lost land of Lyonesse. More an over-grown spotted tabby!

Gerent continued. "Selena stayed here at Carismont while she made her recovery, and in that time I soon fell in love with her. She was beautiful, amusing, charming, and altogether fascinating, and she made certain I was completely in her thrall. Like a fool, I actually believed she was as much in love with me as I was with her, but the truth was very different. Due to the very particular circumstances of that stormy surge in 1806, she had managed to escape from a life she loathed in Lyonesse, and wanted to stay here in my world to enjoy to the full the wealth and comfort I could provide. All she had to do was beguile me into marriage and make sure she never again set foot in the sea, because one drop of seawater would whisk her back to Lyonesse. I did not know that then, of course; I have managed to work it all out since. Anyway, we married in 1807, and right up to the moment of her death she never once went in the sea. She would not go out in a boat, nor would she cross the causeway if so much as an inch of water covered it. For instance, she would have refused point-blank to come to the island as we did yesterday evening, because there was still an inch of water over the causeway close to the island, and that would not have been tolerable for her. I indulged her in all this, putting her fear down as natural and understandable after the terror of the shipwreck." He raised his head and looked at Kate. "If this makes me seem the ultimate gull, then I fear I must own up. I was blind with love, and did not want to perceive anything wrong."

"From what you have told me so far, your conduct seems understandable."

He smiled. "Well, at first we were very happy. Selena adored London, and demanded that we spend every Season there. She conquered society, and was undoubtedly one of its most beautiful adornments. But then, late in 1809, she discovered she was to have a baby. To say that she was displeased would be to make the greatest understatement of all time." Gerent's lips pressed together, and as he leaned his head back against the glass again, Kate was sure she saw tears on his lashes. "She did not want a child at all, and rejected Genevra. Mrs. Pendern became more of a mother to the baby than Selena ever was. I know that childbirth can affect some women in an adverse way, and I tried hard to make allowances, but it was impossible to sympathize with Selena's callousness toward the child she should have adored as much as I did. Our marriage began to deteriorate, not only because of Genevra, but because I began to realize that Selena was putting horns on me, not with just one lover, but with a number of lovers."

Kate was shocked. "But this is so at odds with the marriage as observed by society! Why, even in the sticks of Herefordshire, I read about dazzling Lord and Lady Carismont, and how much in love they were."

He smiled wryly and took her hand. "Oh, Kate, outward appearances can be very deceptive. I think she was unfaithful to me from the outset, and no man worth his salt will endure that, no matter how much he loves. But please do not think I have doubts about Genevra being my child, for that is not so. Even if it were not that my heart tells me she is mine, I have only to look into her eyes, which are so much my own mother's that there can be no question."

So Genevra took after her paternal grandmother, Kate thought.

"However, I was telling you of Selena," he went on. "I issued an ultimatum that unless she remained faithful to me, as our vows demanded, I would seek an end to the marriage. It shook her considerably, and she seemed to change her ways, but it was already too late. I had fallen out of love with her, and when she came to me, I no longer wanted her. Desire had slipped out in the wake of love, and turned the key behind it. Beauty is said to be skin-deep, and never was that more true than in Selena's case." He exhaled heavily. "Anyway, then I discovered that she had not given up all her lovers, after all. There was one she continued to see at every chance, and he was someone I had hitherto regarded as my good friend . . ."

"Denzil Portreath?" Kate said, suddenly realizing that her wild guess had been right after all.

Gerent nodded. "He and I had known each other from childhood. We were on good terms, and he was always as welcome here at Carismont as I was at Polwithiel. What I did not realize was that my wife was even more welcome at Polwithiel! It was April 1816 when I learned the truth from a virtual stranger in London. My informant was another with whom Portreath had once been friendly, but they had fallen out about something. Gambling debts, I think, but I do not really know—or care. Anyway, this fellow was in his cups on the night in question, and I played the Good Samaritan to get him safely back to his lodgings. For my pains I was regaled with the titillating story of my wife's scandalous indiscretions with Portreath."

"Oh, Gerent . . ."

"I can speak of it now, for Selena no longer means anything at all to me, but at the time I was so blinded with anger that I could have torn the throats from both my informant *and* Portreath. But one does not kill the messenger for delivering bad news, so I left him snoring in his lodgings."

"And you still have no idea who he was?"

"No idea at all. I had seen him before, but only actually spoke to him that night, when he was in no state to observe the politeness of telling me his name. He knew me, however, and it was clear that when they had been cronies, he and Portreath enjoyed many a laugh at my expense." Gerent drew a heavy breath. "Anyway, I drove posthaste here to Carismont. It was after dark on the night of May Eve when I arrived, and I came straight here to the island. My intention was to confront Selena first, and then go to Polwithiel to deal with Portreath. However, Selena was already with him, and I found Genevra upset and crying because her mother had punished her for some minor misdeed. As it happened, news of my return from London had already reached Polwithiel, because my carriage was recognized as it drove down through Trezance. Selena panicked, and promptly set off to ride back here, for no matter what delights Portreath could offer her between the sheets, he did not have my title or my fortune. He is in debt to his eyeballs, and I have a shrewd suspicion—unproven—that she was funding him at my expense. However, that is another matter." Gerent paused.

Kate looked at him. "Go on."

"She must have known a surge tide was expected, because the moon was full, the season was right, and local people had heard the Lyonesse bells. She *had* to have heard them too, for there is no mistaking the sound."

"I know. I heard them tonight."

He nodded. "The conditions are exactly as they were then. The moon will be completely full when darkness next falls, so I anticipate a full surge then. Anyway, two years ago Selena was faced with a stark choice. Either she stayed safely on the mainland and hoped to convince me later that she was still a faithful wife, or she risked riding over the causeway in the dark when a surge might sweep in at any moment. She chose the latter course. It was a bad decision, for she was only halfway to the island when the tide came in. The waves crashed over the causeway like a boiling cauldron, she and her horse were swept away, and neither was seen again."

"How dreadful," Kate whispered, able to picture the horrific scene, but then she thought of something. "But, I thought Genevra almost drowned with her mother."

"Yes. She was watching from this very window, and saw Selena ride to the causeway, passing the lights of the Merry Maid. Something made Genevra run down to the shore, but fortunately I saw her, and was in

time to prevent her from going onto the causeway."
Gerent paused and swallowed, then he ran his fingers
through his hair. "Now I come to the point that made
me realize the truth about Selena's origins. You see,
as I struggled to hold Genevra back, suddenly the
surge and the night seemed to disappear. Instead I
saw only a balmy late-spring day, and a woodland
clearing that led to the creek as it was before Trezance
was built."

A tingle ran down Kate's spine, and she got up
quickly from the window seat.

Gerent's voice was soft, almost reflective. "Genevra
and I had just seen Selena swept away by the sea, but
now we saw her waiting on her horse by the creek.
The golden boat was there too, and a maypole around
which people were dancing. It was Lyonesse, idyllic
and inviting, a sylvan world of summer, greenery,
flowers, and medieval merriment. Selena beckoned
and called our names, and the compulsion to go to
her was almost too much to withstand, but I could
feel danger all around, so I fought against it and held
on to my child for all I was worth. Genevra was so
overwrought that she broke free, but as she ran forward, Belerion appeared from behind me, seized her
nightgown sleeve between his teeth, and began to drag
her back to safety. Just as he did with you tonight. In
a flash the sunshine and woodland disappeared, and
there was just the foaming surge of the sea on the
night of May Eve."

18

Kate found she had been holding her breath, and now turned to look at him. "If Lyonesse was—is—so beautiful, why did Selena want to leave it?"

He shrugged. "She was the sort of woman who would never be satisfied. Whatever she had, no matter how costly and rare, it would not be enough. Paradise itself would not have held her for long." Gerent had paused for a long moment, then went on. "I may have refrained from punishing the messenger in London, but I did not show similar restraint here in Cornwall. Within days of Selena's death, I confronted Portreath at Polwithiel. I challenged him, and he accepted. We both once belonged to the same fencing club, so we met with swords at dawn on a knoll by the road from the moor. You may have noticed it as we drove here. There is a standing stone . . ."

"Yes, I noticed it."

"It used to be with its pair at the Trezance end of the causeway, but my father had it moved. I forget why. Anyway, Portreath had elected for swords, thinking himself more skilled in that discipline, but rage made a demon of me. I left him with that scar on his face."

Kate gazed at him. "I . . . I cannot imagine you in a duel."

"Most men will issue or accept a challenge if their emotions are raised to the necessary pitch. Your first husband fought one, did he not?"

"Yes."

"Was he the sort of man you would have expected to indulge in such a thing?"

"No," she admitted.

"My point is proved, I think. Anyway, I thought that the duel, coupled with Selena's death, was the end of the matter. But then, almost a year after she died, I was in the library here going through some accounts when a torrent of tiny sparks spilled out of the fire. Among them was the larger lavender light you have described. Then I heard Selena's voice." Gerent got up and went to lean a hand on the mantel. "As had happened in 1806, when she entered my life for the first time, she came to me again with the new April moon, and she kept returning throughout its waxing. Only when it began to wane again did she leave me alone. I soon realized that she was angry because Genevra had been prevented from going with her to Lyonesse the year before."

Kate stared at him. "She wanted Genevra to have drowned too?"

"It seems that by escaping from Lyonesse in the first place, and then having a child with me, Selena broke the laws of her world. There it is frowned upon for children to be half of that world and half of this, but it is up to the child to decide in which realm it lives. Genevra wants to stay here, and while that remains the case, Selena has to stay in Lyonesse. A man or woman from that world who has a child by someone of this world is doomed to always exist in the opposite world from the one chosen by the child. That is why Selena was so angry to find she was expecting my baby, and why she always resented Genevra. She knew what the laws of Lyonesse decreed, so she took

more care than ever to avoid going back there. But
in the end her greed and selfishness trapped her. She
wanted Portreath *and* she wanted what I could offer
her, so she took the fateful risk on the causeway. It
went wrong, and the touch of the sea meant she had
to return to Lyonesse."

Fantastic as it all sounded, it was also plausible.
Kate had experienced far too many odd incidents herself to cast doubt on a word Gerent said.

He smiled a little sadly. "Before you ask why Selena
does not simply escape again from Lyonesse as she
did before, I have to say that I think Genevra's existence here prevents it somehow. The means of getting
permanently away that could be used in 1806, cannot
be used now, and Genevra is the difference. Portreath
is what Selena craves above all else. He will not go
to her, so she must do all she can to return here to
him. To do that she must change places with Genevra,
but can only attempt to persuade the child when the
April moon arrives. That particular moon has great
significance for Selena, although I do not understand
exactly why. Throughout its waxing she can use her
powers upon her child, but the moment it begins to
wane, she has to resign herself to Lyonesse for another year."

"That is why you wanted to be here in Carismont
for the whole of the last week of April?"

"Yes."

"And Selena has until tomorrow night to succeed
this year?"

He nodded. "Yes."

Belerion grunted in his sleep, and Kate looked at
the bed. "Where does Belerion come into this? And
my cuckoo, which I promise you does exist."

"I do not know about the cuckoo, which I have
neither heard nor seen, but I have come to believe
that Belerion was originally sent to guard me. Now I
believe he guards anyone who is at risk, not just
Genevra."

Kate thought for a moment. "Gerent, why does Selena want *you* to go back? I can understand why she needs Genevra to be there, but why you too? I mean, if it's Portreath she loves . . ."

He nodded. "There are two reasons that I can think of. Firstly, she knows that if I go there, Genevra will accompany me. So in order to lure me, Selena makes wonderful promises, and gives glowing descriptions of the wonders of Lyonesse. The second reason is that when she comes here to this world again, with me out of the way, she and Portreath will be able to enjoy all that is mine. I have no other heirs apart from Genevra and now you—and Justin of course—but as the widowed *first* Lady Carismont, Selena would be entitled to everything, because my marriage to you would appear to be bigamous. Thus, she would step into the entire Fitzarthur fortune, marry Portreath, and live here with him enjoying my wealth. I do not doubt that he would be more than willing to make an honest woman of such a wealthy mistress."

"I cannot imagine any woman preferring Denzil Portreath to you," Kate observed honestly.

"You flatter me, I fancy."

"No. I thought him very cold and disagreeable."

Her glance wandered to Belerion again. "Gerent, there is something you should know . . ."

"Know?"

"About Belerion, and . . . about the cuckoo I have mentioned. The creatures on the coat of arms that you regard as a lioness and a martlet are in fact a leopard and a cuckoo. I know this for a fact because . . . I, er . . ."

"Yes?" Gerent prompted.

She cleared her throat. "Because I can hear them both speaking."

Gerent looked at her. "You what?"

"I think you heard me." She smoothed her nightgown. "For some reason I can hear them. It may interest you to know that Belerion is a very grumpy leopard. He thinks he does all the work, and that the cuckoo isn't doing enough." She caught Gerent's eye. "Don't look at me like that! I *do* hear them."

Gerent put up his hands. "I'm not questioning a word of it. How can I when I have just told you a veritable fairy tale about my first wife? It would indeed be a case of the pot calling the kettle black." He smiled. "I believe you, Kate," he said gently. "Truly I do."

She bit her lip ruefully. "I was afraid to say anything in case you thought me utterly crazy. I sleepwalk, see visions, hear animals and birds talking . . . People have been locked away for just one of those things, let alone all three."

"And I believe in Lyonesse and talk to a lavender light that I think to be my dead first wife. I fancy I would be joining you in Bedlam, don't you?"

She laughed. "I suppose so."

He drew a long breath. "So, Belerion and this cuckoo are on the coat of arms of Lyonesse. Belerion has always been here, and that presumably is why he thinks he's doing all the work. Now the cuckoo comes late on the scene, and . . . seems to have coincided with my meeting you. Ergo, it is your particular guardian."

"Oh, yes, it certainly is." She told him of her encounters with the bird.

Gerent looked sadly at her. "Oh, Kate, it was very wrong of me to involve you in my life. But, at the Pulteney, the need to have you with me suddenly became too much to withstand. The urge came out of the blue, and with such an overwhelming force that I simply *had* to act upon it."

"I'm glad you did." She went to him, and he folded her close. He kissed her damp hair, and she closed her eyes, enjoying the feel of his body against hers, but then a horrid thought struck her, and she looked quickly up at him. "What of Justin? Is he in any danger at all?"

"I am sure he is not. Has he experienced anything untoward?"

"No," she replied, forgetting that Justin had dreamed of being given the golden boat, and that he had also dreamed of Gerent's clothes exactly.

"Then I am certain all is well." Gerent reached in his dressing gown pocket and drew out her ring, which he had found on his bedroom floor. He went through into the dressing room, found a length of pink ribbon, onto which he threaded the ring. Then he returned to tie it gently around her throat. "I know that you believe the cuckoo has come to protect you, but I also know that such emissaries alone cannot be certain of fending off Selena. Belerion deters her, but somehow she got around him to entice Genevra into the water the other night. I do not think that would have happened if Genevra had worn the runes. I am convinced that if you had still been wearing them, you would have been much safer tonight."

He cupped Kate's chin in his hand. "My nurse showed the runes to me when I was even younger than Genevra and Justin. She wrote the charm in my favorite storybook, and said it was effective against wickedness if worn against the skin. She also told me it can be used by any two people who are at risk from the same dark force. So I have protected you and Genevra. Justin I firmly believe to be safe from Selena."

"But what of you, Gerent? How are you protected?"

"I do not fear for myself because I know I am strong enough without aid."

Was he strong enough? Kate recalled his anguished words at Berkeley Street. *For pity's own sake, leave me to live my life! Please!* Selena still had the power to reach him, no matter how much he claimed she did not. Selena also had the power to enter the castle, even though Mrs. Pendern believed it was protected against her. "Gerent, I do wish you had told me everything before," she whispered. "A trouble shared is a trouble halved, and now we can fight Selena together."

He pulled her into his arms. "You are my salvation, Kate," he whispered, kissing her damp hair.

"And you are mine, for until you came into my life,

I did not think I would ever be happy again. You and I, Genevra and Justin, will all live contentedly here, and I will not let Selena steal you from me." She held him close. "Make love to me again, Gerent," she breathed. "On the floor by the fire."

"Has my lady no shame?" he teased gently.

"No shame at all, my lord," she replied, and drew him to the fireplace. They faced each other before the flames. And slowly she untied her robe and allowed it to fall. His gaze moved warmly over her. "You are so beautiful," he breathed, taking off his dressing gown as well.

They lay down together, and she leaned over him so that her long hair brushed his skin. "I love you with all my heart, Gerent Fitzarthur," she said softly.

Later, as they lay sated in each other's arms, the firelight flickering on their bodies, she heard Belerion's sudden low growl. The leopard jumped from the bed to look out of the window. The lavender light pressed to the glass, afraid to come in. Kate leaned up on an elbow. "Look, Gerent, Selena, is here," she whispered.

He sat up quickly, watching as Belerion stood on his hind legs with his front paws on the window seat. The leopard's exasperation was almost tangible as he quite clearly searched the sky behind Selena.

"Come on, you half-witted cousin to a crow! It's your turn now! What's keeping you?"

It was so clear that Kate was sure Gerent must hear it too. "Gerent, did you . . . ?"

"Yes, I heard. This time I definitely heard!"

Then the cuckoo arrived outside in such a flapping rush that it almost cannoned into the glass. *"I'm here, you moth-eaten feline misery!"* it cried.

Kate glanced swiftly at Gerent. "And that as well?"

"Yes. And I can see it too."

The cuckoo recovered swiftly from its near collision with the window, and managed to poke Selena with its beak. She darted out of the way and fled before receiving a second savage stab.

But Belerion was not impressed with the cuckoo's efficiency. *"You'll have to do better tomorrow night, or she just might succeed!"*

The cuckoo sighed theatrically. *"Can't you do anything but moan? By Camelot's carbuncles, you're the most miserable creature it has ever been my misfortune to meet!"* The cheeky bird perched on the outside sill, and waggled its tail feathers impudently just the other side of the glass from the leopard's nose.

"Well, if that's the way you feel, you can do everything for the rest of the night! I'm going back to sleep!" Belerion snorted disgustedly, and went back to the bed, where he lay with his back to the window.

The cuckoo shuffled a little on the sill, then leaned its tail back against the glass to make itself comfortable. If it had pockets it would have thrust its wing tips into them, Kate thought.

19

Kate and Gerent returned to his rooms for what remained of the night. There they lay together, watching the dawn brighten the oriel window, and talking as all lovers do. Belerion, grumbling profusely at being obliged to wake up yet again, stationed himself outside the door, while the cuckoo merely flew from Kate's window to the oriel, where he balanced precariously on the narrow ledge. Vigilance did not appear to be one of his attributes, because it wasn't long before his feathers were puffed up and his head was sunk between his shoulders as he dozed.

At last it was time to get up for the new day. Belerion removed himself from guard duty and went out for a morning stroll in the gardens, and the cuckoo flapped away with a string of loud fluting notes that momentarily silenced the equally rackety seagulls.

Kate made her way back to her own apartment to dress. In spite of the long eventful night, she was full of energy and her spirits were bubbling. It was good to be so helplessly in love again that she wanted to skip and sing as she hurried along the gallery. Being loved by Gerent made her feel exhilarated, restored, rejuvenated, and . . . beautiful. Yes, his ardor made her feel beautiful, and today maybe she was, she thought as she stopped at a window to gaze out at the beautiful spring morning. The patchwork greens of countryside around Trezance shimmered in the morning haze, and the hawthorn hedgerows were so laden with white blossom that they looked like drifts of snow. The moor was ablaze with golden gorse and looked very inviting for the ride she had managed to talk herself into the evening before, she thought a little wryly.

The sea again ebbed between the island and the shore. The next tide would be the first of May Eve; and tonight, the second would come in when the moon was at it's fullest point. As she hurried on, she wondered if there would indeed be a surge, as expected. She wondered too what perils—if any—the tide would bring.

Bessie was waiting in the apartment. "Good morning, my lady. How are you?" she asked, hurrying to attend her.

"I'm very well, thank you."

"You gave us all such a fright in the night. I hate to think what might have happened if Belerion had not set up such a noise."

"I am most grateful to him," Kate replied, in the sort of tone she hoped would convey a reluctance to discuss it.

"Did you see the woods of Lyonesse? Was that what happened?"

The inquiry was so matter-of-fact that Kate thought she might have misheard. "I . . . beg your pardon?"

"Well, Miss Genevra has seen it, so I just wondered . . ."

For some reason Kate drew back from speaking of it. "I simply walked in my sleep, Bessie. I'm afraid it's something I used to do when I was a child, and I've started doing it again," she replied, then pointedly changed the topic. "I believe the first Lady Carismont's clothes are still here?"

"Yes, madam. Do you wish them to be removed?"

"Well, yes, except the riding habits, which I would like to see now."

"Certainly, madam. There are only two now, because her ladyship was wearing the cornflower velvet on the night she . . ." The maid's voice trailed away awkwardly.

"Yes, I understand, Bessie."

The maid hurried away, and after a while returned with the two remaining habits: a misty gray-blue corduroy trimmed with black braiding, and a stylish navy silk that looked agreeably light and comfortable. Kate knew without trying them on that they would fit, and she nodded at the navy silk. "Please set that out. Hopefully I will go for a ride later this morning."

"Yes, madam. What will you wear to go down to breakfast?"

"There is a leaf-green merino day dress . . ."

"I know it, madam. I will put that out as well."

A little later Kate hurried through the castle again. She wore the merino dress, and her honey-brown hair had been coiffed with great elegance by Bessie's nimble fingers. This morning she was too in love to regret the gown's unfashionable style, but in spite of her joy, she was a little apprehensive too, because Justin and Genevra would meet for the first time at the breakfast table, and she did not know how they would get on. If indeed they got on at all! Still, her wonderful new love would carry all before it, and even if the children hated each other on sight—which at least one of them was determined to do!—she and Gerent would still have each other!

Gerent and Genevra were already waiting in the refectory, but Justin had yet to come down. As Kate's gaze locked Gerent's and he smiled, it was as if he touched her physically. The blood quickened through her veins and the sparkle she had exuded since awakening seemed to intensify. Then Justin arrived, and it was not long before Kate's fears were realized, for he and Genevra did not take to each other at all. They glowered as they were formally introduced, and made no attempt at all to be amiable. Yet they both looked angelic, especially Justin with his blond hair. He wore his cream pantaloons and short navy blue jacket, and a shirt with a wide collar that rested across his shoulders.

Genevra's dark coloring did not immediately arouse associations with angels, but she certainly looked very sweet and pretty. Her hair was twisted up into a simple knot on her head, and she was dressed in a white muslin frock with a blue velvet sash. The locket from Gerent was around her neck, and she had brought her pink velvet cat, an impulse she was to regret before breakfast had progressed very far.

It was mainly her fault that tempers became frayed, because she carped at absolutely everything Justin said or did. In the end he retaliated by calling her a baby for carrying a toy animal around with her, and she proved him right by beginning to cry. But no sympathy was forthcoming, and the tears were halfhearted anyway, so she sank into a surly silence. Kate and Gerent exchanged disappointed glances, for they had been hoping their offspring would hit it off. Perhaps it was hoping for too much.

Things were not helped when Gerent mentioned all the estate business he had to attend to with his agent. As he added that it would take up all the morning and a great deal of the afternoon, a mutinous glint entered Genevra's hazel eyes, and her lower lip jutted in such a way that Kate knew a tantrum was only seconds away. So she hastily reminded Gerent of his promise.

"Gerent, I know that you intend to spend some time alone with Genevra before your agent arrives, so Justin and I will take a walk in the gardens. Won't we, Justin?"

That young man was dismayed. "Oh, Mama! I wanted to sail my boat again! Please may I?"

Before Kate could answer, Genevra seized her chance of revenge upon Justin. "If you still play with toy boats, you are as silly as you say I am." With an infuriatingly superior smile, she stroked the velvet cat, which she had placed on an empty chair next to her.

Justin flushed deep red. "A boat is different."

"No, it isn't!"

"It is!"

Gerent was incensed. "That's quite enough. My advice is that the pair of you make the most of your opportunity to play and get on together, because you are soon to have school lessons which will greatly curtail such pleasures. I wish you both to apologize for your conduct. You first, Genevra, for you have been the most disagreeable."

Genevra flung him a resentful glance. "I haven't! He started it!" She pointed at Justin.

Gerent was not satisfied. "No, miss, you started it. You have been decidedly unamiable since the moment you sat down."

"Why are you taking his side, Papa? It's not fair!" Genevra's lips quivered, and her eyes filled with more forced tears.

Gerent held her gaze across the table. "Genevra, it is nothing to do with taking sides. I know you well enough to tell that you came to breakfast with the express intention of not liking Justin."

Genevra's glance slid to Justin. "You shouldn't have poked fun at my cat," she grumbled.

"I only did it because you kept picking at me," he replied, then added gallantly, "I don't really think your cat is silly."

Genevra didn't say anything more on the subject, but it seemed to Kate that her face wasn't quite as rebellious after that. Ten minutes later, quite out of the blue, she said, "And I don't think your boat is silly either."

From then on an entirely different mood descended over the table. They all laughed and chattered together almost as if they had been doing it for years, and Kate saw a side of Genevra that had hitherto been hidden behind tantrums and sulks. The real Genevra was a very likable little girl, toward whom Kate could warm very easily.

When breakfast ended, and just before Genevra went off with Gerent, Kate broached the subject of a possible ride. "Genevra, I was wondering . . ."

The little girl turned. "Yes?"

"I would very much like to go for a ride later this morning, and I wondered if you would like to show me around? Justin could come too. The moor behind Trezance looks very beautiful, and—"

"Go ashore, you mean?" A new note slipped into Genevra's voice.

"Well, yes, but—"

"I can't! No, I truly can't! Especially not today! Papa?" Genevra looked distractedly up at Gerent.

Kate was anxious to reassure. "Oh, please don't think you have to, Genevra, for it really isn't important. Justin and I can find our own way around."

Tears had filled Genevra's eyes. "I can't go over the causeway. Please don't be angry."

Kate hurried instinctively to her and crouched to give her a big, reassuring hug. "Of course I'm not angry."

Genevra hesitated, then returned the hug. "Mama would have been," she explained, and Kate looked up into Gerent's eyes, remembering all he had said of Selena as a mother. Then Genevra took her father's hand and went out with him.

Kate rose to her feet and looked at Justin. "I suppose you don't want to go for a ride either?"

"Not really. I'd rather—"

"Sail your wretched boat? Yes, I rather thought you would. Oh, well, I would feel mean if I obliged you to be my gallant escort, especially as I am soon to rain the intricacies of arithmetic upon your poor little head."

Justin pulled a face. "Oh, no, not sums again."

"Yes, and so it will be until you have mastered the subject. In the meantime it seems I must hie me around on horseback by myself."

"You don't really mind, do you, Mama?"

She smiled. "No." But she realized she was not happy to leave him, even to go for a ride. "Justin, has anything strange happened since you've been here?"

"Strange?" He looked blankly at her, then his eyes cleared. "I say, is the castle haunted? Is that what you mean?"

"No, not exactly. I just wondered . . . I mean, when we were staying at the Pulteney Hotel, you dreamed about the boat . . ."

"Well, now that you come to mention it, there have been one or two odd things."

Alarm leaped through her. "There have? What?"

"There was no wind yesterday evening when I played with my boat in the quadrangle, yet the boat sailed around and around the pool on its own. Lord Carismont saw it too, when he came out with a lantern."

So did I, Kate thought, suddenly realizing why the vessel's progress had seemed so odd.

"Then later," Justin went on, "when I'd fallen asleep on my bed, Mrs. Pendern came up to leave me a tray of supper. As soon as she'd gone I heard a woman singing just outside my window. I was puzzled because my rooms are at the top of a turret, so there couldn't possibly be anyone at the window. I got up to look out."

"What did you see?" Kate asked anxiously.

"Nothing at all. The singing stopped as soon as I looked out." Justin put his elbows on the table, and his chin in his hands. "I've never liked that song either," he murmured.

"What song?"

"The one the man with the penny whistle was playing by the maypole in Trezance yesterday. 'Sumer Is Icumen In.' "

Selena had sung it too. Kate's mind began to race. If things *were* happening to Justin, then she feared for his safety in spite of Gerent's reassurances. She quickly untied the ribbon around her neck. "Justin, I want you to wear my ring."

He was aghast. "On a *ribbon*? Oh, Mama! Boys do not wear ribbons!"

"Well, this boy is going to," she replied firmly, reaching across the table and pressing it firmly into his hand.

"But—"

"Do as I say, and under no circumstances are you to remove it. Do you understand?" She told herself that if Gerent considered himself strong enough to stand up to Selena, then she could be equally as strong.

Unease entered Justin's eyes. "Mama, what is this about?"

"Oh, if I told you, no doubt, you would think it foolish, so I will not say anything more. But I will feel a great deal better if I know you are going to obey me in this. Promise me, Justin."

"All right, Mama," he replied reluctantly, and tied the ribbon around his neck, being sure to tuck it well in beneath his shirt so that no one could see.

But Kate was still a little fearful. She had to warn him about the woods. "Justin, there is one thing more . . ."

"Mama?"

"Again, I am sure you will think this foolish, but it was so real for me that I need to know you are forewarned. I dreamed there were woods around the island. It was a very real dream indeed."

"A sleepwalking dream, you mean?"

"Yes."

His eyes changed as he remembered the book he'd read on the way to Carismont. "You mean . . . you dreamed of *Lyonesse*?" he gasped excitedly.

"It would seem so. Anyway, it was so very vivid that I wanted very much to walk in those woods. If I had, and the tide was out, then maybe it would have been all right, but if the tide was in—or if it came in while I was walking in the woods . . ."

Justin stared at her.

"Something like that has now happened twice to Genevra, and on both occasions she actually had to be rescued from the water."

His eyes widened. "Really? Is that what Mrs. Pendern was talking about when we arrived yesterday?"

"Yes, but you are not to say anything to Genevra."

"I understand, Mama, but if she talks about it anyway . . ."

"Well, that is different, of course. Anyway, the point of telling you now is that I want you to be vigilant for anything similar."

"I promise I will be, Mama."

"Never go outside when you see something you know cannot be there. It is very difficult to resist, but you must try."

"I will."

"And you must be very careful indeed to keep my ring on. Do you understand?"

"Yes, Mama."

Kate smiled at him, then briskly spoke of something else. "Enough of such things. You want to sail your boat, so off you go. But don't go down to the sea yet, just confine yourself to the pool in the quadrangle for the moment."

"Mrs. Pendern said one of the footmen would come with me if I went down to the shore."

"Did she? Very well, but *only* if a footman is with you. Is that clear?

"Yes, Mama." He got up from the table, came to give her a hug, then hurried away.

Kate found herself wondering about the significance of the boat. She glanced at the coat of arms above the fireplace. Belerion and the cuckoo appeared to be guardians of some sort—the heraldic beasts of Lyonesse, perhaps. But what of the boat? Did it also have a part to play?

20

Gerent was closeted with his agent when Kate set out on her ride. There was no sign of Justin, who had gone down to the seashore with his boat, under the strict supervision of a footman. Genevra was reading a storybook in her favorite bower in the gardens. It was the same book in which had been written the runic charm. She also had her locket, and Belerion was with her too, so all in all she was well protected against Selena.

Kate wore the navy silk riding habit, and a black top hat with a trailing white gauze scarf tied around the crown. Little ankle boots, fawn kid gloves, and a riding crop completed the ensemble, so that she felt stylish enough for Hyde Park itself as she rode out of the quadrangle on a fine roan mare. She had declined the offer of a footman escort, and was looking forward to a leisurely ride on her own. Bessie had given her detailed directions for a particularly pleasant circuit of the heights behind Trezance, and she was determined to enjoy it to the full. Bessie reckoned the ride would take two hours.

Kate had not ridden since before Michael's death, but the mare gave her no trouble. The sea was a deep turquoise-blue, and the air was warm and fragrant as the mare followed the winding road down through the gardens toward the gates to the causeway. She saw Genevra seated on a shady bench that was set right beneath the castle walls. Belerion was stretched on the grass at her feet, and was being read a story. Kate smiled, for little girls would always read aloud to whomever or whatever would listen. Genevra waved, and Kate was glad to wave back, for the greeting was a clear sign that Gerent's daughter was already accepting her.

The scent and color of flowers was everywhere as the mare trotted down toward the shore. Justin and the footman were on the landing stage where she had sleepwalked during the night. They were deeply absorbed in the serious business of sailing the model boat, controlling it with a bamboo cane, and did not see her as she passed around a curve of the drive to their right. Their coats lay over a seaweed-festooned rock, and their heads were together as they attended to the serious business in hand.

The gatekeeper opened the gates quickly as she approached, and doffed his hat and bowed as she passed. She urged the mare onto the causeway. The tide was right out, so that the raised granite way led across an expanse of seaweed-festooned rocks and hard, water-rippled sand, where only the occasional pool shone beneath the sun.

From the moment she rode onto the causeway, she could see how busy the Trezance quay was. Tide or not, there was much activity around the vessels moored on the creek. Her approach was soon observed, and she could see the stir she caused. Word about her had clearly traveled through the town, for she could see how fingers pointed and heads were put together. In spite of the riding habit, she knew they did not take her for Selena's ghost, for Bessie had now told her that when out riding, Selena always wore her long red curls loose over her shoulders. It was an affectation that made her very easy to recognize, even at a distance. Apparently Selena had even done this in Hyde Park, where it caused quite an upset because as a rule it was only ladies of a certain profession who chose to wear their tresses thus.

Kate was about halfway along the causeway when she heard the boom of the bells. Muffled and eerie, they tolled four times from beneath the sea somewhere beyond the island, then fell silent again. Everyone on the quay heard, and so did Kate's mare, which capered uneasily. Kate half expected to see the surge tide hours before it was due, but there was nothing, no telltale line of bright water, no ominous incoming roar. Gradually the normal sounds of the seashore and nearby township were restored, and she was able to move the reluctant mare on once more.

As she drew closer to the creek, it was possible to see clearly why Trezance had sprung up where it had. The creek was deep and easily navigable, yet sufficiently distant from the open sea to be protected from both storms and raiders. Kate reined in as she reached it. She was where the maypole had been, and nearby a schooner was moored where she had seen the golden boat. Nearby too was the standing stone with its runic carvings; and when she glanced to the other side of the causeway, she saw the indentation left by the second stone that Gerent's father had moved to the knoll.

A strange feeling shivered over her. It was the same feeling she had experienced when she and Gerent were married at Berkeley Street. Someone was watching her! The people on the quay subjected her to considerable scrutiny, but it wasn't their eyes she could feel. There was someone else; someone malevolent and secretive . . . Suddenly she was only too conscious of being without her runic protection, for the tingle of vulnerability that slid over her now was quite uncanny.

Selena's voice seemed to whisper on the air. *"They'll both come to me, and I will have everything I desire. But you will have nothing, Kate dearest, nothing at all."*

For a split second—almost too quickly to be certain of anything—Kate saw Selena. Not as a lavender light, but as herself. Clad in a dazzling gown that glittered like diamonds, her glorious red hair floating in the light sea breeze, she gazed at her successor with lavender eyes so hard they were robbed of their beauty. Then the image vanished, leaving Kate unsure if she'd really seen it at all. Except that the whisper still seemed to drift on the air. *"They'll both come to me, and I will have everything I desire. But you will have nothing, Kate dearest, nothing at all . . . at all . . . at all . . ."*

Urging the horse up from the causeway to the quay, Kate rode the gauntlet of the staring townfolk. Some men even emerged from the Merry Maid to watch as she rode by, and she was aware of numerous twitching curtains as women studied her as well. The mare's hooves clattered as she left the waterside, where the maypole was ready and waiting, and made her way up through the steep cobbled streets toward the road the carriage had driven along the day before. She was looking for an old holly tree on the left that marked a farm track which led up to the moor. Bessie had told her that the farm belonged to her father, and the track could be followed around behind Denzil Portreath's estate at Polwithiel, to rejoin the road farther on.

At last she saw the holly tree, and the sound of the horse's hooves changed to a dull thud on hard-packed earth as she turned onto the track. It climbed between high hedge-topped banks, and after riding through the yard of Bessie's father's farm, where chickens scattered noisily before her, she emerged onto the open moor. Skylarks sang and tumbled overhead as she urged the mare to a canter, following the track over a terrain that was mostly covered by golden gorse and hummocks of bilberries. The moor sloped down to her right, and several times she glimpsed the chimneys and crenellated towers of Polwithiel among the trees, but she was well away from the boundary, and on land that actually belonged to Gerent.

She found the ride exhilarating, and had almost forgotten other things as at last she passed a fork in the track that Bessie had mentioned. Taking the right-hand branch, she reached the brow of a hill, over which should lie the road back to Trezance. But as she rode over the crest, she found that the pine-clad knoll and the standing stone were directly between her and the road. She reined in sharply, realizing that she had taken the wrong fork, but as she scanned the view it seemed to her that she could reach the road easily enough this way. Besides, she was intrigued by the stone, and wanted to see how like its former companion it was. So she rode slowly down from the moor and then up the side of the knoll, the summit of which was perfectly flat, as if leveled in ancient times.

A light breeze whispered in the Scotch pines, and seemed to murmur around the stone itself as she reined in beside it to examine its runic carving. She saw the protective charm, ᚤᚤᚷᚢ, but there were others she did not know, and that might mean anything. As she dismounted to look more closely, the cuckoo suddenly called urgently.

"Oh, by Tristan's sainted aunt! Watch out! Watch out!"

She looked hastily around, and at first saw nothing, but then perceived the anxious bird in one of the pines.

"He's coming! He's coming!" The cuckoo flew down to the top of the stone, overshot its target, and had to wheel around again in order to land with some semblance of grace. The success of the maneuver drew forth an audible sigh of relief, then it shuffled around to eye her. *"You shouldn't be here! No, by all the bells of Lyonesse, you shouldn't! Don't you know you're on Polwithiel land? He knows, and is coming right now."*

She had taken the wrong fork in the track! Even as the realization swept over Kate, something caught the mare's attention. It whickered slightly, and gazed back where Kate had just ridden. A gentleman was riding toward her on a chestnut hunter. He was dressed in a pine-green riding coat and cream cord breeches, and although his face was shadowed by the brim of his top hat, she knew it was Denzil Portreath.

The cuckoo was anxious. *"Don't trust him! Don't let him put second thoughts in your head! Do you hear now? No second thoughts! Follow your instincts!"*

"But—"

There was no time to ask questions, for the cuckoo took fright at Portreath's approach. *"Oh, by Mordred's armpit! Take care! Take care!"* It flew swiftly away again, leaving Kate feeling very exposed indeed. Instinctively she put her hand on the five protective runes, even though she knew they were only effective for two people, Justin and Genevra.

Portreath reined in at the foot of the knoll. "Lady Carismont?" he said, removing his top hat and sweeping a bow. The sunlight shone on his blond hair as his gaze moved over her, and she felt he recognized Selena's riding habit.

She inclined her head, trying to seem natural and unconcerned. "Mr. Portreath."

"Not that I am one to be petty, but perhaps I should point out that you are on Polwithiel land."

"Am I? I . . . had no idea." To her he was quite charmless, and still seemed as cold as he had at the Merry Maid. Yet Selena desired him to distraction.

"I am not concerned that you are trespassing," he went on, "but I rather fancy your husband would have a thing or two to say were he to know."

She felt the cool green of his gaze. "Mr. Portreath, I did not realize I was on your land. I simply followed the track."

"There is a fork, about half a mile back," he waved an arm behind him. "You should have taken the other way, it stays outside the boundary of my property, and joins the road about two hundred yards farther along."

"I see. Well, I trust you will forgive my incursion on this occasion."

He urged his horse up toward her. "The word incursion implies a certain degree of hostility in your actions, my lady, yet I am sure that is not the case."

"It certainly isn't." She did not want to indulge in conversation with Selena's lover, but at the same time she wished to ask him about Michael. But how to broach the subject?

As he reined in and dismounted, she couldn't help being aware of the scar Gerent's sword had left on his cheek. He gave her a thin smile. "You have come as quite a surprise to the neighborhood, Lady Carismont."

"Why so? After all, it is two years since—"

"Two years indeed," he interrupted, "but even so, it is surprising. You see, everyone thought that the first Lady Carismont would prove irreplaceable. Yet, here you are, proof positive that she was not."

Kate's instinctive dislike began to set. "Mr. Portreath, I do not regard myself as a *replacement* for anyone."

Again, his glance encompassed the riding habit, as if it gave the lie to her words, but all he said was, "Now I have offended you, and that was not my intention."

Wasn't it? She was inclined to take a contrary view. There was just something inherently disagreeable about Denzil Portreath; something that not only made him a puzzling choice for Selena as a lover, but also an unlikely friend for Michael.

"Lady Carismont, I make no bones about disliking your husband; indeed, the rancor that exists between Carismont and Polwithiel is very bitter indeed."

"I had gathered that."

"Have you been told what lies behind it?"

Surely he wasn't going to speak of his affair with Selena? Kate was shocked.

"It is because Selena preferred to grace my bed to his."

Kate was affronted. He thought he was divulging something of which she knew nothing, and he was not concerned about the effect such a startling revelation might have. Nor was he concerned about speaking of such things to a woman with whom he was barely acquainted. If Denzil Portreath had a redeeming feature, he kept it exceeding well hidden . . . most likely between the sheets. He certainly was not a gentleman!

"I have shocked you," he murmured.

"Yes, sir, you have. Is it your custom to be so forward in your conversation?"

"No. I am at fault and must beg your forgiveness. The truth of it is that the whole thing rankles so much that it takes me over the threshold of discretion. I can tell by your reaction now that in spite of your denial a moment ago, Carismont has told you the reason for his quarrel with me."

"Yes, he has," she admitted.

His green eyes were thoughtful, calculating, as if trying to assess her. "But I'll warrant that although he told you I was Selena's lover, he did not tell you the truth about what happened the night she died."

What was he getting at? she wondered. "I'm sure you are about to enlighten me," she replied dryly.

A vague smile played upon his lips. "Yes, I am, although I fear what I have to say does not cast your husband in a good light."

"With you as my informant, sir, I would hardly expect it," she replied.

"Lady Carismont, I loved Selena very much indeed, and she loved me. On the night she died she was leaving him to come to me, but he would not let her. He tried to lock her in her apartment, but she managed to elude him. He was pursuing her when the tide came in and she drowned."

Kate regarded him. "You are right, sir, that is certainly not how I have been given to understand the situation that night."

"Carismont drove Selena to her death, and for that I challenged him to a duel, the scars of which will mark my face forever." He touched gloved fingertips to the white line on his cheek.

"As I understand it, sir, my husband challenged *you*, not the other way around, and he did so because you and Selena persisted in your adulterous affair."

He was a little stung. "If Selena was unfaithful it was because he was a cruel and unfeeling husband. That is something you will soon find out for yourself. Oh, I do not doubt that as yet he is charm personified, and the most gentle and attentive lover you could wish, but that will end, believe me. You will have second thoughts when you see Gerent Fitzarthur for the monster he really is."

Kate had endured enough. Her questions about Michael would remain unasked. "I will not listen to any more of this, Mr. Portreath. I am sorry that I ventured onto your land, but you may be sure it is not an error I will repeat. Good day, sir." She gathered the reins and turned to her horse.

"That is your prerogative, of course, Lady Carismont," he said, "but my conscience is now clear, for I have told you the truth."

She was about to mount, but faced him again at that. "Did you also tell me the truth about my first husband's death?"

The question took him aback. "Your first husband?" he repeated.

"Michael Kingsley. I presume you are the Denzil Portreath who wrote to me about the duel?"

He didn't respond, seemingly cast into confusion.

"Mr. Portreath?"

At last he nodded. "Yes, my lady, I wrote to you. Michael Kingsley was my good friend. I have to say that I am now shocked beyond all belief that you have married Carismont."

"Shocked? What do you mean?"

"Simply that the man who is now your second husband was Michael's opponent in that duel. Michael was unwise enough to tell Carismont about Selena and me. Gerent Fitzarthur believes in killing the messenger, my lady, and that is precisely what he did that dawn on Putney Heath when he deliberately fired before the call was given. Michael Kingsley was murdered by the man in whose bed you now lie so cozily of a night."

21

Kate was so numbed by Portreath's statement that she almost felt she would faint. Flashes of the past lurched sickeningly through her consciousness. She saw the morning Michael proposed to her, their marriage in Hereford Cathedral, their wedding night in Wales, and their joy when Justin was born. She saw her shock when things had first begun to go wrong, her wretchedness when she accepted that Michael would never again be the husband he had been in the beginning, and—lastly—her grief when she learned of his death . . . It was as if the scenes were illuminated by a magic lantern, and she had to grip the pommel of the saddle to remain steady.

Then at last she managed to look at Portreath again. "*Michael* was the man who told Gerent about Selena's affair with you?" she repeated hesitantly.

"Yes, he was. He and I were good friends, and confided in each other."

She remembered what Gerent had said. . . . *I was so blinded with anger that I could have torn the throats from both my informant and Portreath. But one does not kill the messenger for delivering bad news, so I left him snoring in his lodgings* . . . Kill the messenger.

The same phrase, but whose lips spoke the truth? Gerent's? Or Denzil Portreath's?

Portreath was encouraged by her silence. "So, my lady, I think you can now understand my astonishment about your remarriage."

"Gerent had no idea that—"

"That your husband was the man he killed? You may think not, but I beg to differ. I suspect his conscience bade him marry you, for to be sure you are hardly in Selena's class for beauty, and if you are Michael's widow you cannot be a rich woman."

Oh, how cruelly plausible, she thought, reminded again of how very unlikely a Lady Carismont she was, but her every instinct told her it was Gerent who told the truth, not Denzil Portreath. Besides, the cuckoo had warned her not to trust this man. "I do not believe what you say, Mr. Portreath. Gerent still does not know the name of the man who told him about you and Selena, and he left him sleeping it off in his lodgings. I believe him, for he simply would not conduct himself in the way you claim."

"You clearly do not know your new husband very well, my lady. I have already told you the true circumstances of Selena's death, and now I tell you about Michael's as well."

"If you knew the identity of Michael's opponent, why did you not say so in your letter?" she challenged.

"I did not know at the time I wrote, but found out recently. It seems that Carismont was in his cups at the Merry Maid one night, and divulged the sordid tale to someone. The story is well-known in Trezance."

Somehow Kate could not envisage Gerent in his cups at the Merry Maid, or anywhere else for that matter. "If the story is well-known in Trezance, sir, I daresay it is because *you* saw to its spreading."

"Why would I do that?"

"To blacken Gerent's name."

Portreath laughed a little. "He does a fair enough job of that himself," he murmured.

"I'm afraid, sirrah, that I still do not believe you. I speak as I find, and I find you obnoxious. My new husband, on the other hand, has always behaved perfectly toward me."

He searched her face, and then gave an incredulous laugh. "Dear God, you actually love him! I thought it must be a marriage of convenience, but you actually *love* him!"

She colored. "The circumstances of my marriage are no business of yours, Mr. Portreath."

"Maybe not, Lady Carismont, but the circumstances of Carismont's first marriage most certainly *are* my business. Selena was the sweetest, most delightful, adorable creature I ever knew, and Carismont is responsible for her death."

Kate held his green gaze. "Sweetest, most delightful, adorable creature? Sir, you must think me a gull of the first order. The Selena I have encountered is none of those things!"

There was another silence. "The, er, Selena you've encountered? With all due respect, madam, Selena has been dead these two years."

"Well, there is dead, and there is dead, as I think you know full well. Come, sir, let us be forthright here. Selena is of Lyonesse, and on the night she died she wasn't leaving Gerent to go to you, she was striving to *keep* him. She wanted it all, did she not? To sneak off to enjoy your embraces, and at the same time retain all the comforts and wealth of being Lady Carismont. But Gerent had found out, and so she had to go back to Carismont to try to save her marriage. Now she wants to force her daughter to take her place, so she can come here to you again. *That,* sirrah, is the truth of the sweetest, most delightful, adorable creature with whom you had such a passionate affair—"

Portreath's gaze became opaque. "I don't know what you're talking about. Lyonesse is a mythical place, and—"

"Oh, don't patronize me, sir!" Kate cried. "You know perfectly well what I'm talking about. I know you do, because although at the time I didn't understand what you and Gerent said outside the Merry Maid, I certainly understand it now. Selena wants you to go to her in Lyonesse, but you prefer to stay here. So, in order to have you—which God forbid!—she must lure poor little Genevra to Lyonesse. Tonight will be Selena's last chance for another year, for the moon will be full, and the tide will probably be a surge. Look at me, Mr. Portreath, for I know you are acquainted with everything I'm saying!"

He no longer pretended to be mystified. "My, my, how very talkative Carismont has been. I did not think he would wish to court charges of madness by speaking of Lyonesse."

"He and I not only love each other, Mr. Portreath, we *trust* each other too."

"How charming," he remarked dryly.

"Do you love Selena?" she demanded.

He didn't reply.

"Do you love Selena?" she asked again.

To her surprise he glanced away, and then nodded. "Yes, for what it's worth I do love her."

"Then why do you not do the honorable thing and go to her?"

"The *honorable* thing?"

"Yes! For what honor can there possibly be in forcing that other world upon a child who wants to stay here with her father? I think you and Selena are despicable, and fully deserve each other."

Her words found a target. "Maybe we are, but would *you* wish to go to Lyonesse?"

She did not have to think. "If it was the only way to be with Gerent, yes, I would go there. I certainly would not force anyone else into my affairs, as you and Selena do to Genevra and Gerent."

"Easy to say."

"Maybe, but no less true for that."

He looked into her eyes. "And what of your son? I presume the boy is yours? Would you make him go to Lyonesse with you? Or would you give him the choice? And if he didn't wish to go with you? What then? You would go anyway and leave him here in this world, all alone?"

"No, of course not—"

"So you see, my lady, a truth that is easy to say, may not always be an easy decision to implement."

She studied him. "I daresay you are right, sir, but you are not well acquainted with truth, are you?"

"You still persist in disbelieving me about Michael dying at Carismont's hand?"

"Oh, yes, sir, I persist," she said softly. "I know that you are the sort of man who would say or do *anything* to cause harm."

"So . . . you have no second thoughts about marrying him?"

"None whatsoever." She remounted the mare, and Portreath made no attempt to assist her. She gathered the reins, then looked down at him. "You and Selena richly deserve each other, sir."

He swept a cold bow, and she kicked her heels to ride away from the knoll.

His mocking voice followed her. "I'll be on the quayside at nightfall, my lady, and I'll stay there to see what happens! Believe me, I will not leave until it is all over."

She was staving off tears as she rode back down through Trezance, where the children were practicing their dancing around the maypole. The old man with the penny whistle was there again, playing "Sumer Is Icumen In." She rode briskly onto the causeway, still trying not to cry after being so sharply reminded of how Michael had died. A terrible sadness had crept through her as she left the knoll, and scenes from the magic lantern kept flashing before her. Her grief for Michael had been stirred all over again, and with it had come guilt, because she was now so in love with Gerent, in whom her faith had not been even slightly shaken. She may have only known him for a short while, but she felt as if he had always been in her heart.

Portreath's claims about the duel did not give her second thoughts about anything, except perhaps in the matter of who *had* faced Michael that dawn on Putney Heath. She reined in sharply three quarters of the way to the island. Until today she had always believed Michael's opponent to have been a stranger he crossed in a drunken incident. But if, as she was now prepared to believe, Michael died because he divulged Selena's affair with Portreath, who was there with reason to bear sufficient grudge to kill him? Gerent might have been resentful, but he hadn't killed anyone. There was Selena herself, of course, but Michael hadn't faced a woman in the duel, and anyway Selena died several days before Michael. That left Portreath himself. And if ever a man seemed capable of such an act, it was the master of Polwithiel.

An affair such as Portreath's with Selena was not the sort of thing to bandy, and Michael might well have been the only person in whom Portreath confided. If so, there would be no doubt in the latter's mind as to whose tongue had wagged to Gerent. In a rage at having lost Selena and been humiliated in a duel with Gerent here in Cornwall, Portreath had probably rushed back to London to confront Michael.

Kate drew a long breath, for it was one thing to guess all this, quite another to prove it. Justin's voice suddenly drifted on the breeze from the landing stage. "Mama! Mama!"

She shaded her eyes and saw him kneeling up to wave the bamboo cane aloft. The footman was still with him, and so also were Genevra and Belerion. Genevra and the footman were laughing together as they sailed the golden boat. It was a scene so welcome to Kate's eyes that her spirits lifted. The past receded and there was only the present—and the future—in this wonderful place.

A familiar beating of wings sounded close by, and the cuckoo fluttered onto the causeway just in front of her. It folded its wings, shook its tail feathers, then cocked its head to one side to look up at her. *"I think you're right!"* it said within her, for to be sure its beak did not open and close.

"Right? About what?"

"About Portreath being guilty. Yes, by Guinevere's girdle, I'm certain you are."

"Oh, I see." Kate was startled to know the cuckoo could apparently read her thoughts.

"I would have spoken more to you before if I realized you could understand so much. I thought that the best I could do was screech single words over and over, in the hope that one might enter your dim human head. But, by all the mermaids of Zennor, you are very sensitive to my world, are you not?"

"I suppose I must be."

"You walk in your sleep, of course. People who do that can sense Lyonesse more strongly than others." The bird shook its tail again, then opened a wing and stretched both it and a leg. *"Bessie may know something about Portreath and the duel,"* it said.

"I don't think Bessie has anything to do with him now," Kate replied, marveling that she was sitting here in the middle of the causeway conducting a conversation with a cuckoo!

"Bessie's brother Jan works at Polwithiel, and is in Portreath's confidence. Jan and Bessie are close. Ask Bessie."

"Yes, I know about Jan. All right, I will ask Bessie." Kate paused. "Do you have a name?" she asked then.

The bird drew itself up importantly. *"I am called Curnow, and I am one of the two heraldic guardians of Lyonesse. Belerion is the other,"* it declared grandly.

"You are in the coat of arms, I know."

"That is our usual abode."

"What part does the golden boat play in it all?" Kate asked.

"It carries all newcomers to the end of the land. It will take Genevra if Selena succeeds."

"Was Belerion sent after Selena when she left Lyonesse in 1806?"

"Yes. He had to do all he could to drive her back.

there again, but she was too clever. She didn't go near seawater. Then, when she did eventually slip up, he had to remain here to watch over Genevra instead. And now you are here as well, and so I have to help him. He may think he's clever because he's a leopard, but he needs a cuckoo's help. It annoys him greatly, yes, by Camelot's drains it does!" Curnow chuckled.

"Who is Selena? In Lyonesse, I mean?"

"She is no more than a lady's maid who learned too much about magic. You will have heard of the lady she once served. Isolde was her name, and she was supposed to marry King Mark when she drank the magic potion and fell in love with Tristan."

Kate was startled. "You mean, Tristan and Isolde really existed?"

Curnow gave her an arch look. *"Of course they existed! And everyone thinks it was Isolde's other maid, Branwen, who administered the love potion. It wasn't, it was Selena. She wanted King Mark for herself. She still does. She thinks Portreath is King Mark, you see, and I suppose he does look like him."* Curnow gave a long-suffering sigh.

So that was the attraction of Denzil Portreath, Kate thought.

"Ah, well, I have conversed for long enough. By Bedivere's big toe, if Belerion knew I was chattering to you like this, he'd have plenty to say on the matter." With that, Curnow took to his wings again, and flew away, but he called back to her over his shoulder. *"Just ask Bessie about Portreath. Her brother Jan tells her everything!"*

22

Kate moved the mare on again. The scent of flowers grew steadily more sweet as she approached the gates, and seemed to wrap warmly around her as she rode through and commenced the ascent toward the castle.

She found Justin and Genevra waiting where the drive curved closer to the landing stage. The footman remained down by the water with Belerion and the golden boat, which carried the pink velvet cat. The children looked happy and a little untidy, as children should when they had been playing, Kate thought as she reined in. "Do I take it that you are friends now?" she asked.

Justin nodded, and Genevra came close to pat the mare. Her eyes were sparkling, and her cheeks were rosy. "Yes," she said. "I'm glad you've both come here, truly I am. It's much more fun when there is someone else, not just me on my own."

Justin nodded again. "I second that," he declared earnestly.

"Well, I'm truly delighted to see you getting on."

"We don't have to come in for lessons now, do we?" Justin asked, and received a cross dig in the back from Genevra, who was appalled that he should actually remind Kate about lessons.

Kate smiled. "No, not today. Maybe not this week, but next week I'm afraid you will both have to become model students. So, unless you want me to change my mind, perhaps you should return to your play?"

They needed no second bidding, but scrambled back down the slope to the landing stage.

Kate rode on, and as she entered the quadrangle she passed Gerent's agent, who was just departing on his cob. He touched his hat and inclined his head, then rode on by. Gerent saw her returning, and came to meet her, but the moment he took the mare's bridle and looked up at Kate's face, he knew she had been crying. "What is it? What's happened?" he asked, reaching up to put a concerned hand over hers.

"Nothing, honestly," she replied lightly.

"You do not fool me. I know tearstains when I see them." He held up his hands to help her down.

"How eagle-eyed you are, to be sure," she replied reluctantly, and slid down into his arms.

He held her. "Why have you been crying?"

"Oh, just sadness for Michael. It happens now and then. You . . . you don't mind, do you? I mean, it is no reflection on my feelings for you."

"I know that." He pulled her closer. "And it was just that? A wipe of the eye for your lost first love?" She didn't answer, and he drew back, still holding her arms. "There's more, is there not?"

She nodded, and told him about the encounter with Portreath. Anger immediately darkened Gerent's eyes. "Plague take him for the scoundrel he is! Kate, I swear I did not even know Michael Kingsley was the name of my informant, and as for killing him in a duel—!"

Kate put a fingertip to his lips. "I know, my darling, I know, and I did not believe him."

He caught her hand. "You swear it? Kate, I could not bear it if you suspected such ill of me."

"Nothing he said has changed my feelings toward you, but he certainly gave me food for thought."

"In what way?"

"I think *he* killed Michael." She explained her reasoning.

Gerent gazed at her, and then exhaled slowly. "It has the ring of truth," he said softly.

Ring. The word made her feel guilty, and she was glad that her riding clothes concealed her throat, so he couldn't see that she was again without the protection he was so anxious to provide for her.

Curnow fluttered to the top of the barbican, and Kate told Gerent about the conversation on the causeway. "By the way, his name is Curnow," she added.

"The old word for Cornwall," Gerent murmured, then looked at Kate again. "I think it a strong probability that Portreath was Michael's opponent, and I also think it likely that Bessie's brother may know something. But Portreath has accused *me,* and that is something I cannot overlook."

Her heart sank. "You do not mean to challenge him again?"

"Kate—

"Please, Gerent, I beg of you. He isn't worth another duel. He said the things he did because he wanted to give me second thoughts, but it did not work. So promise me you will ignore him. Please, Gerent, for all our sakes here."

"Hear, hear," Curnow remarked from the barbican.

Gerent glanced up at the bird, then at Kate. For a moment he remained undecided, but when he saw the pleading in her eyes, he relented. "If that is what you wish, then it is my command."

"Your word, sir?"

He nodded. "My word, madam."

Curnow breathed an audible sigh of relief. *"No good ever came of duels,"* he observed primly.

Kate smiled at Gerent. "Enough of Portreath, for I want to speak only of agreeable things now. For instance, I have just passed Justin and Genevra playing contentedly together."

"You have?" His eyes lit.

She nodded. "Yes, and a happier pair of rascals you could not wish to see."

He laughed, and lifted her from her feet to whirl her about. Then he pulled her close once more. "Apart from Portreath, did you enjoy your ride?"

"Oh, very much. Gerent, I think Cornwall is the most beautiful county I have ever known, and that Carismont itself is . . . well, perfect."

"And you, my love, were born to be its mistress," he said tenderly, and kissed her on the lips.

But then the bells of Lyonesse sounded again, booming through the air like the knell of doom itself. The noise caught Curnow by surprise, and he almost fell off the roof. Flapping and fluttering, he managed to cling to his perch.

"Oh, my saints, my saints!" he gasped. *"Danger's coming quickly now! Tonight it will be here!"*

Later that afternoon, when the first high tide of May Eve came in without event, and had begun to recede again, Kate sat in the window seat of her apartment. She was dressed in her peach robe, about to rest awhile before preparing to go down to dinner at eight, which was the customary time at Carismont.

She gazed out of the window. A sheet of shimmering blue-green water now lay between the island and the shore, with the causeway vaguely discernible as a pale line beneath the waves. It was a peaceful scene, without any hint of the supernatural that lurked all around. There was no one down on the landing stage, the children and footman having returned to the castle. The wrought-iron gate was closed, and Belerion was lying on the grass beside it, in a narrow patch of evening sunshine that found its way around the contours of the island to this more northerly side. His ears twitched to and fro as he gazed through the graceful ironwork, almost as if he were on the lookout—which he probably was. Curnow was nowhere to be seen. The bells of Lyonesse had been heard again since her return from the ride, but had now been silent for well over an hour.

Behind Kate, the apartment was now very different. While she had been out, Gerent had thoughtfully ordered the furniture in the apartment to be changed, so that she would not feel so keenly that the rooms had been Selena's. She had mentioned to him that she felt like an intruder in what was, after all, now supposed to be her apartment, and so he had ordered something to be done. Now there was a different bed, hung with blue-and-white floral silk, and the chairs and tables were from other rooms in the castle as well. The apartment no longer had the harmonious appearance that Selena had chosen, but it made Kate feel a good deal better. Soon a complete redecoration would commence, and then the rooms really would be hers.

A fire burned in the hearth, ready for the coolness of the spring night, but there was no sign of the sparks. Yet there was something in the air; a silent whisper, or an inner echo. She was aware of a trembling sense of anticipation. The coming hours of darkness would see Selena's last chance for another year, and she was bound to do all she could to draw Genevra into Lyonesse. "But not while I draw breath," Kate murmured aloud.

"Did you say something, my lady?" Bessie came out of the dressing room, where she was attending to Kate's dinner gown.

"Mm? Oh, no. I was just thinking aloud," Kate replied. Then, as the maid turned to go back into the dressing room, she remembered Curnow's advice. "Bessie, I have something to ask you."

"Madam?"

"Did you say that your brother Jan works at Polwithiel?"

"Yes, madam. At least, he did. He sent me a message this morning to say he was going back home to the farm. It seems he can't abide Cousin Denzil anymore, and would rather work his fingers to the bone on the farm than at Polwithiel. I'm pleased he's gone home again, for my father needs the help."

Kate smiled. "It may seem a strange question, but do you know if your Cousin Denzil went to London a few days immediately after the death of the first Lady Carismont?"

Bessie's lips parted, and she lowered her eyes. "Well, as it happens, madam, yes he did."

"Really?" Kate sat up with interest.

"Yes, madam. I remember the time well, of course, for the whole of Trezance was shocked by her ladyship's death, and we all knew . . . well, that she and . . ."

"That she and your cousin were lovers?" Kate finished for her. Now was not the time to pay lip service to etiquette and unwritten rules about what one should or should not say to servants.

Bessie went a little pink. "Well, yes, madam. We all knew that was why his lordship and Cousin Denzil fought with swords. Anyway, a few days after that I happened to go home to the farm to see my mother, and as I passed the Merry Maid I saw Jan sitting inside. This was midday, so I especially noticed, because Cousin Denzil never let Jan away from Polwithiel if he could help it, least of all during the day. So I went in and had a sip of rum and shrub with him. He said he was sneaking out because Cousin Denzil had gone to London in a proper fury about something."

"Do you happen to know what that 'something' was?" Kate asked quickly.

"Only that he said he was going to 'teach someone a lesson he'd never forget.' Leastways, that's what Jan said he said."

Michael. "Did your Cousin Denzil succeed?"

Bessie ventured slowly into the bedroom. "I . . . I don't know if I should say, madam . . ."

"Please do, Bessie, for it's important."

The maid pressed her hands to her apron, and then nodded. "All right, I'll tell you. Cousin Denzil likes his French brandy, and the night he returned from

London he had had far too much and Jan had to get him to his bed. Jan says Cousin Denzil kept saying that 'Michael's tongue wouldn't wag anymore.' And that he'd 'made sure he hadn't lost his second duel. No risky swordplay this time, but pistols at dawn on Putney Heath.' "

Kate closed her eyes. It stretched coincidence too far that this information referred to another Michael and another duel on Putney Heath. Denzil Portreath had murdered Michael by firing before the call. It had been a savage act of revenge because Michael's tongue had wagged. Salt tears pricked her eyes again.

Bessie looked at her in concern. "Is something wrong, madam?"

"No, not wrong exactly." Kate bit her lip as she blinked the tears away. "You have merely told me something I had already guessed. Bessie, do you think Jan would swear to this on oath?"

The maid's eyes widened. "On oath, madam?"

"Yes. You see, I am certain that your Cousin Denzil killed my first husband, whose name was Michael, and who died in a duel."

Bessie's face drained of color. "Your first husband? Oh, madam!"

"I don't know if Jan heard enough to be of certain use in a court of law, but if he could at least testify in front of a justice of the peace? Do you think he would do that?"

"I think so, madam." Bessie nodded then. "In fact, I'm sure he would! He owes Cousin Denzil no favors after the harsh treatment he endured at Polwithiel. Cousin Denzil always made it clear that blood was not thicker than water."

Someone else made it clear too, Kate mused, thinking of the way Selena behaved toward her own child.

Belerion dozed comfortably on the grass by the landing stage. The evening air had not yet lost its warmth, and the scent of flowers from the castle gardens was almost soporific. He was feeling lazy. Tonight he would be busy enough, so it was really agreeable to have nothing to do now. His amber eyes began to close, and slowly he fell asleep.

He wasn't aware of his legs being bound, for whoever did it was stealthy and clever. Nor was he aware of the muzzle being slipped over his jaws. The first he knew was when Selena laughed softly in his ear.

"What now, my fine guardian of Lyonesse?"

Justin was sulking in his turret bedroom. He and Genevra had had their first quarrel, and it had been his fault. Now he was in too much of a huff to make amends, so she was in her apartment and he was in his. They had been getting on so well too.

After being down by the landing stage with the model boat all day, they had come back to the castle to have their evening meal in Genevra's apartment. While eagerly discussing what to do with the remaining hours before darkness fell, they disagreed. Genevra wanted to return to the landing stage for a while. But he wanted to explore the castle instead. She said, reasonably enough, that they would only be able to sail the boat for a short while, after which they had the age until bedtime in which to explore the castle. But he had dug his toes in, insisting on exploration. She had pleaded, but he had been maggot enough to refuse to humor her for another hour. So they had quarreled, and as a consequence neither of them was satisfied. Now here he was, lying on his bed staring at the long evening shadows on the ceiling, and there she was, probably doing the same.

He sighed, and fiddled with the ribboned wedding ring around his neck. Then he yawned. It was comfortable just lying there, and all the fresh sea air made him tired. His eyes began to close, and in a few minutes, like Belerion, he had fallen asleep. But he was safe enough, for no one came to bind and gag him.

In Genevra's apartment meanwhile, that young lady was lying on her stomach on the floor, with her elbows

on the floor and her chin in her hands as she tried
to read her storybook. Outside the setting sun was a
spectacle of crimson and gold.

She had just read *Tom Thumb* and was about to
start *Puss-in-Boots,* when she noticed the five runes
her father's nurse had written in the book all those
years before. She had seen them before, of course, but
hadn't taken much notice until now, when she realized
that they were the same symbols she had discovered
in her new locket. At least she thought they were the
same. Rolling over onto her back, she undid the chain
holding the locket, then rolled onto her front again to
resume leaning on her elbows in order to open the
locket and examine the two sets of symbols side by
side. She put the opened locket on the book. The
penciled symbols in the storybook were faded now,
but discernible in the slanting light from the window.
Yes, they were definitely the same: ᚤᛏᚷ᚜

What did they mean? she wondered, her brows fur-
rowing thoughtfully. She would have to ask Papa. Her
eyes wandered back to the book. *Puss-in-Boots* was
one of her favorite stories, and she *always* read it to
her pink velvet cat. Now, where was it . . . ? She
glanced around the room, and then remembered with
dismay that she had left it in the model boat, which
in turn was lying on the grass in the quadrangle. There
was nothing for it but to go down there and fetch the
cat. With a sigh, she scrambled to her feet and hurried
from the room, leaving the locket lying on the storybook.

On reaching the quadrangle, however, she found the
model boat, but of her velvet cat, there was not a
whisker. She was *sure* she hadn't left it down on the
landing stage. In fact, she was certain it had still been
propped in the boat when she and Justin came in from
play. But if it wasn't here now, the only other place
it could be was somewhere between here and the landing stage. She sighed, for she really did not want to
go all the way down to the shore, but she was afraid
to leave the cat. What if it was lying within reach of

tonight's tide? She would never cuddle her beloved toy again!

She and Justin hadn't come back to the castle by the steps to the postern, but had scrambled up the slope to the drive, so that was the way she'd go now. She began to hurry toward the barbican, beneath which the sunset blazed into the quadrangle, but then she looked back at the boat. What harm would there be in sailing it again for a few minutes? Justin wouldn't know if she put it back exactly as she'd found it. With a conspiratorial smile, she went back for the boat, then ran out of the castle with it.

As she went carefully down from the drive toward the landing stage, there was no sign now of Belerion. But her velvet cat lay where he had been.

23

When the daylight had almost gone and Bessie had been dismissed until the morning, Kate waited to go down to the refectory to dine with Gerent.

She stood in front of the floor-standing glass to admire the way Bessie had pinned her hair. A delightful froth of little curls now framed her face, and the rest of her honey-brown curls had been swept up into a knot from which fell a number of bouncy ringlets. The knot was adorned with ribbons of the same shade of apple-green as the gown, and they floated prettily as she turned her head.

She liked wearing green, for it always made her eyes look handsome, and this shade of apple was particularly becoming. The only drawback to wearing this evening gown was that her naked throat and shoulders were visible to all. Gerent was bound to notice that she was not wearing the ring, and he would not be pleased. Still, she preferred to know Justin was safe.

The soft sound of someone humming "Sumer Is Icumen In" warned her that Selena was near. Then she observed the lavender light reflected across the room. Her blood flowed more swiftly, but she did not turn. Drawing a deep breath, she steeled herself. She had given her protection to her son, and now must stand up to Selena by dint of her own willpower. The coming minutes would be a test, for whatever ill will Selena brought to bear must be resisted.

The humming stopped and faintly, very faintly, she saw Selena herself in the looking glass. Bewitchingly beautiful, her red-gold curls cascading to the waist of her glittering gown, Gerent's first wife met Kate's gaze in the mirror. "Well, now, my fine new lady," she said, speaking properly this time, not somehow within Kate's head. "How very brave of you to forgo wearing the runes that Gerent so thoughtfully pressed upon you. It would seem you are already a disobedient wife. Or at least, a foolhardy one."

"I do not need the runes," Kate replied, trusting wholeheartedly that the words would not go down in the annals of famous overconfidences.

"We shall see, Kate, we shall see," Selena murmured. "You have offended me, you see. It was very presumptuous of you to wear my riding habit today."

"You think I should have asked you first?" Kate inquired, in the sort of tone that cordially implied Selena could go hang if she expected such a courtesy.

Selena's eyes hardened. "Don't think to be clever with me."

Kate turned to face her. "What do you want, Selena?" she asked.

"To see fear in your eyes, my fine lady. You are at my mercy now, and I am sorely tempted to test the strength of your willpower when you are without the runes."

"I am only at your mercy if I fear you, and—runes or not—I do not fear you, Selena." But Kate *did* fear Selena, she feared her very much, although nothing would permit her to let this be perceived. To Selena she appeared all that was strong and resilient.

Selena gave a cold laugh. "I think you fear me sufficiently to listen carefully when I warn you to leave this place. Stay and it will be the worst for you. And your boy."

"My boy?" Kate's heart tightened.

"Such a good-looking child. It would be a shame if anything were to happen to him."

"You can't touch him, Selena, for he wears the runes."

Selena smiled. "Tiresome, but true. Yet, I have to warn you, that is still at risk. There is a rather disgusting saying, that there is more than one way of skinning a cat."

Kate took a step toward her. "What do you mean?"

"Ah, that would be telling. Suffice it that you have brought him up to be an honorable and brave child, a veritable St. George in the making, and because of this he is mine for the plucking."

"Your threats are empty." Kate turned back to the looking glass, as if her hair were far more interesting than anything Selena had to say.

"My threats are never empty, Kate, as you will see before the tide returns tonight. I am not simply going to achieve my desire, I am going to punish you as well. You were very ill-advised to set yourself against me."

The words sent a chill through Kate, but she did not show it. "If you are so clever, Selena, how is it that so far you have always failed? You vowed that you would prevent Gerent from marrying me; you failed. You tried to seduce him; you failed. You tried to draw Genevra into the sea the other night; you failed. And you have tried to dispose of me twice. You failed on Dartmoor, and you have failed here. Oh, and I was forgetting . . . you have failed to persuade Denzil Portreath to join you in Lyonesse. So, all in all, it seems to me that you are a complete failure."

Selena looked savage enough to strike her, but instead went to look out of the window. She saw Genevra down on the landing stage, the pink velvet cat beside her as she knelt to float Justin's boat on the pool by the landing stage. The evening light was muted, with a subtle air of golden enchantment in the dying rays of the sun, and the tide was ebbing fast now, leaving a jumble of glistening seaweed exposed on nearby rocks. Genevra was kneeling on part of the landing stage that at high tide would be covered by the sea. A faint smile appeared upon Selena's lips, and she glanced back at Kate. "You are right, of course, but I have learned my lesson. Tonight I will approach it all in a rather different way, and this time I will not fail."

Kate's unease increased. What was Selena intending to do? Could it really lead to success this time?

Selena chuckled. "Soon I will be happy once more."

"Happiness selfishly and cruelly won at the expense of your own child."

Selena's lavender-blue eyes swung back to her. "Love makes us all what we are," she murmured.

"Love? I do not think you are capable of such a noble emotion!" Kate replied scathingly.

"Oh, how superior you think you are! If you had known a love that reached across centuries, and that consumed your every moment, you would perhaps understand how I feel."

Kate raised an eyebrow. "Ah, yes, I was forgetting—Denzil Portreath is supposed to be King Mark of Cornwall," she said dryly.

"He *is* King Mark! I lost him to Isolde, whose infidelity did not shake him, but now, all this time later, I have found him again. His name may be Denzil Portreath now, but I knew my dear love when I saw him. He has not changed, and is just the same as he was all that time ago."

Kate refrained from saying she saw nothing kingly or admirable about treacherous, devious, murderous Mr. Portreath of Polwithiel.

"There is no Isolde to steal him from me now," Selena continued, "and for him I will sacrifice everything."

"Except, apparently, the title and comfort of being Lady Carismont," Kate remarked dryly. "Be honest, Selena. You could still be with your precious love right now if you hadn't tried to cling to Gerent as well. If you'd been honest, and simply left Gerent to live with Portreath, all would be well. It's your own fault that you are back in Lyonesse, yours and yours alone. So leave Gerent and Genevra alone, and concentrate instead upon how to get your precious King Mark to go to Lyonesse."

Selena gave a sharp intake of breath, not because she saw Kate's words gave her second thoughts, but because there came a scuffling in the chimney. Then Curnow's voice raised in outrage. *"Get out of this place, you vile sorceress, you stain on the honor of Lyonesse, you . . . you unnatural mother! Leave, I say! Get back beneath the sea, where you belong!"*

Soot showered down over the hearth, making the fire smoke, then came a string of cuckooing squawks as the unfortunate Curnow tumbled the rest of the way. He gave another squawk as the fire scorched his posterior, obliging him to leap smartly out. There was a distinct smell of singed feathers as he stood by the hearth and shook himself fiercely.

Selena had changed to her light form again, and was skimming desperately around the room, trying to find a way out, but the windows were closed, and there wasn't space enough beneath the door. Her only hope was the chimney, and Curnow was between her and that.

The cuckoo watched her panic-stricken progress. *"Not quite so clever now, are we?"* he remarked, enjoying her discomposure.

"I hate you, you mangy bird!" came her reply.

"Mangy? I'll give you mangy!" He launched himself into the air as she unwisely came a little too close. In a second he'd caught her in his beak. Kate heard Selena's squeals as she tried to pull free. So ferociously did she wriggle and squirm, that suddenly she managed to wrench herself away. Within the space of a heartbeat she had gone, dashing up the chimney as if her life had depended upon it, which it had, of course.

Curnow had no hope of scrambling after her quickly enough to hope to catch her again, and he was so annoyed with himself that he landed on the floor once more and hopped up and down. *"Oh, by the damnation of Dumnorix! By Lancelot's loins! By Peredur's pox!"* Realizing his language was perhaps a little strong in the presence of a lady, he stopped hopping, and cleared his throat in no little embarrassment. *"Er, forgive me, I fear my rage had the better of me."*

"I'm sure it's quite understandable."

"That's twice I've had her now, and twice I've let her escape. By all the powers, you must not tell Belerion. I will never hear the end of it."

"He will not learn anything from me," Kate promised.

Curnow shook himself again, and more soot showered over the floor. Then the clock on the mantel began to chime. It was time for Kate to go down to dinner. The cuckoo gave a heavy sigh, then made his way to the hearth. He glanced back at her. *"I fancy you did well against her, considering you are without the runes. But you must still take great care, for she is up to something new. I do not know what it is, but I can feel it in my quills. Tonight is going to be very hazardous indeed, and I fear the outcome may go either way."*

With that he launched himself up the chimney, and with much soot-scattering and disgruntled cuckooing, managed to climb up to the open air.

Kate had just reached the entrance to the refectory when she encountered Mrs. Pendern coming out. The housekeeper had just made certain the dinner table had been set exactly as it should be, and halted with a respectful curtsy as she saw Kate.

"Good evening, my lady."

"Good evening, Mrs. Pendern. I trust all is well?"

"Oh, yes, indeed, madam. I was checking the table, because some of the maids can be a little lax. His lordship is waiting, and dinner will be served in five minutes."

Kate was about to continue into the refectory, when she paused. "How are the children, Mrs. Pendern?"

"They are in their rooms, madam. I fear they had a little spat earlier on, and are at present not speaking to each other."

"Oh, no . . ."

"Please do not worry, for it was not a terrible quarrel, just a silly falling out over what to do after they'd eaten. They will be as right as rain come the morning."

As right as rain come the morning? Oh, how Kate hoped that would prove to be the case! Never before had she so vehemently wished a night away, but wishing did not mean the thing was done, and so the hours of darkness and likely peril stretched interminably ahead.

The prospect suddenly daunted her, and she caught up her silk skirts to hurry to Gerent, who was by the fireplace, pushing a fresh log down with his boot. He wore the deep-purple coat again, and white silk pantaloons that clung to his hips and legs. Firelight blushed the sheen of his white satin waistcoat and turned to copper the pearl pin fixed to the intricate knot of his lacy neckcloth. He was the picture of fashionable elegance, and might have been on the point of setting out for Almack's.

His smile of welcome faded as he saw her agitation. "What is it, my love?" he asked, coming toward her to take her hands and draw them both to his lips.

She inhaled deeply, determined to quell the sudden panic. "I . . . I just wish the night was over and done with," she replied, her trembling fingers twining through his.

"Soon it will be." He kissed her forehead.

She closed her eyes, loving him so much that she could almost understand how Selena felt. Almost, but not quite, for no matter how deeply and eternally Kate loved Gerent, she could never, *ever* sacrifice her child's happiness on account of it. She drew back, and looked up into Gerent's eyes. "I have a confession to make."

"I trust it is not too dastardly?" he replied, smiling.

"It concerns my wedding ring."

"Ah. Well, I had noticed that you did not appear to be wearing it. Where is it?"

"I have made Justin wear it." She told him what

Justin had divulged at the breakfast table, then finished, "So it means he is experiencing some of this as well, Gerent, and I need to know he is safe. I decided that if you are strong enough to stand up to Selena without protection, then so am I."

He smiled and pulled her close once more. "My darling, I understand exactly. Have I not taken the same precautions with Genevra? But you will take care, will you not? Strong or not, without such a shield, you are vulnerable."

"Ah, but I have already encountered Selena, and emerged safe and sound from the experience." She related the confrontation that had just taken place in her apartment.

"Oh, my darling, if I had known, I would have come to you . . ." Gerent let go of her, and turned to lean a hand on the mantel of the chimneypiece. He gazed at the coat of arms. "She said she has something new in mind for tonight?"

"Yes, although I have no idea what it is. She may even have simply been talking for effect."

He shook his head. "No, she meant it."

"Gerent, I don't think we should let the children sleep in their own rooms tonight. They should be with us."

"I agree." He looked past her as Mrs. Pendern, a footman, and a maid entered the refectory with the dinner. "Ah, I'll attend to it right now. Mrs. Pendern?" he called to the housekeeper.

She came to him. "My lord?"

"For reasons you can no doubt hazard, we have decided that the children are to sleep with us tonight. Will you see that two extra beds of some sort are placed in my bedchamber? Any beds will do. Actually, I imagine there are still some of those old trundle beds somewhere in the castle . . . ?"

"Oh, indeed there are, sir. The children are in their rooms right now, do you wish me to send them to your apartment immediately?"

"No. Just attend to the trundle beds, while her lady-

ship and I dine. We will speak to the children our-
selves directly afterward. The tide will not start to flow
again for some time yet, so they should be safe enough
for the moment."

"Very well, sir."

But Gerent was wrong to imagine the tide was necessary for Selena's preliminary activities, for as he and
Kate sat down to their first course of Palestine soup,
flavored with artichokes, things were already happening outside.

24

The soup course had just been set before Kate and Gerent in the refectory when Curnow gave up his pursuit of Selena. Well, that was perhaps not the truth of it, for he gave up trying to find her again, having lost her as she fled to safety among the oak trees of Lyonesse. He had searched high and low, but her whereabouts eluded him.

Espying the brook that wended its way from the spring at the foot of the island to the creek, the cuckoo glided down to the bank to have a drink. He had to stretch right forward, tilting his rather cumbersome tail up in the air, and just as he was taking a draft of the cool, sweet water, someone's foot gave him a kick. As he catapulted into the brook, a net was thrown over him!

Squawking with alarm, he struggled for all he was worth, but escape was impossible. Curnow considered himself to be the cuckoo to end all cuckoos. How could he have been so unguarded as to stick his fool tail up in the air like that? It had been just *asking* for trouble!

His captor was Selena, and she laughed as she gathered him up. She was in her human form again, wearing the gown of diamonds, but her loveliness was spoiled by the set of her mouth and the hardness in her lavender-blue eyes. She bundled him into a wicker cage. "I already have that lazy leopard, and now I have you as well," she murmured, and carried him along the bank of the brook. Her shimmering hem brushed through the grass and wildflowers, and the sun glanced brightly on her red-gold hair. She ducked her head to avoid the low-hanging branches of hawthorn blossom, which come the morning would be gathered in armfuls to decorate homes. Curnow could see the creek ahead, and the maypole awaiting the May Day revels. The golden boat rocked on the quiet water, ready to convey any newcomers to Lyonesse's farthest bounds.

People and children emerged from the ramshackle dwellings by the creek to watch Selena approach. They regarded her as a witch, and had always feared her. Now they were more afraid than ever, because she had overcome Belerion and Curnow. The guardians had always been stronger than her, and when she escaped from Lyonesse it was only through guile that she had managed to remain at large. Now it seemed the guardians had fallen into her clutches.

She ignored the watching people as she walked toward the golden boat, which was moored close enough to the bank to be easily boarded by way of an oak plank. She carried Curnow on board, stepping past a sadly bound and tethered Belerion, and went to hang the wicker cage on a nail on the mast. Curnow hunched in the cage, the picture of dismay and self-reproach for having so failed in his duty.

"What a useless pair you have proved to be," she said to them both. "Oh, I grant that you kept me on my toes for quite some time, but in the end you were ridiculously easy to catch. You should be ashamed of yourselves."

As the leopard and cuckoo looked wretchedly at her, she gave a laugh. "I could not believe that fate was being so generous to me. Belerion falling asleep when he should have been on guard, and Curnow with his tail so high in the air that he was an easy target for my foot. Thank you both." She gave them an insultingly deep curtsy. "Now there is nothing in my way. Soon I will have Genevra where I want her, then when the tide comes in next, I will go to my dear love."

Shortly afterward, Genevra was still to be found kneeling on the landing stage, using the bamboo cane to tap the golden boat as it sailed on water that was still and smooth. The pink velvet cat lay beside her, and the evening shadows were now so long they blended together. The western sky was a dull red, and the seagulls, usually so noisy, were strangely silent. The causeway stood above a waste of sand, pools, and seaweed-draped rocks, and the sound of music drifted from the mainland as the children of Trezance practiced their maypole dancing one last time before May Day.

Suddenly the music changed. The tune remained the same, "Sumer Is Icumen In," but it was no longer played simply on a penny whistle, instead there were more instruments: a flute, drumbeats, jingling bells, and something that sounded like a form of violin.

At first Genevra paid no heed, for she was too intent upon the boat as it slid across the mirrored surface of the water, but then she noticed another sound closer at hand, the gentle tinkle of water. The sun seemed to have come out again too, as if the approaching night had changed its mind and gone into retreat, so that when she glanced toward the sound of playing water, she was surprised to see sunshine dancing on a spring among the rocks. Then she realized she was no longer kneeling on the landing stage, but on a mossy bank where primroses bloomed. At last the change in the music dawned upon her as well, and she sat back on her heels to look toward Trezance.

With a shock, she found herself gazing along the clearing amid the woods of Lyonesse. At the end lay the creek, where the real golden boat was moored.

She could see children in strange clothes dancing around a maypole, watched by adults. The men were wearing costumes that reminded Genevra of the illustration of Robin Hood and his merry men in her storybook, although some of them had antler headdresses that were very peculiar indeed. The women might have all been playing Maid Marian, and carried garlands of hawthorn blossom.

Selena stood among them, in her jeweled gown. She was beckoning, and Genevra heard her voice. *"Come to me, Genevra, come and join in the maypole dancing."*

The little girl's lips parted fearfully, and she scooped up the velvet cat and scrambled to her feet, leaving the model boat to glide away out of reach of the bamboo cane.

"Come, Genevra. We're having such fun here. The children want to play with you."

Genevra's eyes filled with tears, and she clutched the cat close. "Papa?" she whispered. "Papa, I'm frightened."

Selena seemed to hear, in spite of the barely audible whisper. *"It's all right, Papa will not mind. You can go back to him afterward. Oh, do come on, sweetheart . . ."*

Genevra began to back away toward the steps carved out of the castle hill, but suddenly a swarm of little lights barred the way. They wouldn't let her pass, and the only way she could go was into the clearing; indeed, they began to drive her that way. The notes of the music seemed suddenly very sweet and enticing, and some children who weren't dancing started to wave and shout to her. She could hear their laughter, and the eager way they called her name. Surely there would be no harm in going to them? She wished Justin were with her to help her decide, for she would feel much more safe holding his hand.

The children called again, and seemed to be having such a wonderful time that suddenly she wanted to join them. She began to walk along the clearing, stepping through the grass and wildflowers of the Lyonesse woodland, where only a moment before had been the exposed sand, pools, seaweed, and rocks of present-day Cornwall.

Justin was still fast asleep on his bed. He was dreaming of the Tower of London, when suddenly he was disturbed by Genevra calling him in the distance. His eyes opened, and for a moment he wasn't sure where he was, but then he remembered it was the turret bedroom at Carismont. He must have slept in his clothes all night, for it was daylight again outside! Running a hand through his blond hair, he sat up, aware that the ring around his neck was hot against his skin.

"Justin! Help me, please!" Genevra called again.

Where was she? Down on the landing stage? Puzzled, he slipped from the bed and went to lean out of the window. He expected to see the same scene he had looked at the night before, but instead he saw a vista of greenwood. Oak trees in the freshness of new leaf and a long clearing that was bright with spring flowers. He saw bluebells, cowslips, celandines, violets, speedwell, primroses, ramsons, and along the fringes of the clearing, creamy frothing boughs of hawthorn that sweetened the air. It was Lyonesse, just as his mother had warned him he might see.

Now he could hear music as well. That same awful song as before. It was coming from the far ending of the clearing, where Trezance should be. But the town had gone, and in its place there was a medieval settlement. People were watching maypole dancing, and nearby he could see his boat. At least, it wasn't really his boat, for it was far too big, but it was identical.

He scanned the clearing for Genevra, and at last picked her out on the edge of the crowd by the maypole. A woman in a brightly spangled gown was holding her hand, and wouldn't let her go, even though she was struggling. "Please help me, Justin! I'm frightened!"

"Genevra?" he breathed, unsure what to do. The ring was burning him, and he wanted to take it off, but he knew he must not. Why could he hear her so very clearly, even though she was at least a quarter of a mile away?

"Justin! Come to me, please!" Genevra's voice caught on a sob as she dropped her velvet cat and it was trampled underfoot by the maypole dancers.

Justin was torn, partly wanting to rush to Genevra's aid, partly remembering what his mother had said at the breakfast table. *"Never go outside when you see something you know cannot be there. It is very difficult to resist, but you must try."*

Genevra began to weep. "Why won't you help me, Justin? I'm so frightened!"

"I . . . I'll tell Mama, and your papa . . ." he began.

Suddenly the voice of the woman holding Genevra's hand broke into his thoughts. *"No, Justin, don't do that. There is no need. Why don't you simply come and join us? We're having such fun."*

Mistrust burned through him, whom he knew was Genevra's mother, although he wasn't sure *how* he knew. "I think I should tell Mama and Genevra's papa," he said again.

"No!" The woman's voice hardened suddenly, and the sparkling lights in her gown seemed to fly up into the air, snaking along the clearing toward him like a flight of angry bees.

Alarmed, Justin stepped nervously back from the window. "I'll get help, Genevra!" he cried, then fled from the bedroom.

He stumbled down the spiral steps of the turret, and when he reached the bottom he was sure he could see the dazzle of the lights in the room above. He ran through the castle for all he was worth, making for the refectory, although again he was not sure why. "Mama!" he screamed, stealing another fearful glance over his shoulder. The lights were twisting and diving behind him, like a serpent made of diamonds. "Mama!" he shrieked. "Mama! They're trying to catch me! They want me to go to Lyonesse!" Suddenly his eyes opened. The ring was no longer burning his skin. It was nighttime, and there was just the glow of the candles on the refectory table. In a tearful blur he saw Gerent and his mother rising from their chairs.

Kate's napkin fluttered to the floor as she hurried to him. "Justin? My dearest darling boy, whatever is wrong?"

"Mama? I . . . I think I was dreaming," he stammered, bewildered tears welling down his cheeks. Had he been sleepwalking? Hadn't he really seen or heard anything at all?

"It's all right, sweeting, you're safe now," Kate said, kneeling to take him in her arms. Her perfume filled his nostrils, light, delicate, and more reassuring than she would ever know.

He glanced fearfully back again, but the lights had gone. "The diamonds in her gown were chasing me, Mama," he whispered.

Kate and Gerent exchanged dismayed glances.

Justin put his arms tightly around his mother and hid his face against her bare shoulder. "Genevra called me. She was in Lyonesse. I saw her from my window. The woman—her mama—had hold of her, and didn't want me to tell you anything . . ."

With a stifled oath, Gerent turned on his heel and dashed away. He ran to Genevra's apartment, and found it empty. Then he saw the open storybook on the floor, and the precious locket lying where she had left it. He closed his eyes. Selena had succeeded in her heartless aim. Genevra had been lured to Lyonesse.

25

It was completely dark, and the tide had ebbed its farthest. Soon it would turn and begin to flow again, drawn in by the silver orb of the full moon, which shone from a cloudless sky filled with stars.

Torches bobbed all over the island as the servants combed every inch in case Genevra was lying injured somewhere. It was a vain hope, of course, but Gerent did not intend to leave anything to chance. That was why a search party had been sent to Trezance as well, but it seemed very unlikely indeed that she had simply walked to the mainland. Not Genevra, who was terrified to leave Carismont.

Fishermen were still working on the upturned vessel on the quay, and if the little girl *had* walked along the causeway or simply across the sand and rocks, someone was bound to have seen her. As time ticked relentlessly by, however, it became increasingly obvious that the worst had happened. If Genevra wasn't on the island and hadn't gone ashore, then there was only one other place she could be: Lyonesse. Justin would clearly have been taken there too, had it not been that he wore the runes and was able to resist.

Now he was asleep on a trundle bed in Gerent's apartment, with Mrs. Pendern watching over him. The housekeeper had encircled his bed with protective greenery, and scattered pieces of paper upon which she had written the runes. And to make absolutely certain that he could not be lured away if she happened to fall asleep, she had tied a few yards of ribbon to his wrist, with the other end tied to her own. Now if he moved from the bed, she would be alerted.

Kate and Gerent stood at the top of the drive just outside the barbican, where they could look down the slope at the ongoing search. They still wore their evening clothes and held hands as they watched the torches moving below. The moon was so bright and strong in the heavens that Kate could almost feel it tugging at the tide. She felt Genevra's abduction keenly, and hated to imagine how desperately frightened and unhappy the little girl must be right now, wherever she was.

Gerent drew a heavy breath. "Why, when I want more than anything to suddenly see Lyonesse stretching before me, do I only see the present?"

"If you saw Lyonesse, what would you do?"

"Enter it, search for Genevra, and bring her back."

"You think that would be easy? You think that Selena would simply permit you to take your daughter and leave again? Oh, Gerent, she would *never* let that happen. She would be delighted to have you in her clutches as well. She'd make you both stay in Lyonesse, while she came back here to enjoy all she had before. The widowed Lady Carismont, and her lover, Denzil Portreath, living in luxury beneath your roof, with your fortune."

"Nevertheless, I need to be able to try, Kate. You do understand that, don't you?"

She hugged him tightly. "Yes, of course I do, for I know I would feel the same if it were Justin she was holding." She glanced up and saw in the moonlight that there were tears on his lashes. His pain brought her own tears closer, and she looked away again, needing to distract herself. She had to be strong for him now.

Her gaze followed some of the Carismont men as they rode back along the causeway. Then she looked at the waste of sand, seaweed, and rock pools between the island and the main shore. It was impossible to believe that Lyonesse was there right now, no longer drowned and lost, but somehow existing alongside the present. There were trees and flowers down there, and a village of huts where the lights of modern Trezance glowed.

Her glance came to rest upon the Merry Maid. A gentleman was there, leaning back against a window-sill with a tankard in his hand. Beside him, tail swishing idly, was a chestnut hunter. Denzil Portreath! She remembered the mocking words he'd called after her as she left the knoll. *I'll be on the quayside at nightfall, my lady, and I'll stay there to see what happens! Believe me, I will not leave until it is all over.*

Suddenly Gerent noticed him as well. "That damned cur!" he breathed. "Is he a ghoul that he must feast upon my anguish?"

"Gerent—"

"I'll have none of it! None of it!"

Before Kate realized what was happening, Gerent had let go of her hand to dash away down the drive.

"Gerent! Come back!" she cried anxiously, but he took no notice. She saw him meet the returning horsemen, one of whom swiftly dismounted and handed over his reins. In a moment Gerent had leaped onto the horse, turned it, and kicked his heels to urge it back down the hill again. Kate watched in dismay, putting shaking hands to her mouth. Please don't do anything rash, she thought. Denzil Portreath simply isn't worth it.

Oh, where were Belerion and Curnow? Why hadn't they come? If ever the guardians were needed, it was now.

The man who was both Michael Kingsley's murderer and Selena's lover straightened warily as he saw Gerent's headlong gallop along the causeway. He did not doubt the reason for that gallop, and a nerve moved at the corner of his mouth as he carefully set his tankard down and stepped across the cobbles to face Gerent as he rode up onto the quay.

Gerent reined in on seeing his adversary standing foursquare across his way. "Well, Portreath? Does it please you how well Selena has done?"

"I have no opinion one way or the other. Your daughter matters nothing to me."

"She matters a great deal to me!" snapped Gerent, wanting to hurl himself from the saddle and grab the other's throat in his hands.

"All I am concerned with is avoiding Lyonesse. If Selena comes to me, all well and good, but I have no intention of going there."

Gerent was contemptuous. "Haven't you the stomach for it? Well, I suppose that is all I should expect of a coward and a liar."

Portreath's cold blue eyes sharpened in the light from the Merry Maid's lanterns. "Have a care now, Carismont, for I am not in the mood to meekly accept your insults. Besides, I am not the one who will shortly go to Lyonesse. That honor is yours, dear fellow. If you want Genevra back, you will have to rescue her. Not that you will succeed, for Selena wants you both there. Once she has you in her grasp, you and your daughter will soon sail for the ends of the lost land. And there you will remain, while Selena and I enjoy your wealth."

Seeing the blaze of rage kindling like a furnace in Gerent's eyes, he reached slowly inside his coat. "Don't be foolish now, for although it suits me to have you dead, we mustn't forget poor little Genevra, must we? What will she do without you? Lyonesse will be very lonely for her." Calmly he cocked the pistol and leveled it at Gerent. "I suggest you turn around and trot back to your island lair. Off you go, there's a good chap. Then wait for Lyonesse to beckon."

Gerent didn't move. He was so filled with loathing,

fury, and utter contempt that he considered taking the ultimate risk. But he had to think of Genevra. "Just answer me one thing, Portreath. Will you really accept Selena back in your bed, even though she is monster enough to have done this tonight to her only child?"

Portreath smiled. "Yes, I will accept her. I'm of a mind to be master of Carismont, with access to your bottomless coffers."

"May God have mercy on your vile soul," Gerent breathed, lowering his glance for a moment. To his astonishment he saw an open canvas bag the previous rider had tied over the horse's withers. Just inside it lay two old pistols, both of which appeared to be loaded.

He wasn't about to question why one of his men should be riding around with armed pistols, for right now those pistols were of inestimable use. Without seeming to do anything in particular, he slid his fingers over one of the guns, but did not draw it. He continued speaking. "If you had an ounce of honor, you would tell Selena to go to blazes for what she has done. Instead you have made the goal worth playing for, and that makes you as guilty of the crime as she."

"Go back to your island while you still have it, Carismont, for I am tired of this idle chatter."

Gerent pretended to do just that, but as he turned the horse he used the clatter of its hooves to mask the cocking of the pistol, which he then drew out and fired at Portreath, not to hit him, but to knock the pistol from his grasp.

Portreath cried out in alarm as the gun was struck from his fingers. It scuttered across the cobbles to the edge of the quay, then slithered over and fell with an audible plop into the water of the creek.

The shot brought people pouring out of nearby buildings, especially the Merry Maid. Everyone saw as Portreath sank to his knees to beg Gerent not to shoot him. Gerent discarded the spent pistol, and purposefully drew the second, which he cocked in front of everyone. "My, my, did I fire without due warning? How very ignoble, to be sure," he murmured.

"You'll never defeat Selena, Carismont, so you may as well give up the fight. She is going to come back from Lyonesse."

"She will find you dead," Gerent breathed, coolly leveling the second pistol and directing it toward Portreath's forehead.

"For pity's sake . . ."

Gerent's finger tightened on the trigger, and he fully intended to squeeze, but then something changed his mind. A sixth sense told him that Portreath was more use to him alive than dead. Abruptly he turned the pistol away and uncocked it again. "You may live for the time being, Portreath," he said softly. Then he replaced the gun in the canvas bag, and urged the horse back onto the causeway.

As he rode away, the dull tolling of the Lyonesse bells commenced. It was a signal that the tide was about to turn.

Genevra sat on the deck of the golden boat, her knees drawn up, her head bowed so that her dark hair fell forward, hiding her face. She was frightened and miserable, and her eyes were red and swollen from weeping. She raised her head as the bells rang out. In the distance above the trees she could see steeples and towers. Belerion still lay bound close by, and now and then she heard a sigh from Curnow, in his wicker cage on the mast.

The cuckoo was deep in thought. He could not— *would* not—believe that Selena was within an inch of wicked victory. There had to be something that could be done to spike her vile guns. But what? He had a niggling feeling that an obvious solution was within grasp, and he sighed again as he willed himself to concentrate. Gradually the germ of an idea began to form, and a new light crept into his eyes. Of course! Why hadn't he seen it before! He shuffled excitedly, then began to plot.

Selena lounged impatiently on a golden chair by the boat's prow. Her slender fingers drummed, and her foot tapped. She had to wait for the tide, because only then could she leave and return to her love. And there was Gerent to wait for as well, of course. She knew he would come, because he loved his child so very much, and once he was here, he and Genevra would find themselves sailing for the remotest reaches of Lyonesse.

Genevra looked tearfully at her mother. "Please let me go home, Mama," she pleaded.

"Lyonesse is your home now."

"But I don't want it to be."

"Your sniveling is beginning to irritate me."

Genevra blinked as hot salt tears pricked her eyes anew. "Please. I want to be with Papa, and with Justin and his mama."

"Well, I cannot give you Justin and his wretched mother, but your papa will be here soon enough. He will think he can rescue you, but all he will be doing is entering my web. It is as good as done."

Curnow spoke slyly from the wicker cage. *"Don't count your chickens, Selena, for they are far from hatched."*

"Oh, shut up," she declared, and rose angrily from her chair to toss a cloth over the cage.

The cuckoo wasn't cowed. *"Kate will triumph, Selena. She has it within her power to deny you the chance of ever being with Portreath, either here in Lyonesse or any other place."*

"What do you mean?" Selena demanded, snatching off the blanket again and eyeing the cuckoo.

"I'm not going to tell you," Curnow replied, aware that Belerion was stretching his neck to look at him in astonishment.

Selena was in no mood to play cuckoo games. "I'll pull your tail feathers out one by one unless you tell me," she threatened.

Curnow backed away nervously. *"She'll still defeat you. It's already done, you see, and only if she undoes it will you have your lover with you at Carismont."*

"If she undoes what?" Selena asked testily.

"I'm not going to say, but I will say that what she has done will make certain that you do not enjoy Portreath for long if you go to him, but on the other hand, it will certainly make him eager to come here to you."

Selena became very still. "Explain."

"Let me go to her, and you will see."

"I'm not *that* much of a fool!" Selena cried.

Curnow pressed his tail against the mast, meaning to preserve it at all costs.

Selena's lavender-blue eyes were sharp and shrewd. "You seem very sure of yourself."

"Oh, I am, Selena."

She gave a cold laugh. "And *I* am sure that I can have everything I want—my lover, Carismont, London, and all the fashions and influence I crave so much. Nothing your precious Kate can do will stand in my way."

"Her actions already bar your way, Selena," the cuckoo replied. *"Leave Lyonesse, and you will sleep in a lonely bed, because Denzil Portreath will soon be dead."*

Belerion stared at the bird in the wicker cage. Had the cuckoo lost what few wits it had?

"Dead?" Selena repeated.

"Oh, yes. Without a doubt."

Selena turned slowly away, unsure whether to believe the cuckoo or not. Somehow she did not think Curnow was fool enough to pretend anything at a juncture such as this. Which left the uncomfortable probability that he was telling the truth. But what could Gerent's dearest Kate have done that would have such a profound effect?

Curnow watched her. *"Kate can persuade him to come here to you."*

Selena whirled back to face him again. "Maybe I can see to it that she sends him to me anyway! Maybe, runes or not, I can get at her through her boy!"

"Then you must do it tonight, before the moon changes, and I doubt if even you can achieve anything

in so short a time. No, either you follow my advice, or you resign yourself to another year of waiting. By which time, of course, Portreath will be no more, in any world."

Selena swallowed. "Very well," she said, "but woe betide you if you are trying to trick me!"

"I may be a cuckoo, but that doesn't mean I'm cuckoo as well," Curnow replied, breathing out with relief.

"What must be done?" Selena asked.

"Go to Kate, and ask her about the letter she wrote."

"Letter?"

The cuckoo nodded. *"Promise that if she will send Portreath to you, you will release Genevra. It must be an honest promise, now. No trickery and Morgan le Fay meddling."*

Selena regarded the bird for a moment, then turned and left the boat.

Curnow winked at Belerion, who still had no idea at all what his feathered companion was up to. *"I'll explain to you in a moment,"* the cuckoo whispered, *"but first I must see how far I can cast my thoughts and be heard by Kate. Let's hope I can reach her from here in Lyonesse to the castle in modern times."*

Belerion rolled his eyes. The cuckoo was becoming more addled all the time, he thought.

But Curnow was confident he had perceived a way to bring satisfaction all around. Even for Selena and Portreath, who most certainly did not deserve it. All that was required was for Kate to know what was in his mind. He knew she was sensitive to him; it just remained to see *how* sensitive.

26

Kate and Gerent had just returned to his apartment, where Justin and Mrs. Pendern were still fast asleep. Gerent went to the oriel, but there was no sign of Lyonesse, the bells of which sounded eerily across the bay. The night continued bright and clear, illuminated by the clarity of the completely full moon as it hung low above the western horizon. To the east the sky bore the first hint of approaching dawn, as yet the merest stain of ice-green.

There were still lights in Trezance, especially at the Merry Maid, for the entire town knew that something momentous was bound to happen with tonight's tide. Denzil Portreath was still there. He was now sitting on the edge of the quay, with his legs dangling above the water. It seemed that not even humiliation made any difference to his determination to witness what occurred.

"That damned mongrel is still there," Gerent murmured.

"It is the sort of contemptible thing I would expect of such a man," Kate replied.

"I feel so helpless, Kate. I am Genevra's father, I own this island and most of the town, yet I cannot do anything to help my own child."

"There is still time . . ." Kate began.

"Time? An hour or so, that is all. Then the surge will come in, and Selena will be released. She will go to Portreath, and he is waiting to welcome her. They may not have everything they want, but they will have sufficient. Oh, I should have punctured him between the eyes when I had the opportunity."

"Why didn't you?" Kate asked curiously.

"I don't know." Gerent turned to face her. "I had him in my sights, and all I had to do was fire, but something stopped me. I found myself thinking he was of more use alive than dead. Dear God, the man killed your first husband and helped my first wife make a cuckold of me, yet I let him go."

"Kate? Can you hear me?"

Curnow's voice suddenly sounded distantly in Kate's head. With a gasp she caught up her apple-green skirts and hurried to the window. "Curnow? Where are you?" she cried.

Gerent watched her. "What have you heard?" he asked.

"He's speaking to me from somewhere. I can hear him inside my head."

"Kate, can you hear me?" the cuckoo's voice asked again. *"If you can, think your thoughts back to me."*

She closed her eyes, and concentrated with all her might. *"Yes, I can hear you."*

"And I hear you! Oh, excellent! Now, listen very carefully . . ."

Gerent watched her as she stood there with her eyes tightly closed, then his attention was drawn to the window. Lyonesse was before him at last, the clearing silver in the moonlight. Selena was walking toward the castle, her shimmering gown dragging through the ghostly wildflowers.

He put a hand on Kate's sleeve. "Look, Kate. Look!"

"One moment, Curnow's telling me something very important . . ."

"There isn't time. Lyonesse is here, and so is Selena. I have to find Genevra."

Kate smiled at him. "And find her we will. Gerent, Curnow has just told me a plan that I am sure will work!"

"Plan?"

Kate looked out at Selena, who had almost reached the pool where the spring played. "Are we awake or asleep now?" she whispered to herself, then said to him, "We will go down to meet her. Just follow what I say, and back me up, no matter what."

He nodded. "If that is what you wish of me, then of course I will do it."

"Oh, Gerent, I do love you so," she whispered, and linked her arms around his neck to kiss him tenderly on the lips.

He caught her to him, so their hearts beat close, then he took her hand. "Come on, then, let us confront her."

They hurried through the castle to the postern, and emerged at the top of the steps to see Selena waiting by the pool. "Well, now, how very perceptive of you both to know I have come to speak to you," she said.

"Have you come to bargain, Selena?" Kate said, lifting her hem to descend the steep steps. The chill night air touched her skin through the thin silk and gossamer sleeves of her gown, but she was hardly aware of it. The blood was pounding through her veins in a wave of suppressed excitement that almost made her rash. No, she must be prudent now. She had to think very clearly, and do exactly as Curnow had said.

Gerent went down the steps as well, praying that the cuckoo's plan was indeed as clever as Kate thought. Was it ever wise to trust a bird whose name was synonymous with foolishness?

Selena glanced at Kate, then looked at Gerent. "It is a pity you are so handsome, for sometimes when I am with you I almost desire you again," she murmured.

"My passion for you is long since at an end," he replied.

"Really? Oh, I think I could have you if I really put my mind to it."

"You flatter yourself, Selena."

She laughed, and tossed her wonderful red-gold hair. "Well, you are here in Lyonesse now, Gerent, and willingly so, if I am not mistaken."

"What do you want of us?" Kate asked, even though she already knew.

"Curnow informs me that I must ask you about a letter."

"I have written one, yes."

Gerent tried not to show surprise. A letter? To whom?

Selena's eyes flickered. "Am I to presume it is of consequence to me?"

"If you love Denzil Portreath, then yes, it is," Kate answered.

Selena turned away, her rich gown winking and flashing as she moved. "You already know that I love him."

The bells boomed out again, and Kate saw that the eastern horizon was paler than before, a vague splash of blue, green, and turquoise that made the stars seem brighter than ever. A stir of wind moved through the hitherto still trees, the grass and flowers rustled, and ripples moved across the pool. The tide was coming.

Kate smiled. "Yes, you love him, Selena, but you're not going to have him. I've seen to that."

"I don't believe you." Selena's hair lifted in the breeze, which carried with it the tang of the sea.

"Oh, he may be waiting for you right now, but what he doesn't know is that the law is about to catch up with him. I'm afraid I have proof that your Mr. Portreath murdered my first husband in a duel, and—"

"Michael Kingsley was your husband?" Selena gasped.

"Yes, and I have written a letter that sets out in detail the circumstances of his death. Right now it is on its way to my lawyer in London."

"You're lying!" breathed Selena.

Gerent shook his head. "No, she isn't. I have read the letter, and I personally sent it to Charles Carpenter by special courier. You remember Charles, don't you, Selena? I believe you once called his competence into question in front of the Prince Regent. I fear Charles has been no friend of yours since then."

Selena flushed.

Kate addressed her again. "I wonder, given the stark choice, whether Portreath would prefer to stay where he is and hang for murder, or be with you in Lyonesse?"

Selena didn't reply, but Kate could see how her mind raced.

"Selena, I am prepared to speak to Portreath, to tell him word for word what the letter contains. He will know that his days are numbered, and he will come to you rather than swing from a gallows. But if I do that for you, I want something in return."

"Oh, I'm sure you do," Selena murmured. "Genevra, I suppose?"

"Yes. And Belerion and Curnow," Kate replied, having learned from Curnow that they were also prisoners with Genevra on the golden boat. "Time is running out, Selena. You have to decide."

Selena's skirts swished as she resumed her pacing.

Kate watched her anxiously, then glanced at the ever-lightening sky. She had no idea when the surge would come. Maybe minutes, maybe an hour yet. But it *would* come, and then it would be too late. "Selena, you have to decide how much you want Portreath. Believe me, the only way you can have him is if he comes here to you. Capturing Genevra and changing worlds with her will avail you of nothing, because the man you love will hang for his crimes."

Selena regarded her. "I underestimated you, did I not?"

"We are both prepared to fight for the man we love," Kate replied.

"It would seem so." Selena's lavender-blue eyes sharpened. "How can you be so certain that Denzil will listen to you?"

"I can be certain," Kate replied, but her fingers were crossed behind her back. Curnow's plan was excellent, but was it infallible? What if Portreath called her bluff and decided to take his chance? The letter could indeed be belatedly composed, and Jan Portreath could give evidence, but who was to say the case would be proved? It was all in the lap of the gods . . .

Selena nodded suddenly. "Very well, you go to Denzil right now, and tell him what choice he has. And when he decides to come to me, tell him to walk onto the causeway as the surge comes in. I will walk onto it from here, and we will be washed to Lyonesse together."

"And what of Genevra, Curnow, and Belerion? How will I know they are safe?"

"I will bring them here to the steps, safely above the level of the tide. But if you try to trick me—"

"There will be no trickery," Kate promised.

"Go, then."

But Kate was uneasy. "How can we go back to the present? We are here in Lyonesse, and neither of us knows how to get back to our own world!"

Selena smiled. "You are both asleep. All you have to do is awaken. This pool is here in Lyonesse and also exists in your world. The cold of the water will achieve what you wish." With that Selena disappeared, and they both saw the lavender light skimming away toward the creek and the golden boat.

Gerent and Kate knelt by the pool, and dipped their hands in the chill water. The air seemed to spin, and the trees faded, leaving the expanse of sand and seaweed-garlanded rocks of the present. The lights of Trezance shone in the early dawn light, and they both saw Denzil Portreath among the crowd on the quayside. Gerent caught Kate's hand. "Come on, we have very little time."

They ran as fast as they could across the hard, tide-rippled sand. The first seagulls were stirring, and the eastern sky was growing lighter by the second. Beyond the muffled booms of the bells, Kate was sure she could hear the bubbling, rushing sound of the incoming tide, just as she had first on the balcony at the Pulteney. But this time it was only too real.

Portreath rose warily to his feet as he saw them coming, and as he made his way toward his horse, intending to put distance between himself and Gerent, Kate called out anxiously.

"No, please! Wait, Mr. Portreath! We have something to tell you!"

He hesitated.

"Please!" she begged again. "There is so little time, and it's desperately important!"

He turned, and came back to the edge of the quay, just as they reached the steps that led up to the waterfront where the solitary standing stone marked the beginning of the causeway. Everyone heard the bubbling, gurgling sound of the tide in the distance, and as they looked, they saw the first foaming white wave appear around the far edges of the island. Breathless and with a heart that pounded as if it would explode, Kate faced Selena's lover.

"Mr. Portreath—"

"You have nothing to say that can possibly be of interest to me," he interrupted.

"Oh, yes, I have. Unless you go to Selena in Lyonesse, you are going to hang for murder here."

"I think not," he said with a dismissive laugh.

"I can prove it, and a letter is this very minute on its way to London. Hanging is all that awaits you here, sir, so your only hope of survival is to escape to Lyonesse." Kate turned. The tide was sweeping in now, roaring and frothing over the sand and rocks.

Gerent pointed to the landing stage on the island. "Look, they're all there!"

Sure enough, Selena stood there, her gown still dazzling with lights, and with her stood Genevra and Belerion. There was a wicker cage on the steps, presumably containing Curnow. Yes, it *did* contain the cuckoo, for suddenly Kate could hear his frantic voice in her head.

"Hurry! Oh, hurry! You only have a minute or so now!"

She faced Portreath again. "All you have to do is walk into the causeway. Selena will walk from the other end, and when the tide clashes over it, you will both be swept to Lyonesse."

"I will be drowned, you mean!" Portreath cried, his face ashen as he watched the sea racing in.

"You will live on, in Lyonesse. You and Selena together."

Gerent grabbed him by the lapels suddenly. "Damn you, Portreath! Can't you see that this is your only hope? If you stay here you're going to swing by your scrawny neck! Now, much as that thought appeals to me, I have my child to consider. So get onto that causeway and start walking, or I'll kill you here and now with my bare hands!"

Kate gazed at the sea. "Please, Mr. Portreath, for all our sakes."

Suddenly he nodded. "All right, but I despise you, Carismont, and I always will. Believe me, if I find a way of making your life a misery from Lyonesse, I will!"

"You don't frighten me, Portreath."

The roar of the water was all around now, drowning the tolling of the bells. The crowds on the quay were silent as Portreath walked down onto the causeway, and began to slowly make his way toward the island. At the other end, Selena walked in her wonderful gown. Shimmering with diamonds, she seemed to almost glide as the sea crashed against the raised granite way. Spray scattered over everything as the waves met, and all around the water seemed to boil for a moment as the conflicting currents fought each other.

Where Selena and her lover had been, there now rose serpents of the little lights that Kate had first seen at the Pulteney Hotel. They twisted toward each other, twined together, and then dove down into the sea and disappeared. The bells were silenced as the causeway disappeared from view beneath the ferocious deluge.

Water splashed up onto the quay, making the onlookers step hastily back, and when the sea settled a few minutes later, there was no sign at all of Selena or Denzil Portreath. They were both in Lyonesse.

"Mama!"

"Papa!"

Childish voices hailed from the island, and Kate could have wept with joy as she saw Justin and Genevra jumping up and down and waving excitedly. Mrs. Pendern was with them. Belerion gave a roar that was clearly one of satisfaction, and Curnow's protests resounded through Kate.

"By Bedivere's big toe, will someone please let me out of this plaguey cage?"

Later in the morning, when the sea had retreated sufficiently, Kate and Gerent walked hand in hand back to the island. The sea was calm and blue-green in the early sunshine of May Day morning. People had already been out to gather hawthorn to decorate their homes, and the children of Trezance were dancing around the maypole. The churning notes of "Sumer Is Icumen In" rang along the quay as Kate and Gerent made their way down to the causeway.

Justin and Genevra were waiting at the other end, watched over by Mrs. Pendern, but Belerion had escaped and was dashing through the shallow water still covering the causeway to join Kate and Gerent. Curnow had been released from his cage, and fluttered overhead, cuckooing, squawking, and talking all at the same time.

"Cuckoo! Hey, nonny! Squawk! Tra-la! What a wonderful May Day! By Arthur's ankles, I've never felt better!"

The causeway was only covered by an inch or so of calm sea, just as it had been the evening the carriage carried Kate to her new home, and now she laughed as her wet hem, so unfashionably long, floated on the shallow water.

Gerent halted in order to draw her into his arms. "I love you, sweet Kate."

He kissed her on the lips, and there was a distant cheer from the onlookers on the quay. Kate flushed a little, and drew back. "Perhaps we are a little public here," she murmured.

"Maybe, but as it all belongs to me, I think I may flout sensibilities just a little." He smiled, then became more serious. "Do you regret marrying me, Kate?"

"Regret? Certainly not. I haven't had a single second thought."

"Good," he whispered, and pulled her close once more.